THE WOVEN SKIRT

Fran Steinmark

Author's Note

All of the characters, organizations, and events portrayed in this novel are either products of the author's imagination or are used fictitiously. Any resemblance to actual persons, living or dead, is purely coincidental.

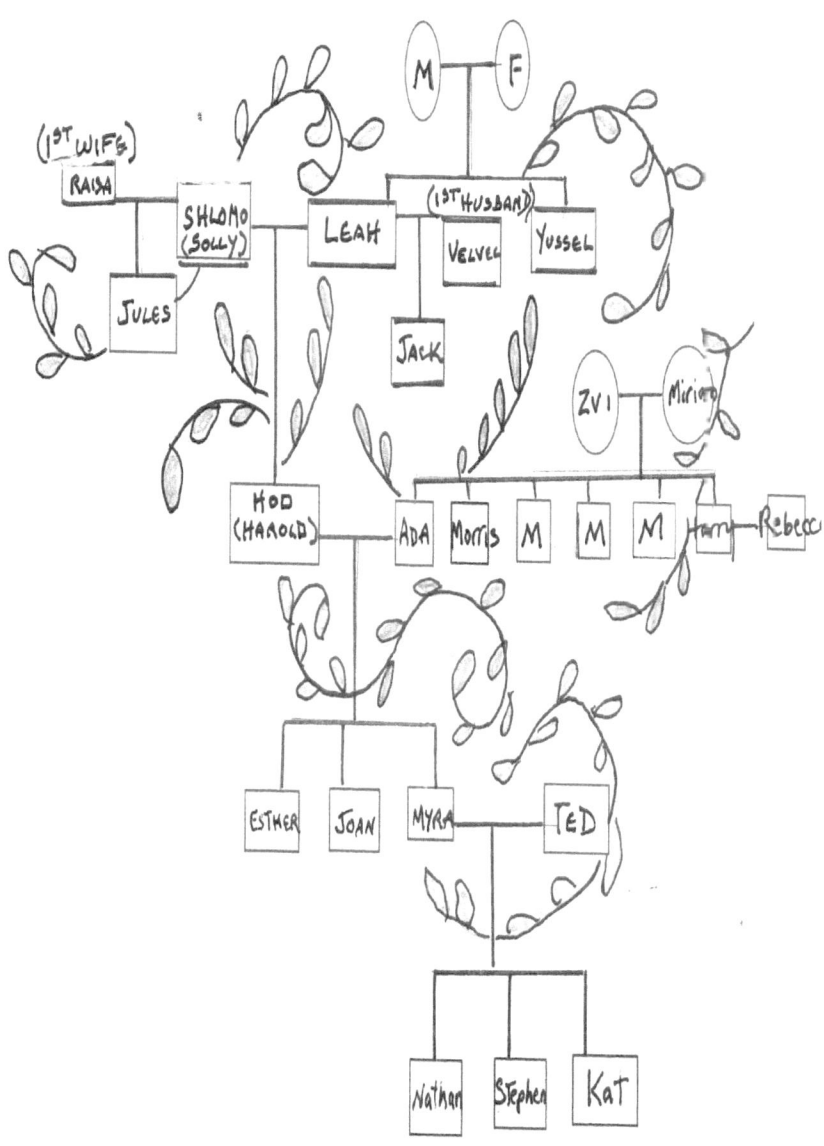

Chapter One

KAT

Try to imagine something as annoying as wind-borne cockleburs or yucky spider webs with multiple, invisible drag lines that might entrap you. Picture them sticking to your hair or clothing—or even worse: getting entrenched in your inner ears, the same way some fears often do. No matter how hard you try to shake those little pests off—flailing, cursing, or throwing a hissy fit—they persist in holding on. In fact, the more your feathers become ruffled, the more intent those buggars are at digging in for the long run.

I have had too many first-hand experiences with these kinds of irritations. I can tell you, though, that when they do occur they are not as insignificant as they might seem on the surface. What's really going on is that you are battling Mother Nature—no minor-league opponent; I can vouch for that. That's who you are actually going up against. She's throwing her darts at you, trying to trip you up, only in a much less subtle manner than an undetected, broken sidewalk or untied shoelaces.

According to my ever-philosophizing, real-life mother, who is in her sixties and eons past her hippie years, the thing to remember is that these discomforts are inconsequential compared to the overall scheme of life. She says that the key is to "Learn to accept what is beyond your control to change. In so doing, you'll be free to tackle the greater challenges in life." She seems to get off quoting the self-help, New Age gurus' version of how best to survive in this world.

So, if you ever inadvertently step on haphazardly discarded chewing gum, don't bother wasting your time scraping away at every piece of gook stuck in the crevices of your shoes. Try to remember that gum on one's shoe is really petty, even though itsy-bitsy amounts will forever remain in your sole, forcing you to lug around someone else's trash for all time. No matter how infuriated you may be, what you're supposed to do is drain your mind of all concerns and simply move on. Put your two feet squarely on the ground and walk away. I know. I know. The sidewalk will keep on feeling tacky and your gait will be completely off. It isn't easy to do, for sure.

"Un-cling yourself," she advises me over and over again, her honey-blond, bleached curls bouncing on her head. "Eliminate the superficial clutter of negativity. Concentrate on the glory embedded in each precious moment and everything will look and feel much better."

My mother's advice generally sucks. She lives a short step away from la-la land. She hasn't a clue as to what challenges most people face, but more specifically, s*he has no idea what kind of crap I have to deal with every single day of my life!* And yet, she still insists on telling me how I should be living, constantly insisting that I need to meet with a therapist. Her unsolicited comments jab at my brain like a jackhammer. Oh, please mother, give me a break and look for someone else to save.

I'm twenty-eight years old, and all the frivolity and enthusiasm of my youthful, once optimistic years have already vanished. If you must know the truth, I was thrust into adulthood way before I was ready for it, hastily waving adios to a carefree life of dating, clubbing, and incessant yakking with my BFFS—Best Friends For Sure—when I wasn't busily investigating pedophiles and deadbeat mothers for the county's justice department. Nowadays, I feel more like I'm forty, but when I look at myself in a mirror or store-front window I can up that number to forty-five. Oh, where did that zany, awesomely ridiculous, fun-loving, not-having-to-answer-to-anyone girl go? How did the skin under my eyes grow to be so puffy? When did my hair begin to thin out? Where did those gullies protruding on either side of my nose come from? I assure you, they're not laugh lines.

My ordeals (or nuisances), are emblematic; they simply cannot be scraped away like burrs, gum, or spider's gunk. It's like I'm knee deep in a cesspool, and since I've had all the gumption pommeled out of me, moving ahead is impossible. If I tried really, really hard, I might be able to maneuver just a short distance, but what would be the point? I'd still be in the middle of a cesspool!

This is why I choose not to go on a diet to lose a ton of weight: all the fatty deposits are eventually going to find their way back to me. This is why I choose not to clean my house: there will always be a shitload of dirt waiting in the wings to make it filthy all over again. This is why I do not do everything under the sun to try to please Craig, hoping to get on his good side when he doesn't

4

have a good side and probably never will. For what feels like an eternity (but in actuality is only a little less than two years—hell, did I just say "only"?), I have been stuck in a lousy, unfixable marriage with absolutely no decent way out. If I ever tried to divorce Craig, the trouble I'd be in would be far worse than what I'm facing now. I'm talking major doo-doo. So, because of that, I do a lot of grinning and bearing and muttering under my breath and engaging in a lot of sex without the pleasure and intimacy I truly crave. After being pricked, prodded, and bothered all the time by things that really unsettle my nerves and hurt terribly—I'll confess the "hurt part" to you but no one else—I'm supposed to make believe that none of this is really happening? Really? *Really?*

It would be great if I could snap my fingers and not be Mrs. Baxter anymore. That would be my very first wish if I ever ran across a genie like the one in *Aladdin*. Wouldn't have to think twice about it. No hesitation at all. "Unmarry me," I would direct the purplish-blue genie, assuming it would be the Disney version standing before me. "And while you're at it, kindly send Craig on a one-way trip to the moon."

Craig's constantly picking on me and calling me names; not the endearing kind, so don't even go there. He has no problem telling me how stupid I am any chance he gets. Putting me down is a game he must enjoy tremendously because he does it often enough. Once in a while, he gets a little slap happy. There, I've said it, but I'm not going to elaborate further about it because I'm just not. That's supposed to be our little secret. I'm better off keeping it that way. Craig and I were married shortly after my brother, Nathan, died two years ago, when he was just thirty-two years old. The marriage was a mistake right from the get-go.

Quite suddenly and unexpectedly, *kapoof!* Nathan left the planet. Dead. Gone for good. Nathan's illness hit me, my brother Stephen, and the rest of my family like a lightning bolt destroying the main electrical line to our house and knocking us all down. Talk about being in a battle. Nathan's autoimmune disease came at him with the intensity of an atomic bomb, triggering a drug-resistant renal disease that extinguished his kidneys as well as any possible future, however bright that might have been. We three kids grew up being very close, even though we had our fair share of fights and disagreements. It was incomprehensible to believe that our trio could ever be reduced to two, which is exactly what happened. Death comes to old people and victims of freak accidents, but not to someone you know really well, let alone a brother! It shouldn't have to be faced until you're older; much older like when you yourself are sufficiently decrepit and infirm.

Nathan was my super-hero; he was unlike anyone else I knew. He had no problem stating whatever was on his mind and didn't give a rat's ass what others thought of him. Without question, he left a lasting impression on everyone he met.

Nathan pissed people off (me included) all the time, but he still managed to be loved and admired immensely. Man, he pulled some crazy shit in his short lifetime like when he fabricated the name of a novel, its author, and all the characters for an A+ on a book report in eleventh grade English. Then he had the audacity to convince Stephen to submit the same fake report three years later, and it still pulled in the very same grade.

When Nathan was a sophomore in high school (he must have been about fifteen-ish and I was close to nine), he entered the tail end of a major cycling race. He said it was by accident, but if you knew Nathan like I did you would have had your doubts about that. Nathan's keyed up recitation of his marathon experience came gushing out of him the minute my mother and I looked up from the stovetop to acknowledge his presence in the kitchen. I was being taught the intricate technique of making sweet and sour meatballs when Nathan appeared flushed, sopping wet, and anxiously pacing back and forth, causing his clipless pedal shoes to tap incessantly on the terracotta floor. The ugly mole on his right upper lip—that I have the same misfortune to have inherited from our family's gene-pool—glistened like a full moon, making it stand out even more than usual.

"I began cycling as fast as I could possibly go in the same direction they were coming. There was nothing else I could have done. I swear, I was afraid they were going to trample me to death."

With hands full of egg, matzoh meal, and chopped shoulder steak, my mother took a break from manipulating the mush to make sense of Nathan's frantic rambling. "All right, I'll bite. What happened this time?"

"My body was dripping from sweat," Nathan excitedly shared, "but I managed to keep a fair distance ahead of the biker behind me. When I crossed the finish line, I was whisked away. Just like that, someone came and grabbed me right off my bike. I had no idea what was happening, and it turned out I was being brought to be examined by a medical doctor. *They assumed I was the winner!*"

"The winner of what?" my mother asked, plopping each formed meatball into the simmering sauce, mindful not to splatter.

"Weren't you listening to me? You never listen to me!" he yelled. "I just told you that I won a bike race. It was the Nassau to Suffolk County Bike Challenge."

"But you never formally entered that race," my mother announced with a look of hesitation. I could tell she was afraid that Nathan was going to jump down her throat for saying so. He had a habit of acting that way with practically everything she said to him back then.

"Mom," Nathan continued, "I didn't enter that race. I told you that I got into the middle of it just by accident."

"By accident. Purely by accident? I find that a little hard to believe. Where were—"

"Oh, you're impossible to talk to," Nathan interrupted. "The doctor couldn't get over how well I had endured the race. He said my stamina was remarkable."

"Of course, it was remarkable," my mother interjected. "You hadn't been racing from the start. Or had you?"

Nathan pulled out the desk chair and sat down noisily, extending his legs far out in front of him and kicking me in the shins as he did so. I squeaked out an "ouch," that went ignored.

"They gave me a water bottle and placed a wreath about my neck. It was hysterical," he said, chuckling enough to make his belly bob up and down. "They broadcast my name over the loudspeakers. They said I was a part of the Lowenbrau team. I was interviewed on public radio. Crowds gathered to take photographs with me. Some people even asked me for my autograph. I'm famous. You have a famous son. How do you like that?" He stretched back in his chair, brushed aside some wet strands that had fallen on his forehead, and then clasped his hands behind his neck with a grin of immense satisfaction.

I gawked at Nathan, eyeing the tight, yellow biker's shirt he wore with the word "Lowenbrau" printed in the middle, while my mother wiped her brow with the dishtowel. Some of what Nathan was saying was starting to sound pretty neat.

Placing the lid on the saucepan, my mother asked, "And then what happened?"

Nathan's face grew serious. "Well, you know Mr. Barkley, my English teacher?"

I twisted my head back and forth from Nathan to my mother, making sure I could capture every word in their exchange.

"Uh huh," she said.

"Well, it turns out he was there."

"Where? At the finish line?"

"Not at the finish line. In this big tent in the general area where all the festivities were taking place. Evidently, he heard the announcement with my name and came running to see me."

"To congratulate you?" I asked. "Do you think he'll give you a really good grade now because of this?"

"No, you idiot!" Nathan shouted. "Just keep your trap shut."

I looked to my mother to intercede on my behalf, but she appeared worried and preoccupied.

"Mr. Barkley stepped up and told someone in charge that I was a student of his and not officially a part of any team."

My mother leaned against a stool. "Go on," she uttered, sounding throaty. The zig-zagging lines deepened on her forehead.

Nathan's tone was less joyful than it had been. "I kind of got the feeling that I was in some kind of trouble because the man in charge said, 'Take off that f-ing wreath and get your f-ing conniving body out of this winner's tent before I have you f-ing arrested!'"

As young as I was then, I knew what the "f-ing" words really stood for. I stared in astonishment at Nathan, wondering if he had tempered his words so as not to offend my mother or if he had repeated the man-in-charge's words just as Nathan had originally heard them. Either way, my brother wasn't modifying his speech for my benefit. Plenty of what my mother had termed "inappropriate ways to express yourself" had come barreling out of his mouth in my presence before.

Nathan finished his tale, sighing with relief. "Phew. I ran out of there before the cops were called and came right home to tell you what happened."

"That really was something," my mother responded. "Hmm." She lowered her head, focusing on the red sauce stain on her apron as she rubbed her nose with her fist. "I don't know quite what to say."

Nathan didn't hang around to hear anything else. He ran off to jump the stairs leading to his bedroom two at a time, and I watched my mother then put the kettle on to make two cups of tea: one for her and one for me. "The meatballs will take about thirty minutes more, and then they'll be done. I think we should take a tea break and have some chocolate chip cookies while we wait. Don't you agree?"

The story of Nathan's bike ride and his winning feat became embellished each and every time he related it to someone new. Overhearing him, I could pinpoint the exact moments where he was going to break out into a loud guffaw. That's one of the things I miss most about Nathan.

His laugh was so authentic and contagious. It enveloped everyone who heard it and immediately put you in a good mood. Unlike me, he had quite the gift of gab, keeping his audience fascinated and spellbound for hours on end. I swear that he could sell someone the hair off of their own head. He was some crazy, funny kind of guy. Now, he's not anything at all.

My mom would say that you could drop Nathan, penniless and blindfolded, in the middle of Africa and he'd find his way home in no time. That's another one of her fancy predictions she got wrong. His very last journey—his most challenging one; the one that counted more than anything else—took place nowhere near Africa. Despite his limitless ingenuity, inexhaustible resourcefulness, and putting up a really good fight, he didn't have anywhere near what was needed to make it back to us.

Chapter Two

When I found out that Nathan had died mysteriously in the hospital, I screamed for hours in disbelief. It seemed like my bones were caving in on my stomach and intestines. There is not a horrible enough word to describe how badly it felt. I fell to the floor and crawled into a bedroom, where I was curled up in a corner. I didn't ever want to get out of that corner. I wanted the earth to stop spinning and reverse its direction. I wanted everything I had heard about to be undone. Everyone in the family knew enough not to coax me out. My world had fallen apart. I felt terribly alone and afraid. I felt abandoned. I wanted to change Nathan's storyline and rewrite that horribly gruesome ending.

My brother had gone into the hospital two days prior for minor surgery which was intended to correct scar tissue on his abdomen. Instead of feeling relieved that just one more phase of my brother's kidney disease had reached a satisfactory resolution, our plans for a celebratory dinner had to be scrapped and burial arrangements had to be hastily made.

In the funeral parlor, summing up all the guts I possibly had, I reluctantly peered in the halfway opened casket at the face and body that had belonged to Nathan, but my brother—my crazy, genius older brother—was nowhere to be found. His ever-present gusto and *joie de vivre* went painfully missing. His skin looked like that of a painted doll's, only expressionless. That corpse, stuffed and dressed in a ritual shroud, was not him. He never was into organized religion. He thought it silly, contrived, and out of sync with the postulates of a scientific universe. Why didn't they bury him in his Yankees T-shirt and cap, for goodness sake? *That was what he was really into!*

In the days that followed Nathan's funeral, my parents and Stephen had to deal with their own unshakable grief, so I didn't want to burden them, but I desperately needed to find someone I could lean on. At the time, Craig and I had just started dating. We were at that stage of our relationship when he thought everything I said was cute and whatever I had on was sexy. He would tell me things like, "Those leggings are hot," or "Pink is a good color on you," or "How did you get to be so pretty?" He was ever so kind and mellow, acting like the kind of guy who planted flowers and took care of stray animals. His six-foot frame had made his shoulders appear more solid and broader than they actually were. I ran to him, hoping to get lost in a different reality, and he made himself readily available, surrounding me with his giant muscular arms. It was where I could feel safe and protected.

My parents' home had been packed wall to wall with people throughout the days of the mourning period for Nathan. Friends and relatives had flown in from all over the States. There were also plenty of others who appeared to be dropping in just for the meals. I identified them as the "mooching freeloaders" the minute they crossed our threshold, wearing the same every day, hungry expressions as patrons entering the Cheesecake Factory or

14

P. F. Chang's at the mall. What did these people truly know about my brother and our loss? Who needed them? Their words of comfort seemed shallow and artificial. Some of the visitors had faltered upon seeing me, not knowing what to say. I made it easier for them by ducking out of their way or ushering them directly to my parents. No matter how many prayers were being offered, sitting down or standing up, facing Jerusalem or facing the dining room table loaded with whitefish salad, pastrami sandwiches, and rugelach, nothing was going to bring Nathan back to the living.

Craig and I sneaked away from the house full of mourners and long lines of never-ending sympathizers. We hooked up in hallways, elevators, bathtubs, in the back seat of his car, and anywhere else we happened to find ourselves, out of earshot of the muted Kaddish prayers. We had torn off each other's clothing and dove into each other's bodies with an urgency that was almost vicious. I had ridden him the same way he had ridden me, neither one of us giving a second thought to the consequences.

A few months later, the plus sign on a pregnancy kit explained why my period had been a no-show. Craig never uttered a word about an abortion. He just asked me when and where I wanted to get married. We made the plans for me, Craig, his parents and mine, and Stephen, to assemble at the rabbi's study to cement the union. Since it didn't seem appropriate to buy something white or new for the occasion, in deference to Nathan's recent demise, I wore one of my fancier red dresses from my closet. My parents, alternating between acting anxious and

15

pensive, floated off to the side several feet from where Craig and I stood holding hands. My mom kept scratching her arms. My dad's jaw was clenched tight, his eyebrows knitted close together. The toe of his right moccasin tapped up and down arrhythmically. The atmosphere was not too dissimilar to the one in the bereavement room when that same rabbi had slashed little black ribbons with a razor blade and then pinned them onto our chests.

Craig's mother and father, not doing too good of a job at hiding their anger, spoke over my head to their son, treating me like someone who didn't understand English. His mother kept her arms crossed against her navy suit jacket, which was buttoned all the way, and sat herself in the chair by the rabbi's desk. They had entered the room saying a "Good Morning" to the rabbi and no one else, but Craig's father did give an abrupt nod to Stephen as he passed him on his way to the bookcases in the corner. My brother stared ahead, not focusing on me or anyone else, as if he was at the edge of a station platform waiting for a train to pull in and whisk him away.

Before we could get started, the rabbi indicated we needed another witness to make the marriage contract official. While we waited for one of his administrative aides to join us, my mom turned to me and tugged at my skirt. *Please stop this now,* her eyes pleaded. I jerked my head sideways and peered out the window, zeroing in on a gecko slithering across a pane of glass. The bulbous appendages of its four feet stuck to the surface like suction cups. When the ceremony was about to begin, Craig kissed my cheek and drew my attention back into the room. Noticing a downward droop to my jaw, he squeezed my hand and whispered, "Everything will turn out to be wonderful. I promise you."

At that time, it seemed like our getting married was the perfect antidote for the heavy, nonsensical fog I had been existing under—the ideal diversion from all that oppressive sadness and despair. Figuring Craig would be considerate and supportive of me for all the days, months, and years to come, I was hoping that I had found my true love and that we would turn out to be each other's soul mates.

Boy, was I wrong. I was clueless—a numbskull! What a half-baked, harebrained, boneheaded, plain-out dumb thing to do! In my defense, though, who *can* think clearly at a time of such tragedy?

Every time Craig and I now have something to discuss it feels like I'm in a boxing ring. He's either got his back up or he's ready to throw a punch at me with his mouth. What's the point of raising my voice as well if I am never going to be heard? When we have sex nowadays, it's all about what turns him on and how he likes it. My needs are not in the equation. There's no tenderness, no stroking, no sweet talk. The faster he comes, the better it is. He rolls off of me without caring if I reach an orgasm, wipes himself, and grabs the TV remote. I turn over and pretend to fall asleep while I hear snippets from every sport show airing highlights of teams he's interested in.

I fantasize about being courted on a Greek Isle by the son of a rich tycoon. He tells me that my figure is sensual and perfect. He says, "It's exactly how a woman should be." He's turned on by my excess weight, and he caresses my breasts. His fingers and tongue massage my nipples, making me feel wet between my thighs. I imagine him penetrating me with a gentle rocking, but in truth, there is nothing now for me to hold on to at all. I try to not shake too much. I don't want Craig to suspect what is happening beneath the covers on my side of the bed. I don't want him laughing at me. I don't want to be further embarrassed.

So, if Craig and I have had a blowout over something I've said or done (because it's always going to be my fault), the next day I act as if nothing has happened between us. I'm too afraid to leave him right now, as I haven't quite figured out the mechanics of how to live somewhere else. It would be torture having to live under my mother's thumb again. I don't have much money saved up, and I can't expect my parents to foot my bills, especially after everything they've been through. Nathan's illness had a severe impact on their finances. I suspect they're still suffering from the interminable, emotional wounds of losing a child, although my stoic mother does a good job of hiding it. How would I ever be able to raise my son, Noah, by myself? How could I put my family through so much pain again? I just couldn't.

Once a week, I get to spend a little time with some of my friends on the evenings that Craig has his poker game. Craig does not hide how he feels about my friends; he's quick to point out something they've said or done as being really stupid, and then I won't want to be seen around them anymore. He says that I am exposing our son to riffraff.

Craig reminds me, "Water sinks to its own level," and "When you lie down with fleas, you get up with them." As far as I'm concerned, he's probably the one with the biggest number of fleas.

Craig and I have become enemies, sharing the same address but barely tolerating each other—unless, of course, he's feeling turned on (Not by me, mind you. He has stacks of videos and magazines to accommodate that purpose). "Only weirdos and desperate men are into fatso, jumbo women like you," he says. "Don't ever count me as one of them."

I've gotten used to tuning out Craig's yelling and constant put-downs. Craig says that it's my thin skin rather than his words that are doing any damage. He wishes my entire body could be that thin.

It is unfortunate but not one female in my family is anorexic or has that sunk-in look with the well-defined cheekbones. Chunky and chubby would be fairly accurate ways to describe us. In fact, several of the extra pounds I gained during pregnancy still persist in hanging around my stomach and chin, which of course gives Craig ample ammunition. I keep reminding him that I'm stuck with this bulging excess due to my genetics and *his* baby.

"You wanna be stupid, then continue to be stupid, but don't think that *I'm that* stupid," he emphatically responds and then shrugs and walks away. "And you wonder why I look elsewhere," he mutters to himself but audibly enough for me to hear.

My mother, on the other hand, is quick to pipe in that such an excuse for flab is hogwash and suggests that I should work out once in a while, as if I have all the free time in the world.

"I want you to be healthy," she says.

"That's because you'd rather have a cute, petite daughter with whom you can shop and show off to your mahjong buddies," I tell her.

However, not even my mother, who strenuously works out at the gym and regularly eats nothing but morsels of fiber—I swear she must own a ton of stock in chia, flax, and hemp seed companies—escapes the bulging thighs syndrome ordained by our inherited chromosomes. Even when she's sporting her tummy-control, spandex tights that she's so overly enamored with and tries to constantly hawk to me, the excess padding sitting below and around her hips is pretty apparent.

"You need to drop some pounds," she tells me practically every time she sees me. I, of course, am counting to see if a new record has been set before these words come bursting out of her mouth.

"Here you go again, Mom. Why not stop before we have yet another argument?"

I must be an embarrassment to her; otherwise she wouldn't always be seeking to improve me. There were times when I would have traded everything I owned just to be a thin, blonde Scandinavian babe with six-foot legs, but my having Noah is well worth every extra inch around my waist and hips. And what's more, I'm keeping a tight hold on Noah, notwithstanding the Sturnberger propensity for large Rubenesque figures and Craig's threats to take him away if we ever get divorced.

When I observe how comfortable and loving my parents are with each other, the contrast between the two marriages rattles me. It's as if the truth is obstinately staring me in the face and saying, "This is how it's supposed to be. If you keep living with Craig, you might as well get used to being angry, jealous, disappointed, fearful, unappreciated, tired, and lonely." The list can go on even longer; I could insert every negative emotion that a human being can possibly suffer.

My mother is the kind of woman who excels at everything she sets her mind to, so it's no wonder that her marriage is as wholesome as it is. Me being constantly subpar, never able to reach her lofty standards, and not having the desire nor the means to exert myself to try, it's no surprise that my shipwreck of a marriage is lingering on the rocks. It will never be as wonderful as what my mother and father have together. Not by a long shot. They're still living like newlyweds on a round the world luxury cruise.

My mother tells me that this doesn't have to be my destiny. Ask me if she has any idea how bad things really are between Craig and me. The answer is *no!* Furthermore, why can't she ever talk to me in plain English? Why can't she talk to me like regular mothers talk to their daughters?

"The universe is setting you up to work through certain issues before you can move on. You must accept the reality of the circumstances, take control of your own life, and shape it into the way you *choose* it to be!"

Move on to where, exactly? The only thing I see moving is the needle on the scale telling me my weight keeps going up and up. One day, I will explode and all my problems will be resolved. At that point, I'm hoping my parents will dive right in and take control of Noah, with or without the legal right to do so. Naturally, Craig will fight them on this maneuver until he jumps onto some other hot topic with which to amuse himself. Currently, he's been harping that Noah has to learn respect and that I mollycoddle and spoil our child way too much. Noah's not even a toddler yet. How can any child be spoiled by receiving too much love?

So, this is my plan: I will continue to ignore Craig's "fuck you" attitude and will look away from the ugly truths that persistently jump up in my face. I will continue to apply makeup and Band-Aids to cover up the side effects of his ambushes and assaults.

Does Craig have a girlfriend on the side? I don't want to know about it.

Do I eat too much? Do I really care?

Are my girlfriends lame-brained? I will do a better job of weeding out the smarter ones and keeping them around.

I will continue to endure my life, which is one long pain in the butt. I will watch over Noah, my sweet, precious, most adorable son, and protect him with all that I've got and all the while, I will keep telling my parents and my brother, Stephen, that everything with Craig and me is just hunky-dory. "Yes. Today is a good one so far. We're fine. Just leave it at that."

Chapter Three

One of the earliest "sticky gum" situations I ever had to endure occurred way back when, before I was even married to Craig. The year was 1980 and my parents made the terrible mistake of branding me "Kat Sturnberger" when I was born. In so doing, they burdened me with a horrible handicap and an exasperating fate. Since my mother, nee Myra Kaufman, came of age midway between the era of Betty Crocker and Women's Lib, it never occurred to her to hyphenate her name as many married women do nowadays. For that, I am most eternally grateful because I dodged the "Kat Kaufman-Sturnberger" bullet, which would have been deadly. Yay for me for not having been born at a different moment in time.

I have always hated my name. The "Kat" part didn't bother me at all; people think it's short for Kathy or Kathleen, but it's not. It was that stupid surname, with all three of its annoying syllables, that was the most problematic. It hung over me like it was Miracle Glued to my body and there wasn't a chemical made strong enough to pry it off. It subjected me to a barrage of unflattering stereotypes and tied me to connotations and a history that made me feel uncomfortable and out of place. It was as if I'd been given the name of a family that I really didn't want to belong to.

Going back through the generations, my relatives had such names as Shlomo, Zvi, and Hod. I can't imagine those names were as whacky-sounding then as they are now. There's not a John, Mary, or Paul in the bunch, but Shlomo and Zvi have almost a biblical ring to them. Perhaps they were very religious, learned men like rabbis, but no one I know has ever mentioned this before, so I seriously doubt it. I once looked at a photographic essay of Eastern European Jews by Roman Vishniac. It horrified me to think that these were pictures of *my ancestors*. Everyone and their surroundings looked dull, grimy, and poor. I never wanted those dismal images to be a reflection of my personal heritage.

Plenty of immigrants with unusual-sounding names Americanized them to better blend in with their new culture. Why couldn't our last name have been changed to something totally neutral, like Sturn, or Styne, or even Baxter (which is my married name now)?

Since Sturnberger begins with the letter "S," I always had to sit in the back row of every one of my classrooms, along with the T's, occasional Z's, and all of the annoying, weirdo misfits—the ones with the countless zits and metal rings punctuating their faces. For someone who actually enjoyed learning, this was just one more cross to bear, so to speak. Anyone's free to use this metaphor, right? I once toyed with the idea of getting my own tongue pierced right after a particularly nasty run-in with Mrs. Myra Bossy-pants, but eventually nixed doing it because it would have bothered my dad much more so than it would have my mom.

As a teenager, my name wore very heavily on my back. It embarrassed me. I resented how it made me feel pigeonholed.

Every morning in school, I used to sweat profusely just hearing my name called for attendance. The stupid class morons never missed an opportunity to snicker at me. They were the so-called in group and believed it was their privilege to look down upon everyone else. It was their favorite pastime; making fun of me, my hair, my clothes, and humiliating all those they considered geeks.

I was three years old, in 1983, when my family moved from our protected enclave on the South Shore of Long Island into a more Christian neighborhood on the North Shore, where we were enrolled into prestigious private schools typically reserved for Protestant kids. This move was intended to expose us to a multi-cultural, richer environment. My mother had constantly complained of living in a ghetto-like community with the sameness of materialistic values and unimaginative neighbors. My brothers and I, on the other hand, had no idea what she was talking about. We seemed to be happy with our lot in life, enjoying our schools, our friends, and the many hours of playing tag on the street or board games at our friends' homes.

On the very first day of the new school year, the principal at the elementary school in which Nathan (age 9) and Stephen (age 6) were enrolled, smiled assuredly at my mother, convincing her it was okay to temporarily relinquish custody of her sons into his care. He committed to personally escorting my brothers to their new classrooms to meet their second and fifth grade teachers, Dr. Cohen and Mr. Granger. Stephen spent a great deal of the morning crying, and kindly Dr. Cohen did his best to comfort and integrate him within the class environment. Nathan's experience, however, had played out quite the opposite to Stephen's, and we were subjected to the detailed, obsessive recounting of it during the car ride home and during each and every evening meal for many months to follow.

According to Nathan, when his teacher first heard the name "Nathan Sturnberger" being pronounced with dragged out emphasis on *Sturn-ber-ger* by the principal, his entire demeanor and facial expression changed so much that Nathan could sense how bothered his teacher had become. Mr. Granger had immediately sent Nathan on a bogus mission to all the other classrooms. "Go bring me back a bacon masher," he had demanded. "I'm not sure which teacher has it in their possession." Naturally, Nathan came up empty, and another teacher had even sent Nathan looking for a pork flipper as well.

At the same time that this was going on, a gang had overrun a site for a new home being constructed on our street, spray painting swastikas on every support beam and bashing every pipe that was in plain sight. Naturally, both my parents were dismayed by these events. They had hoped that such discrimination was a thing of the past.

When my dad would try out for Little League in the predominantly Italian Catholic neighborhood in Queens, New York where he grew up, all the other candidates were told to stand on the pitcher's mound, but the rules had been different for Teddy Sturnberger, who wore a mezuzah around his neck. He had been directed to throw from the outfield, always pitching up hill. Each year, the results would be the same: "Your skills are not up to the level we're seeking. Sorry, kid. You'll probably have better luck next year."

Teddy's friends, with names like Vinnie, Anthony, and Johnny, had no problem whatsoever in making the team. Heck, Anthony even threw like a girl and still got in. Teddy could out run them, out throw them, and out bat them all. However, no matter how hard he tried to impress the coaches with his athletic abilities, they would make it perfectly clear that they did not want him on their team.

His application for Cub Scouts didn't fare any better. He could just as well have thrown it in the garbage instead of submitting it to the troop leader. The scouts would meet at the back of a church, and that was where Teddy would go to drop off his completed forms. Perhaps they had witnessed him run through the aisles, failing to kneel and cross himself before the statue of Jesus Christ. Possibly, they had noticed how uncomfortable he felt being in a structure where he had heard his family being called a "bunch of kikes."

"We don't want you," the den mother would say, not mincing her words. "We have too many kids already." Every boy from Teddy's class was in that troop. There was room for them, but not for the boy with the weird, Jewish-sounding name.

What gives people the right to act superior over others and make assumptions based upon the way a name sounds? When I was younger, I wanted to be seen and appreciated for who I was: an intelligent, spirited individual. I wanted to shout, "Hey, world! Look at Kat. I'm special, even with my dark chocolate tight-knit curls and in spite of my family's tendency to be overly endowed, or *zaftig* as they say in some circles."

Besides bringing Noah into my life, the only other benefit from my marriage to Craig that I can think of is that people now refer to me as Kat Baxter. What movie celeb wouldn't want a name like that? It's short, precise, and doesn't give off too much information straightaway. There's no hint of ethnicity, nationality, or any connection to widespread condemnations.

Included within the duties of being Mrs. Craig Baxter, however, is my required attendance at one or two office cocktail parties a year. Despite experiencing major stress due to what others may term my inherent, anti-social behavior, Craig demands that I accompany him, insisting that I behave friendly and outgoing so I don't embarrass him any more than I already have. "I expect you to look halfway decent, if that's even possible. Try putting something on that isn't a tent and don't go off by yourself sulking in a corner like the village idiot." I dare not say I don't feel like going because then I would be committing a terrible offense, chiseling away at the ideal, family-man image he's hoping to impress upon his co-workers. Staying home alone would only cause me more grief because there'd be plenty of hell to pay when Craig finds his way home afterwards—*assuming he could find his way*—tripping and reeling about, totally smashed and incoherent.

Craig ditches my company with the first handshake of a familiar pal or with the beckoning smile of an attractive woman he can slip his arm around. It does not bother me to be abandoned on these occasions. I'm perfectly okay with being un-noteworthy and blending in with the scenery. I pick up a glass of iceless water to keep my hands busy and make a point to grab just two carrot sticks from the hors d'oeuvres tray. I can tell that others in the room expect me to go scoop up gallons of the dip, but to everyone's disappointment I typically bypass the sour cream concoction and seat myself in a corner, preferring to sit in a single chair rather than a loveseat or couch and eliminating the guesswork as to whether someone else has room enough to sit alongside me. I know they can plainly see that I'm supporting at least three women's bodies in my one expanded frame. After a short while, the other guests stop pointing their fingers and sneaking peeks at me, which I pretend not to notice.

Nothing I can do or say at these parties will have an effect on Craig's mood if and when we return home together; our rides are never pleasant. He gets nasty when he gets drunk, and he's always getting drunk. He finds fault with everything I did or didn't do; the complaints roll over to my outfits and the way I wear my hair. "Why can't you look more like Audrey? She's what I call 'attractive.' Are you aware that your ass took up most of the room? Try keeping your mouth shut: less food can go in and less nonsense can come out."

I stop hearing him after a while because I can mentally picture myself driving a different car in the opposite direction. By the time we've pulled into our garage, his bellyaching has ceased and he looks at me as someone he's resigned to fuck. As far as I'm concerned, all I want is the strength to survive each day as best I can and to continue being Noah's mother. I'm way too exhausted to fight any other battles.

Chapter Four

Craig and I moved into our new Spanish-style townhouse right after Noah was born. The tree-lined streets in our gated community are sprawling with bike riders, roller skaters, joggers, and baby strollers. We have a backyard just big enough for a barbecue, a couple of outdoor chairs picked up for a steal from a garage sale, and a Costco-purchased water table for Noah to get soaked in. I've been asking Craig to fence in the property so Noah can't wander too close to the canals, but he just shrugs me off and says that I'm too much of a worry wart. His honey-do list keeps getting longer with chores that I add with full awareness that they are never ever going to be completed. We have a broken towel rack in the downstairs bathroom. Four slats of the vertical shades in the living room have fallen. A screw came loose in the seat of a kitchen chair. He yesses me to death. "Christ almighty, I'll take care of it. I've told you a million times that I'll take care of it! Get off my back, why don't you?" If I suggest hiring a handyman instead, he berates me for spending all of his "goddamn, hard-earned money."

This is Florida and kids drown in backyard pools and water spots all the time. I have investigated enough of these cases to know that ignoring the perils of drowning is pure negligence and, in some situations, a crime. Last month, thankfully, a good Samaritan neighbor ironically named Sam, clad only in rubber boots and shorts, dug through the sandy soil to plant small ficuses, which I've been told grow very rapidly in a southeast climate. He had noticed the twenty containers bought by Craig at Home Depot three weeks earlier and stacked up on our brick patio. They were looking a little sad and hadn't been budged an inch since, so Sam was nice enough to offer to do the job himself.

"Oh, you don't have to do that," I told him. I was holding Noah in my arms, and Sam was tickling his belly.

"Really, it's no problem at all. I can get it done in no time." Sam has the kind of face that always looks friendly and accommodating, with no sinister "out-to-get-you" thoughts under wraps in the background. When he smiles, he throws his whole self into it, and you get a generous showing of most of his teeth.

I answered him quickly before a sense of modesty prevented me from accepting the gallant gesture. "Well, I sure would appreciate it. You'd be doing me a tremendous favor."

"High-five me, bud," he said, raising his hand, expecting Noah to respond accordingly, which he did not do. Sam gently lifted Noah's hand, uncurling his fingers and giving it a soft tap. "There you go. We've got to keep you safe, right buddy?"

As he plunged the spade into the dirt, I stared at his bare chest and well-defined six-pack, wondering what life would be like if this kind guy was my partner. *I could so do him.* If I ever got loose from Craig, however, I would swear off men forever. Just maybe, though, Sam might be the one exception to the rule.

Hopefully, the white fly infestations will not destroy the newly planted shrubs and there'll be a decent natural border to keep Noah safe. My dad had planted a white clump birch in our garden when I was two years old, and each spring we would see how far I had grown compared to the tree. It will be interesting to periodically measure the height of our new fence against Noah. As of now, the ficus hedge and Noah are just about even.

It was only until the last week of my ninth month of pregnancy that I gave up my paying job as an investigator, and ever since Noah was born, I've been a stay-at-home mom. It's not that I wasn't satisfied with my career choice in social services—I still care an awful lot about the well-being of all children—but since I've become Noah's mother, not only do I totally enjoy being with him, I devote a great deal of my time to meeting his needs and ensuring his safety. Craig thinks that I go way overboard with this and that I'm a classic example of a "helicopter mom."

All the years covering child abuse and neglect, however, has made me aware of just how important and difficult good parenting can be. To my disappointment, though, working at home has proven to be much harder than working in an office; there is never any "off" time, the pay is lousy, and the lack of vacation days stinks. I get lonely, tired, and fed up often, but there is no one who will stand still long enough to hear me complain about it. My husband believes that I am spoiled rotten and living a life of luxury. Opening up to my mother will result in a torrential outpouring of "You should be doing this" and "You should be doing that." There'd be enough criticism streaming out of her mouth to drown me. Many of my friends do not have the economic freedom to make the same choice I did. They simply cannot afford to stay home, and as a result, they're not totally dependent upon their husbands for financial support like I am. I wouldn't have a single penny if Craig didn't give it to me, and he's not shy about reminding me of this any chance he gets. He enjoys being in control of our finances as much as he enjoys being in control of me.

You might say that I have become obsessed with Noah, but in a good way, and you'd be right. Even before I was old enough to babysit or be a camp counselor, I knew that I loved being around kids. Noah's adorableness makes parenting him that much easier. I photograph him a million times a day to capture his progress and growth, so anytime a camera appears before his face he goes into automatic grin mode. It's impossible to choose which of the thousand pics of him I like best, so I post them all on Facebook.

I'd rather spend time online, surfing the web or catching up with the latest posts than seeing to the house cleaning, which is an impossible task with the pile up of puzzles, balls, and plush toys all over the floor. If you step the wrong way, you're likely to hear ten different renditions of "Old MacDonald" or "Twinkle Twinkle." With every doll and stuffed animal wired to the hilt, Noah has become a musical maestro just by squeezing the hands or bellies of his play friends.

Noah is fourteen months old and just started walking. He's not that steady on his feet and kind of looks like a miniature Frankenstein monster when he maneuvers his way across a room. Minus a few wisps of fine, blond hair gently falling over his prominent forehead, he is still quite bald, making his large blue eyes pop from his cherubic face. He's at that stage where he prefers crawling over walking because he can get around faster that way. Show him a bag of goldfish crackers, and he drops on all fours like nobody's business. When he hears the sanitation trucks coming down the street, he makes a mad dash to the front door so I can take him outside to watch the workers unload the cans. "Oh, wait till he starts walking," unsolicited comments come at me in various aisles of Target when he's loudly whining and trying to reach all the bright objects on the shelves. "Life becomes impossible once they're on their feet."

Craig keeps saying that he'll start to enjoy Noah when he's older; he plans on turning him into a real jock. "Changing diapers and making 'goo-goo' faces is only for girls." The guy knows the stats and key players from all the major ball clubs, he can name each of the Super Bowl contenders going back to year one, but he can't be bothered to watch his only child stack blocks or play doctor with his dolly. "All he did was place the cubes on top of each other; what's the stinking big deal? And I've told you time and again, boys don't play with dolls! We want him to grow up being a man not a wimp. He acts too much like a fraidy-cat already!"

Craig wishes that I invested as much enthusiasm in my home management skills as I do in amassing stuff for Noah. "It wouldn't hurt you to lift your fat ass away from the computer and clean up the filth once in a while." He tells me there are piles of dust all over the place, but I don't see it. "I can write your name on the dining room table. I–D–I–O–T. Only a moron wouldn't be able to read that!"

Craig also says I slaughter every bit of food I touch. He has had something negative to say about almost every dish I've prepared. "Did the salt container fall into this? This chicken is still raw. Are you trying to poison me? I almost just choked on a peppercorn. For someone your size, I would have assumed you to be a better cook." The steaks are too well done, the fish is too rare, the lettuce leaves are wilting, and the soups are all watered down. After the first few months of what he called disastrous meals, Craig decided to commandeer our kitchen. Between you and me, I'm not too enamored with the food he prepares either. He seems to go overboard with what he likes to call his "nouveau cuisine," and then he adds these hot Mexican sauces to it, which, in my opinion, really don't go with it at all. However, I'll never tell him that.

"Voila," he announces, placing a finished plate on the table. "This is how the real cooks and high-end chefs do it." Usually tied around his chest is his black, he-man apron; the one that says BAD HOMBRE in orange embroidery. His face is ruddy and flushed from the heat of the stove, making it difficult for me at these moments not to picture horns coming out of his head. I don't say a word and eat whatever he has given me, whether I like it or not, but I doubt he should quit his day job to become a five-star chef. More often than not, our meals are excessively spicy, but then again, from the sight of me, it's not like he's necessarily starving us.

If Craig treated me nicer, our home could be a whole lot cleaner and I wouldn't mind tackling a sink load of dirty bowls and pans from cooking up a batch of brownies or cookies every once in a while. If he just paid me a little more respect, I might even make him his favorite peanut butter bars.

When my mother is about to visit us, I will make a half-hearted effort to straighten up the mess, quickly shoving supermarket receipts, grocery bags, and store catalogues into drawers and the scattered shoes and socks littering the base of the staircase into the garage. No matter how tidy everything seems to me, she will inevitably grouse about my "disrespecting property" and the bad messages I am sending my child. "How can you expect Noah to learn to take care of things if you leave so much garbage lying around? I'm having trouble finding an empty spot where I can put my feet." I don't bother responding with "Yeah" or "Whatever" anymore; she's way too familiar with that routine. Ignoring her comments infuriates her even more.

There are days, however, when I reach my limit with Noah's incessant baby talking and Craig giving me the cold shoulder. That's when I feel even less of a person and more like a dried-up pile of autumn leaves, waiting to be swept into the gutter or thrown into a Hefty bag. At my mother's urging—which she harped on and on about for seemingly forever—I signed up for a nighttime drama course at the local high school. I can't tell you how many times I had to hear, "It will give you a little more stimulation outside of your home," or "Maybe you'll meet some interesting people," or "Perhaps it will breathe some life back into you."

It pained me to follow her advice, but it turns out her suggestion, as maddening and tedious as it was, wasn't such a bad one after all. In case you've gotten the impression that I am a total dud, I would like you to know that I am a pretty decent singer—not that my voice is exactly star quality.

We meet on Wednesday evenings, so supper is a rush job on these nights. I won't leave the house until the baby's in his crib for the night so Craig has less to complain about. He wouldn't know the first thing about properly seeing to Noah anyway. I could pump out a bottle's worth of milk during the day but wouldn't trust Craig not to throw Noah in the crib with it at bedtime and then just walk away.

My theater group is presenting a production of *Fiddler on the Roof* in two months. I play Golde, Tevye's wife. It's a great role, and I'm glad I got it. I definitely looked more like a "Golde" than the size 2's and 4's trying out for the part. So while I feel I am the more talented one, typecasting was definitely at play here, as it should be. On Thursdays, I typically sing all of the show tunes to Noah while we're playing in his toy room. I can't help it, but I always get choked up when I sing "Sunrise, Sunset." Imagining Noah as a grown man leading his own life shatters me. Babies grow up to be kids. Kids grow up to be young adults. There's driving, smoking, drugs, alcohol, illness—much too much for me to worry about. How do I even know that he'll make it past Nathan's age?

Chapter Five

Since I've given birth to Noah, my wardrobe has consisted mainly of stretched out chinos, sweatpants, and old t-shirts. I have yet to be able to button the waistband on my old jeans—bridging a five-inch gap of protruding flesh makes it difficult to do so. I've tried pushing the bulge back toward my midsection and closing the zipper lickety-split, but it's a hopeless situation. That blubber has nowhere it wants to go but beyond the surface of my pants where it can flop and jiggle around freely. As a quick fix, I've fashioned a chain of safety pins to hold the two flaps together or I've opted to wear my used maternity clothes with their elasticated panel fronts. Not exactly what the gorgeous, skinny models don in the slick pages of *Cosmopolitan* or *Vogue*. You won't see them wearing any of the outfits hanging on the XX and XXX racks at Dress Barn and Lane Bryant either, which I have often gone rummaging through as a last resort.

At times, I've been splattered with spit-up, pee, and projectile vomit, so it doesn't pay to wear decent clothes on a day to day basis. Needing to come up with a costume for my role as Golde, I asked my mother if she had anything in her closet that I could borrow for the part, and while she seemed insulted that I would even think we'd be the same size, she said that she would take a good look around. One morning, she called to say that she came up with the perfect solution. She had found an outfit in a box stored in the attic. I told her that I didn't want to wear old musty stuff.

"Kat, don't be ridiculous." She used the same tone as when I was an eleven-year-old and had asked her to please not make me attend the Valentine's Dance at school. I had ended up going and Lawrence Fisher totally humiliated me by pinning a corsage on my chest the size of a football field. "Mom, I hate you. I hate you. I hate you!" I had shouted afterwards. "I was totally embarrassed in front of the entire sixth grade class. Every single kid made fun of me!"

"I'm telling you, this is just what you need for Golde," my mother repeated into the phone, ignoring my protestations. "It's the skirt that Poppy's mother used to wear."

"Mom, I said No. No thank you. What part of that don't you understand? Anyway, that skirt has got to be ancient. How in the world did you happen to have it in your attic? I thought you got rid of a ton of stuff each time you moved."

"Somehow, I kept this one box with several things in it." Her voice grew thin at the end of her sentence and her focus seemed to trail off in another direction. Where her mind had wandered off to I had no idea, but then, in all of an instant she came back to me. "Kat, just so you know, the skirt will be here if and when you want to wear it."

Sighing with frustration, I told her, "I'm not going to wear something with mold all over it."

"There's no mold."

"It's not what I had in mind."

"Once again, you're making a huge mistake."

"It could be all ratty and contaminated from other things," I responded quickly. We had a kind of verbal jousting match going on.

"It's not ratty. I never said it was ratty. I wouldn't use that word in any case. Actually, it's in pretty good condition. They made things really well back then."

Poppy was my mother's father. They had a lousy relationship, and I was surprised that my mother would hold on to anything connected with her father—even something somewhat remote as an old skirt. When he died in 1992, the overriding sentiment shared by our family members was one of relief. The kind of relief that a relative gets when they see their loved one released from a long-term jail sentence. The official cause of Poppy's death was lung cancer, but he wasn't the one who was being freed; it was everyone else.

When the rabbi had arrived at the house to gather information for Poppy's funeral, there was a lot of laughter and chatter around the dining room table. It seemed to me that neither my aunts nor Nanny had been overcome with tremendous sorrow, but my mom did keep to herself, appearing somewhat agitated and sullen. Obviously, no one was around then to give her the advice that she dishes out to everyone else nowadays: "If you bury your feelings, they'll turn septic inside. Why carry an extra load if you don't have to? Speak out; share what's on your mind. Your body will communicate it anyway in spite of yourself."

I can recall when I would have sleepovers at Nanny's house seeing a painting of Poppy that my mother had made. The portrait hung over Poppy's armoire and I would stare up at it before it was "lights out," giving me a good dose of goose bumps and nightmares. In the painting, Poppy was wearing a shirt, jacket, and tie, looking somewhat imperial and distant; my mom had used sharp brushstrokes and a cold palette. Usually when Mom paints, she stands in front of a blank canvas and has no idea what's going to come out. This portrait was based upon a photograph, however, and Mom had tried to make it as realistic as possible. It's funny how emotions come through, even when we don't want them to.

Poppy was a tall man. With his mustache, balding head, and thick English accent, he cut an imposing figure. My mother hardly has a British accent except when she says certain words. My brothers and I would make fun of her whenever her accent used to come out; this quirkiness was so out of character for her. She tries so very hard to do and say everything just right. Other than knowing she is the youngest of three sisters and was born in England, I'm in the dark about a lot of her past. I don't know anything about her parents' parents—where they lived or how they made a living.

After my mother started to endlessly obsess over me in my teen years, I did my best to avoid her attention as much as possible. I had ducked out on most of her conversations and had refused all her subsequent invitations to learn how to cook alongside her. It's silly how little I know of her personal history, but that's more of my doing than hers. One day, Noah might want to learn the names and legends of our family tree and I am going to come up short. I should make an attempt to gather this information for his sake and share it with him when he's older—only the good parts that is.

Chapter Six

My mother's home is a short twenty-minute ride from where I live. On the days when Noah and I drive to see her, he becomes excited as soon as we approach the entrance to her community, squealing with delight at the prospect of seeing his beloved Nana.

"Lunch is all set," she announced on one such visit, wearing a tie-dye tunic over green stretch pants and running like a mad woman who had just won the lottery to greet us by the curb. Noah was so eager for my mother to lift him from his car seat that he tugged at his seatbelt and then his little legs and arms shot out in every direction. I had purposely dressed him in the expensive navy and white Ralph Lauren polo and matching shorts she had bought him. Typically, I get his clothes at Target or wherever I can find a good buy on clearance.

Observing their mutual joy reminded me of how wonderful my own mother-daughter relationship had been in my early years. However, when I had entered my double-digits, for some unknown ridiculous reason, she became overly controlling: "Where are you going? With whom? What time will you be home? That skirt is too short. Make sure you do up your top buttons." Our relationship had nowhere to go but south.

We proceeded into the kitchen, and Noah was positioned in his high chair clutching his Elmo bib, prepared to eat the goodies my mother had prepared. A bowl of cooled down macaroni and cheese and homemade pea soup were waiting for him along with a sippy cup filled with chocolate milk and a strawberry doughnut dowsed in sprinkles. When it comes to Noah, my mother's concerns about eating healthy seem to go flying out the window. There is no limit to how much sugar and carbs she can parade in front of him just to elicit a smile from his face. Shoved before me was a plate of mixed greens, a salad piled high to my eyeballs, and a full glass of Crystal Lite. The absence of carbs was obvious and her passive aggressive behavior hit me right in the gut.

I wanted to start right off the bat by yelling at her, but instead said, "So, I was thinking about talking to you today about family stuff." Even I was surprised by my businesslike tone.

My mother was busily popping blueberries into Noah's open mouth like a carnival game. You would think there was a giant stuffed panda bear prize waiting to be won. Each time a berry fell to the floor, she let out an exaggerated gasp to fuel Noah's amusement. I wondered how long she could keep up the charade of "oh, oh" and "clumsy Nana!" It was becoming annoyingly tiresome. How different it had been when Nathan, Stephen, and I had been children at the dinner table. The eating habits she was now instilling in her only grandson deviated considerably from that strict code she had exacted upon us. We had been rigorously taught to keep our elbows off the table and our utensils placed vertically on an emptied dinner plate. No, Miss Manners' suggestions for dining etiquette had not gone unheeded in Myra Sturnberger's household, but when it comes to Noah, my mother's rules have vanished.

47

"What family stuff are you talking about?" she asked, not turning her face, but I could still tell it was plastered with a larger than life grin. I gave her a nasty look. *Oh, so you're aware that I'm here as well?* I had purposefully worn my hair down in a style she prefers, but she hadn't said a word about it. *Why did I even bother?*

"I've been thinking about Nanny and Poppy a lot lately, Mom. And about what you were like as a child and about Aunt Esther and Aunt Joan." With her clown-like gestures and her working so hard to keep Noah entertained, I wasn't sure if she had heard me.

"What dragged this up?" she finally asked, sounding confused, which was understandable. Here I was at 28 years of age and I had never inquired about this before. "Oh, I know," she said, bobbing her head. "It's because of the skirt. It's got you thinking. Hasn't it?"

I finished chewing on a piece of iceberg lettuce, thinking it would have tasted a whole lot better with blue cheese dressing. I knew enough, though, not to ask for some and I didn't care for the low fat/low calorie dressings she typically had shelved in her refrigerator with expiration dates at least six months overdue. "Those dressings are still good," she likes to say. "You can't go by everything you read. It's a crime to throw food away. I used one of them yesterday and it didn't hurt me." Yes, I've heard all about the poor children in India and Bangladesh, but that doesn't mean I have to be a sucker for her food poisoning.

"Mom, you've had this box in the attic that you must have moved with you every time you've changed houses and you've never mentioned anything about it to me before. I've seen every one of Dad's old toys, stamp books, and collectibles, but you've never showed me a thing from *your* past."

She shot me a quick look. I couldn't tell whether she was more stunned or annoyed by my question or just disappointed she had run out of blueberries. I bit into a cherry tomato and stared back at her.

"Kat, I tried to have discussions with you, but you didn't seem to be interested in me or what I had to say. What you would do is run off all the time and slam the door to your bedroom with either the TV or music blasting."

"You're talking about when I was a young teenager," I defended. "All girls go through that stage."

She slapped the table loudly with her open palms and gave me such a condescending look that Noah jerked out of his reverie and began to whimper. "Well Kat, it doesn't seem like you ever came out of that stage." She then proceeded to tickle Noah under his arms and chin until she could observe an abrupt change in his mood. "Is your Nana being silly? Is she? Tickle. Tickle. Am I being silly?"

"Mom, I'm asking you nicely, which you know is so hard for me…so please, tell me about the box."

She tossed out, "It's just a box with a few nostalgic things in it from England," and then hid her eyes behind two sets of fanned fingers. "Peek-a-boo," she cheeped to Noah. "Eat your quiche before it turns cold," she barked at me.

I looked down at the food in front of me just to make sure it was her and not me who was acting bonkers. "I don't have any quiche. There's just rabbit food on my plate."

"It's there all right," she corrected. "You just have to dig beneath the surface."

I was hoping to prove her wrong, but I did manage to spear a fork-load of spinach/cheese pie that I discovered hiding beneath the lettuce. Adding to my disappointment, it actually tasted delicious. "Firstly, this portion is big enough for an ant, and secondly, where did this recipe come from?"

"I just love experimenting with different ingredients," she bragged. "It wouldn't hurt you to try doing the same once in a while. After all, it's in your blood. That portion is perfectly adequate, by the way. We're supposed to eat no more than a fistful."

"You've given me a thimbleful," I grumbled, but my complaint could just have well stayed locked inside my head for the lack of response it elicited.

Yet again, she was totally wrong. Nothing about cooking is of interest to me now. Nathan was the only one of her offspring who enjoyed being creative. My mother began to ramble on about a quiche she once made for a friend while she stood to grab the sponge from the sink to wipe off Noah's tray.

"She asked me what I had added to give it a 'tang'. After I told her it was mustard, she said 'what a great idea.'"

I couldn't imagine what in the world my mother was talking about. I rose to fill my glass with ice water from the fridge and eyed Noah bend over the tray to grab my mother's hand.

"Ooh, no Noah baby," my mother yelped. "Don't lick the sponge. It's dirty." Noah broke out laughing and tried to lick the sponge again, then my mother's hand, and then the tray itself.

Mom's immature chant, "Yucky, yucky poo-poo," inspired him to carry on misbehaving even more.

"As an adult, you're supposed to be discouraging this kind of behavior," I advised sternly, pulling my hair back into a ponytail. "You are reinforcing inappropriate conduct."

"Kat, to this day, I remember feeling flustered because the woman paid me a compliment and I hadn't ever received one before that point."

I finished my drink and gaped at my mother. Didn't she realize how dopey she sounded sometimes? I had absolutely no interest in finding out what woman and which compliment she was talking about. I had other things on my mind. For the rest of our visit, she wouldn't tell me what all the contents of the box were no matter how much I tried. I even promised to diet for a week straight if she would just stop being so cryptic about it. However, she did eventually send me off with a sleepy, thoroughly sated Noah in tow with the box propped up against the stroller in the back of my minivan, giving me a strict warning not to throw away any of the contents.

"Take it home. Look through it as much as you like. Try on the skirt. It really is ideal for *Fiddler*. You'll be surprised at how much it can boost your confidence."

The motor was running with the air-conditioning turned on, but I had not rushed to pull my car away until that final zinger arrived. For the most part, I had actually been thinking the visit was a quasi-decent one. Mom's doting on Noah had been overindulgent, but then again it always was. He could have parachuted down into her house all by himself and her reaction to our visit would have been the same. My presence added nothing to the experience; it never does. But then she had to go and stupidly infer I suffer from a lack of confidence? Whether I do or I don't, that was not the time to raise the issue. Oh, why does she always have to throw her two cents in and ruin everything?

Chapter Seven

When we arrived home, I set the box on the dining room table, intending to look through it after Noah went to sleep for the evening. The box was light, but I'm guessing whatever was in it had an emotional weight on my mother. Why in the world would she make such a big deal about the contents? Despite the strain between us, I have to admit that I genuinely do love her and was curious to discover what had been stockpiled inside.

Our mother-daughter relationship certainly has had its rocky slopes, but it was made that much worse when I decided to run off and marry Craig, resulting in a disaster of catastrophic proportions. I understand she sees me as a failure and is disappointed; I get it. Her jabs, however—about my weight or her interjecting proverbial quotes regarding the path to my inner peace—are really getting old. I should be doing this; I should be trying that. "Dress up a little more. Why don't you fix up your hair? Try putting on makeup once in a while." Nothing she says can be straightforward or direct. It always has to be layered with hidden innuendos. Is she actually saying she wants me to be more attractive for Craig or for somebody else? I'm struggling to stay afloat in a no-win situation and I need her support, not for her to continuously knock me down.

For sure, my mother is one tough cookie. At the funeral service for Nathan, she was the only one among us who rose to speak. We remaining three sobbed uncontrollably in our seats, too overcome with grief to share a significant anecdote or a poignant childhood memory. To date, she has never ever cracked or broken down that I'm aware of. I've seen no tears running down her cheeks or tons of moistened tissues tossed away in my presence. I have to ask myself time and again if she is even human.

Craig didn't have too much to talk about when he came home late in the afternoon. His indifference was a little unnerving. After dinner, he commandeered the remote and watched ESPN while I bathed Noah. I hurriedly read Noah his favorite Eric Carle bedtime story *Brown Bear* while rocking him in the glider so I could grab some quality alone time before joining Craig. Noah's eyelids closed heavily as I breast-fed him; I loved hearing his sweet purrs of contentment. As classical music was gently lulling him to sleep, I lowered him down into his crib and he stirred just a little, emitting a weak, ineffective whimper. He looked so angelic in his footed pajamas that I had a fleeting desire to pick him up again and engulf him. This was such a safe, sweet haven.

So often, I have wished to stay in the nursery alongside Noah all night long. There have been nights when I wake up and find myself being dragged by Craig back into our bedroom. Resisting his advances would only make matters worse. He talks about having more kids one day. This, I cannot comprehend. Why, for heaven's sake? He barely notices the one child he already has. God forbid I should accidentally skip taking my daily birth control pill because right now, I already have too much on my plate to worry about.

I knew the skirt, the box, and its other contents were waiting for me and because it was impossible to linger in Noah's room forever, I forced myself to leave, but not before delivering one more kiss softly upon his cheek.

When I entered the den, I found Craig and his interest glued to the Tampa Bay Buccaneers game. Usually, that's a signal for me to use the time to memorize more lines from the *Fiddler* script, but it was the box that my mother had given me that now vied for my attention. Something about it really piqued my interest. I don't why; it was just a worn, medium sized mover's carton that had frayed corners and smelled stale. Two side panels had the markings "Master Bedroom" and "286/286" in black ink. This box must have been the very last one packed and hurled into a moving van. To me, its exterior spoke of insignificance.

"C'mon *defense*," Craig yelled with the crescendo of roars emanating from the TV. I pulled out one of the dining room chairs and started to look inside. *Tell me something I don't know.*

Chapter Eight

Warily, I lifted out a manila envelope that was stacked inside the infamous moving carton. It was bulging with unknown contents, although the words "My Story by Myra Sturnberger" were stenciled across its front panel, reminding me of my mother's painting of the same name, which hangs in my upstairs hallway. I may have forgotten to mention that she's an artist. Oh, but I did previously mention her father's portrait—the one that's all foreboding and mean-like.

It was three months after Poppy's funeral when Nanny called my mother in Florida from her home in Long Island. My parents and I were sitting at the kitchen table. They were huddled over spreadsheets, bar charts, and phony income statements while I was drinking hot chocolate. They were helping me put the finishing touches on a seventh-grade budget report that was due the next day. If I had not been procrastinating all week long, the project would have been completed at least two days earlier and I would have been snuggled in bed fast asleep like Nathan and Stephen instead of having to hear my mom reiterate, "I'm never doing this again," and my father threaten, "This is the last time, young lady, that I'll be helping to do work that should have been done by you." It was five minutes past midnight, and my mom immediately grew alarmed that something was terribly wrong when she heard the phone ring. As soon as my Mom picked up the receiver, she could hear Nanny crying. She told her to take a deep breath while she ushered me away.

"Get into bed now," she had ordered. "You'll have the report bound and ready for school in the morning. I hope this teaches you a good lesson."

After brushing my teeth, I had jumped into my bed but then snuck back down the hallway to overhear my mother share the details of Nanny's conversation with my dad.

"Please forgive me. Please forgive me. Please forgive me," Nanny had sobbed repeatedly.

"Of course, I forgive you," my mother had said in the calmest voice she could muster, "but what have you done?

"I'm afraid to tell you," Nanny had whimpered. "You'll never forgive me."

"Please try and compose yourself," my mom had advised. *"Tell me exactly what it is that you have done!"*

Nanny explained, "I cleared all of Daddy's closets out and found every gift you ever gave him, still in the original packaging. None of them had ever been worn because Daddy thought everything you gave him was either stupid or not good enough. Afterwards, while I was lying in bed watching the television, I noticed the portrait of Daddy that you made him. Do you remember which one?"

"Yes, I do. Go on," my mom had replied.

Nanny continued, "Well, he's always placed it above his wardrobe, even though he said it wasn't any good."

"Okay. Go on," my mom encouraged.

Nanny had to blow her nose and wipe her sniffles before she could speak again. "I opened the drawer to my side table and took out my manicure scissors." Her tone grew even more somber. "Are you sure you want to hear this? I am so ashamed."

My mother had been losing her patience and had to yell, *"Just tell me what you did!"*

"Don't yell at me. Please don't yell at me," Nanny had pleaded. "I'm going to tell you everything now. I got out of bed and went over to the painting. I took the scissors and stabbed him in the face. And then I stabbed it and stabbed it and stabbed it. I kept on stabbing it until there was nothing but shreds hanging on the wall. Can you ever forgive me for killing your painting?"

Mom told Nanny not to worry and that what she had done was a good thing. She told Nanny that she needed to start doing more things of this nature. My mom had then asked Nanny if she wanted her to paint another portrait, this one with Poppy's face in the center of a bullseye, and she could score points depending upon where she hit it. This part made me chuckle, or rather snort, which is an obnoxious habit I have retained into adulthood. I became terrified that my parents had heard my laugh so I raced back to my room and threw the covers over my head.

The painting I have hanging in the hallway opposite my bedroom is the largest of ten that my mother loaned to us for our townhouse. Noah sees scary monsters in some of its shapes and has to be held whenever we pass by. I see nothing but Egyptian hieroglyphics in it; because it contains so many images and there are sections that I don't understand. If it wasn't for the bright orange and green coloration that goes so well with the décor, I would have given it back to her ages ago. As if it isn't enough for me to be miffed by my mother's evasiveness, I have to be confronted by it each and every day in her art. Again, I'm in the middle of one of those stubborn "sticky" situations, which repeatedly and obstinately stare me in the face as if to say "We're not going anywhere, so you might as well just get used to our hanging around."

A string was tightly wound around the clasp on the back of the manila envelope; it took several revolutions to undo it. Whoever sealed this envelope did so with a vengeance. I withdrew a pile of papers squeezed together tightly by a paper clip. The clip's tension was so taut it was as if the papers had been inside a pressure cooker for decades. I wondered who had compiled the contents. "My Journal" was typed across the cover page of one set of papers, and then I found another set with the title, "Black Bubbe." As I wasn't in the mood to probe further into this topic, I dropped the envelope and its papers on the table and looked deeper inside the box. I extracted a miniature red hardcover book loosely held together by an unraveling spine. Several of the tissue-thin pages had become completely unglued. The little book opened from left to right and was titled "Prayer Book for Jewish Sailors and Soldiers." Uniformed blocks of black Hebrew letters filled some of the tawny spaces, while some areas appeared to be completely worn away.

On the front page, there was an inscription written by someone whose penmanship was impeccable, indicating that the author might have been a perfectionist and extremely mindful of his thoughts and actions. Each word slanted at the same precise angle. Each loop was the same shape and length. I could tell that the exact amount of pressure had been placed on each letter, keeping the flow of ink uniform throughout.

Next, I discovered a small gold circular charm. It was inscribed to the "Captain of the Cricket Team" and dated 1926. It occurred to me that this might be something to bring to the *Antiques Roadshow* the next time it came to Miami. Then, I pulled out a ballpoint pen that had the word "Cunard" going down the side. There was a teeny plastic replica of a cruise ship in a yellowed capsule that was part of the body of the pen. When the pen was new, the ship probably sailed through fluid in the capsule each time the pen was tilted. *A menu from the Titanic reaped a nice chunk of change in on one episode of the Antiques' show. This pen might be worth really big bucks!*

"Yes!" Craig's voice bellowed from the den. I truly hoped the team scoring was the Bucs, or else I would be burdened with further grumblings about my and the team's shortcomings when it was time for us to go to bed. There is no question that I'd rather have him in a good mood because of the Bucs' game—or any other game for that matter—so he would be less of a bully and more considerate towards me later on. There is a definite correlation between some game outcomes and Craig's level of aggression. He forgets he's just a spectator. He forgets that I'm a person and not a ball to be thrown around.

As Craig jumped up, so did his red T-shirt with the Jolly Roger logo spanning his premature, middle-aged torso. He shot his arms triumphantly into the air and spun around, noticing for the first time my presence by the dining table.

"Where have *you* been hiding?" he asked as if someone had just shot him with a dose of epinephrine. He lifted his matching red cap to smooth down his hair and then replaced it on his head.

"I've just been going through some things my mother gave me." My tone was neither enthusiastic nor disinterested. "How's the game going?"

"Fantastic. I've got some money riding on these boys, and they're not letting me down. It's putting me in a lovin' mood, if you catch my drift." He raised his eyebrows and his whiskey glass in unison.

I turned back to the box and muttered, "There's quite a bit more to sort through. Don't count on me going to sleep so soon."

He said, "I never do," as he shrugged and gulped his drink.

I plunged my head deeply into the box as if I was trying to reach something beneath the table, the flooring, and even the foundation of the townhouse. I heard the clink of ice cubes falling into a glass and the rattle of liquor bottles. Craig muttered something and I pretended his words were not intended for me.

Perhaps I could find a solution or some solace to this hellish predicament beneath all of the relics in that damn box. I dug up an old rubber ball that looked like it might have belonged to a dog. Its irregular surface had multiple chewed off sections; some of the material crumbled as I held it in my palm. I felt as eroded as the object I was holding.

Next came the skirt. The woven skirt my mother seemed so desperate for me to reinstate into the world. The charcoal gray material was coarse, filthy, and, frankly, was about one inch of burlap short of a potato sack. What could possibly have gotten into my mother's brain that she would even call that a skirt, let alone suggest that I might use it? Who would want to wear something so disgusting? My grandmother's life must have been miserably poor. I wanted no part of it. *Mom, you are so off track with this suggestion. If this doesn't clearly indicate you've lost your marbles, I don't know what does.* When I finally unraveled all the tons of fabric, it resembled a wiry web.

The box, however, had still not been completely emptied. An official-looking document appeared to be tucked into the bottom, held in place with masking tape. It was labeled "Fetal Death Certificate" and was dated 1967. The name "Myra Kaufman" had been entered in the section labeled "Mother." I did a quick calculation, and this indicated my mom must have been just 17 at the time the certificate had been created. *She got pregnant as a teenager?* Wow; this was news to me.

"Get up here already," Craig called from our bedroom. "I'm ready to bring the term 'rough sex' to a whole new meaning." His words came out slurred.

Chapter Nine

The next morning, during Noah's first nap of the day, my mother called to ask me how the skirt fit. I was in the middle of catching up on the last few shows of *The Bachelorette*, trying to release some space on my DVR. I told her that I had not even tried it on. It had looked diseased and atrocious. Again, she stressed that it probably was just like the skirts the women wore in Anatevka. No kidding. I replied that this was Community Theater and the costumes didn't need to be that authentic. I wasn't so sure that I wanted to go near it ever again. My mood was bitchy, and I was taking out the discomfort experienced from last night's episode on her.

"So, what's with all the junk that was with it?" I asked.

"I don't look upon that as junk." From my mother's tone, I could tell she was put out. "Did you see the envelopes?"

"Uh huh."

"Did you read anything?"

"No. Was I supposed to?"

Mom's comment, "It wouldn't bother me either way," really irked me. I definitely do not appreciate her being so indirect and devious. I clicked over to speaker mode and sauntered into the bathroom, carrying the phone in my bathrobe pocket. Taking out a bottle from the vanity, I pumped some moisturizer into the palm of my hand and began to massage my legs and arms. Craig's notion of rough play had left sores on my wrists and shins.

"Why didn't you just come right out and tell me to instead of playing games?" I asked. "What exactly is in the envelopes? Are these legal documents I'm supposed to be holding on to?"

"Not at all. They' just some stories I had written and thought you might enjoy reading them." My level of unease was already zooming off the charts; I didn't need her to be that aloof and cagey.

"Ugh. Just stories? About whom and what? Can you be a little more precise or is that asking too much?"

"Just stories about my family—well, in a way you could say the stories comprise a sort of journal," she explained further in an excruciatingly impassive voice.

"How long have you been doing this? I've never heard of you writing a journal before. This is all news to me!"

She told me that there wasn't anything to get so stirred up about. "You recently complained that I haven't shared much with you from my past. Now I'm doing it. There are anecdotes from my childhood and those from a few generations back imparted to me throughout the years. Perhaps you may find something quite powerful in them."

A wave of fear shot through my body. I purposefully refrained from mentioning anything about the death certificate I had found. Was there something sinister lurking in our family history that she was now trying to bring to light? What took her so long to inform me of this?

"Shouldn't I have learned about this when I was pregnant with Noah?" I asked. "What if he becomes seriously ill? How does all this connect with Nathan's illness? If there is something specific I need to know, can't you come right out with it and just tell me? I don't have a whole lot of time to sit down and sift through your old stories right now!"

I could hear my mother let out a long deep breath, indicating her patience was growing thin. "Kat, I'll take the box back when I come over during the week." She sounded just as annoyed as she typically did, not bothering to mask her irritation. "I'm sorry now that I even gave it to you in the first place." When she ended the call, I was happy to go back to my TV viewing.

So, Noah ate his lunch and played with his fire engine and other cars. In the afternoon, we took a quick ride to the supermarket, where he was fascinated by the lights and various shapes and colors on the stacked shelves. Pretty soon, however, he was squirming to get out of the cart, so I Velcroed an anti-spill container to his wrist. He munched on his organic puffs and forgot about wanting to be held. When we got home, there was a message from Craig letting me know that he would be coming home late. The day seemed to drag on forever. Noah and I played with his drum set and activity centers. He dropped some balls into his plastic pint-sized basketball hoop and I applauded each time he scored. Pretty soon, he was pretending to score a point just to see if I would still respond.

"No, buddy. The 'yay' has to be earned," I told him.

The regimen of dinner, bath, bedtime story, and final "top off" was followed without disruption. Upon hearing his heavy breathing, I headed to the kitchen to fix myself a quick meal.

When Craig's away, I usually read the newspaper or a current parenting magazine while eating my dinner. This night, I chose to retrieve the large envelope from the box; the one labeled "My Story." Turning to the very first page of what appeared to be a diary or journal of some sort, I was relieved to see that it had been typed. I was glad that none of the many other entries had been handwritten either. Hardly anyone writes in cursive anymore, but that wouldn't deter my mother from continuing the practice. She believes using internet slang, like OMG, LOL, or PCM, is turning humans into an impolite society.

I decided that my mother's story had to be far more upbeat than what's been filling the news lately. With so much fighting and political unrest going on around the world, I welcomed what I presumed to be a pleasant fictional account of a chubby little girl growing up in merry old England. I anticipated learning about rope skipping, tea and crumpets, and visits to the Tower of London.

Chapter Ten

My parents wanted to attend the opening night performance of *Fiddler on the Roof*, and Craig was insistent that he stay home to babysit Noah. So much for supporting me in my endeavors. To be honest, I didn't need him there if he was going to sit with a disapproving scowl on his face all night long. With no one acting as a buffer between Craig and my parents in the seating section, the atmosphere between them would have been hostile and extremely tense. We haven't used many hired babysitters in the past, so his staying home wasn't such a terrible idea. I took my time giving him the okay, though, because I wasn't sure if I'd have a one hundred percent sober and alert adult on child patrol. I didn't dare share this thought with him. I didn't need him to become more tee'd off than he generally was.

The show played to a full house, which was great since most people I know have seen *Fiddler* performed umpteen times. Most of the audience was familiar with the lyrics and sang along to many of the songs. It was a feel-good experience. No, Golde did not wear my great-grandmother's skirt. The fabric was too pitiful and cumbersome and would have weighed me down too heavily on stage. I didn't even want to touch it again after the first time I saw it. If it had been a rental costume, I suppose I wouldn't have resisted wearing it as much, but the skirt was an authentic link to the unattractive, ancestral past from which I was trying to distance myself. Why my mother kept it, I can't even hazard a guess. She must have seen some value in it; otherwise, it would have been tossed out ages ago. And what would be her convoluted reason for giving it to me now? What power or magic could it possibly hold? What could I learn from the threadbare skirt of an old, uneducated, Eastern European woman who was probably as vulnerable, powerless, and overly burdened as the characters in *Fiddler*?

After the curtain call, my father presented me with three full bunches of sunflowers. He chose these over the carnations and tea roses because he said he wanted the bright, warm colors to make me especially happy. Craig used to bring me flowers and chocolates when we were first dating. It was his attempt to impress both my parents and me. "How sweet of him," my mother would say, but then would point out, "They're from a supermarket", "some of the buds appear to be dying", and "chocolates will go right to your thighs." The three of us sat in a diner eating dessert before we took our separate cars home. I ordered a loaded, fudge-topped cheesecake and watched my mother fume over her fruit.

I almost tripped as I made my way in the darkness from the den into the kitchen. Discarded Johnny Walker bottles and two of Noah's sippy cups, smelling sour from left-over milk, were lying on the floor. After I climbed the stairs, I fortunately found Noah fast asleep in his crib. Standing outside the door to my bedroom, I heard Craig turn over and punch his pillow. My preference was to wait until Craig fell into a deep sleep before I got into bed, so I tiptoed down the stairs, biding my time and hoping I wouldn't be discovered. It seemed like an opportune time for me to just chill out and unwind after the night's performance.

As far as the box was concerned, my mother never did come to retrieve it as she had defensively vowed to do, although it's not like her not to follow through with a threat. She was a strict disciplinarian when Nathan, Stephen, and I were growing up; Nathan constantly tested her mettle in those years.

The following day, my mom called to compliment me again on my portrayal of Golde. Had she hung up the phone immediately afterward, things would have been fine.

"You're too fat, Kat."

This business about my weight never ends. Nothing fits me because I am still breast-feeding, and even though I keep telling her that, my mother just continues with the eye rolls. It's unhealthy to diet; the baby needs his nutrition. My priority is Noah and I don't care about being a size four Boca babe.

"There's something not healthy going on here," she said. "I think you're hiding behind your excess weight."

My mother loves to play pretend psychologist.

"You're a mess; your house is a mess; there is dirt and dust piled high on every surface."

So what if I haven't had my haircut in a year and a half and the vacuum cleaner is still unopened in the box it came in? I picked up a pen and pad from the counter and wrote, *U can KIMB.*

"Nothing is going to improve on its own. Unresolved, the patterns will just repeat themselves in future lives."

Why don't you G2H? I added on the same piece of paper in block lettering.

"The body retains fat to defend against threats. It's a primordial defense."

I begged off the conversation, pretending that Noah had woken from his nap. "Yeah, yeah, yeah, gotta go…Noah's crying for me."

At lunchtime, I placed a call to Craig in his office, but he could not be reached. He didn't pick up his cell all afternoon. When he finally pulled up in the driveway, I practically dropped Noah on the hood of his car. It was still pretty early in the evening, so I presumed that Craig had come straight home instead of making a detour at the local bar.

"Take Noah for a bike ride," I said before making an about face for the front door, feeling my stomach churn. I needed to be alone and I didn't know what do with my nervous energy, but I couldn't believe how brazen I had been with Craig.

Craig locked the car door and grabbed Noah, holding him sideways under his arm with the child almost upside down and facing back towards the street. "Always such a *lovely* greeting from my wife. I see you're in that *wonderfully sweet, happy* mood as usual."

"How *wonderful* would you feel with pee and spit-up all over you?" The urge to cry rose in my throat, but I did my best to shove it right down. Hearing Noah emit a prolonged "Whee", I asked Craig how long he was going to let the blood rush to our son's head.

"You always look like a mess," he replied snidely while Noah kept twisting to turn himself around. "All I ever see you in are those sweatpants. Why would tonight be an exception?"

"Just take your child for a goddamn bike ride, okay?" I waited for some nasty put-down to come spewing out of his mouth. Maybe even he was a little thrown off by my rare assertiveness. I certainly was. This spurred me on to add, "God knows I do everything else for him around here. And could you please hold him like he's a human being instead of a package?"

"That's right, *your highness*. I forgot I'm married to *Wonder Woman*." The volume of his voice then turned up and he sounded all nasally. "When was the last time you came home from a full day's work, after sweating all day in a stuffy office, trying to earn a decent wage so there would be food on the table that you do a whale of a job ingesting? Don't you think I'm entitled to a little R and R? I had him all last night—or did you forget that?" At this point, he finally brought Noah upright and swung him forward to rest against his chest. Noah's dampened hair was pasted to his forehead and he seemed a little dazed. I didn't like the way Craig had just manhandled our son.

I ignored his last remark and headed into the house, not bothering to call him out on the "being in the office all day" lie either. Fear forced its way from somewhere in my insides and nudged at my conscience. *Would Craig ever hurt Noah? No. Not intentionally. Never. Don't be so ridiculous.* I sighed with relief when I entered the house and heard the rise of the garage door instead of my husband's footsteps thumping toward me. Next, I heard the recycling bins being dragged across the garage floor and Craig's bike being rolled out onto the sidewalk. Standing in the dining room, I stalled long enough to hear Craig tell Noah, in not too harsh a tone, that the helmet was going on whether he liked it or not. Noah was probably tensing his back and vehemently swerving his cheeks in opposition the same way he does when he's about to eat a green vegetable I'm foisting on him. I was glad that Craig cared enough to make sure Noah was properly protected.

On my way to the bathroom, I grabbed a new bottle of bath oils that I had picked up at the supermarket and then I grabbed my mother's so-called journal. I planned on taking an infinitely long soak in the tub and not resurfacing from the bathroom until after Craig and Noah had finished with their dinners. There was zero possibility of Craig letting me get away with something like that. The only thing I had going in my favor was that he loathed my presence that evening as much as I hated to be around him.

Chapter Eleven

There are times when Craig can be awfully affectionate and sweet. After many of our fights, when he's remorseful and contrite and pleads for my forgiveness, my heart goes out to him. That's when I truly believe he intends to change for the better, but as it turns out, his promises are very short-lived.

"I'll do better. I will."

"How can I believe you?"

"Because I'm standing here in front of you, begging for you to forgive me. We're a team, you and I. We made Noah together. You know how great a kid he is—you say it all the time. We must have done something right. Let's put some ice on your cheek. It will help the redness and swelling go down. I honestly didn't mean to hit you so hard. It was an accident. You could see by your own eyes it was an accident. I want a chance to get us back on the right track again. We love each other. Come on babe, one more chance. That's all I need."

Much of Craig's problem is due to his not having played pro-ball. When he is able to finally work through this issue, I'm absolutely certain that he will be back, full time, to being nice again. I hope against hope too that when Noah's older, Craig will be encouraging him to play sports and will surely want to spend a lot more time with him. Yes, that's definitely when the father-son bonding will take place. I can see it clearly happening. I can.

When my mother tells me that she's concerned I might have a heart attack or develop diabetes, that's a cop out. She's really afraid that I'll succumb to the illness that Nathan had. She doesn't know it, but a few months after Nathan died, I had a ton of blood work done. The endocrinologist said there was nothing wrong with me other than the fact that I needed to lose weight, but by then I was already pregnant. Since then, I've been on a ton of diets and have lost loads of pounds. Unfortunately, they've all come back to find me again. At least I make sure that Noah eats right. I don't want him having weight or body issues when he grows up. Nothing but home cooked organic foods for him.

My mother claims I'm angry all the time—that I'm constantly judging and dumping on others. When I explain to her that I am suffering from backaches, she tells me these are all connected to my mental and emotional states. She hands me books on the subject written by famous doctors only she has ever heard of, which I toss in the stacks of clothes in my bedroom. "No, I didn't get to reading them yet," I tell her over and over again until the she finally stops asking which chapter I'm up to.

She brought me to see a pain management specialist who put a ton of needles into my neck and back. "Of course, you know," the specialist pronounced, "that losing weight will definitely have a profound effect in lessening your back pain." *And I had to pay for that advice?* I did not heal, and everything hurt a great deal more! Even after six sessions, there wasn't a tiny bit of improvement in my condition and my body had as many holes in it as a sieve.

She brought Nathan to see a psychic doctor when he first got ill, and what good had that done? This quack told Nathan he had parasites and gave him a truckload of herbs to take, which Nathan complained stunk to high heaven, but my mother, who seems to know something about every subject in the world, had corroborated that herbs had extreme healing qualities. Where did she come off professing to be an expert in this area as well?

The so-called doctor had intoned to Nathan over the phone for over thirty minutes. I can't believe my brother actually listened to that drivel, but he wanted to get better so badly, he would have tried any remedy at that point. I can imagine Nathan's face mocking the doctor on the other end. The doctor had said he wanted to speak to Nathan's kidneys directly. It's no mystery where Nathan probably placed the receiver. Nothing helped. If my mother is such a genius and knows so much, then she could have—should have—saved Nathan. It's that simple.

At some point, my mother needs to let go of her quixotic flightiness and come back down to earth to face reality with the rest of us! This is where people get sick. This is where people die. This is where *we are hurting*. Instead of cockamamie remedies, an old skirt, and little anecdotes—which stupid me actually reads in every one of my spare moments to find out more about her crazy past—I wish she'd give me something I could really use.

That evening, Craig had an appointment to sell a joint Long-Term care policy to a middle-aged couple who were referred to him by a friend I had never heard of before. The possible commission, being quite sizeable, justified Craig treating the clients to an elaborate, lengthy meal. I got to stay home to toss yogurt melts into Noah's mouth and play tag with a rambunctious and overly tired child, who surprisingly gave me no trouble when it was time to go to sleep.

Chapter Twelve

When you choose to live in a gated community in South Florida, you have to abide by the enacted rules. Craig, of course, believes that these regulations are written for everyone else but him. Without consulting with me first, Craig bought a motorcycle, which was a direct contradiction to the covenants governing where we live. It was one of those noisy, in-your-face, chrome-splattered, souped-up ones—with handlebars fittingly called *ape hangers*—that the homeowners' board of directors were hell-bent on keeping out of our neighborhood.

He and his buddies had collectively decided to purchase Harley Davidsons and black, leather jackets—the virile, *Weekend Warrior* kind with ample built-in armor—and belted, buckled, iconic boots that went along with their bad boy theme. I had arrived home early one evening from the *Fiddler* post-production cast party, slipping past the card-playing group without Craig even noticing my return. There was a more than usual oomph to the vibe in the room; a lot of raucous whistling and snickering in the marijuana-tainted air. The men spoke—or rather whooped it up— about an upcoming trip to the Keys with their choppers and *old ladies*. They mentioned a hog parade along I 95— aka *the big slab*—with the curvaceous legs of their women snuggling tight, flanking the guys' sides and the women's delicate arms squeezing their middles.

"Nothing but hardware between us and the thrill of danger."

"We should all grow beards."

"It'll be the perfect combination of awesome and cool."

The testosterone was flying high among the cave men.

I had purposely stayed awake to ask Craig about the biker trip when he came to bed. "How am I supposed to get away? What am I going to do with Noah?" He was as equally surprised by my conscious state as he was by my questions.

Standing outside the bathroom door, he submerged his hand beneath the waistband of his plaid boxers, vigorously scratching his pubic hair. "What? What did you just ask me?"

"Your biker trip. Who's going to take care of Noah while we're away?"

He ceased scratching and lodged his hand on his hip. "Ah, I knew we wouldn't be able to ditch the kid for the trip, so I just figured I'd go stag."

"What if my folks could watch him?"

"Oh, hmmm. That's an idea for you." Lifting up the edge of the sheet, he slid in next to me and cupped my breast. "I'm serious now. Do you think you will fit?"

"Fit on the bike or fit in with your friends?"

He didn't answer me. I hated myself then. I hated myself for ever having confided in him, for once trusting him enough to share the most painful, intimate memories of my youth, for telling him about not fitting in and feeling like an outsider. He lowered his head and was sucking on my nipple.

"I'm not in the mood for this," I had told him.

"Too bad. I am."

I wished I had gone ahead and bought one of those inflatable sex dolls that I'd read about in a pop-up ad on my computer screen. "Shanteen" came with three penetrable holes to provide "ultimate pleasure." Craig would not have cared or known the difference if he was banging Shanteen or me. *Maybe Shanteen can be strapped to Craig's back when he rides his bike down to the Keys.*

It turned out that Noah ran a temperature the weekend of the jockstrap mini-vacation, and I ended up having to stay home to nurse him anyway. Not for a second did I buy into the notion that Craig had it in his mind to go solo. I never asked him who, if anyone, shared his seat, or if he had a good time. A few days later, we received a letter from the association's management team directing Craig to either immediately dispose of the bike or else face fines of $100 a week leading up to a maximum of a thousand dollars. Again, without any discussion with me, he got rid of the bike.

During my middle and high school years, I did have one really close friend named Beth who felt just as much an outsider as me. We spotted each other on the first day of seventh grade in the hallway by the lockers and knew instantaneously that it was going to be "us" against "them" for the balance of the school year. Beth and I would talk on the phone for hours (texting had yet to be invented), and shared a passion for surreptitiously eating entire containers of cake frosting right out of the can while we complained about how unfairly the world was treating us.

At the end of the school day, we would often choose Beth's house as the spot to crash and hang out. Beth had total freedom to come and go wherever and whenever she wanted. Her mother, unlike my beady-eyed one, was pretty cool, quite possibly because she used to be in show business, singing with a traveling folk music group. She had an arsenal of outlandish hats, sequined mini dresses, and feathered boas in her closet, which Beth and I would gather and bring into Beth's bedroom. We strutted and pranced around like world famous divas while puffing on cigarettes pilfered from Beth's mother's purse and laughing ourselves silly.

Getting fully into character, we would make random phony phone calls, trying to engage unwitting responders into lengthy fabricated scenarios. The test was to see how long we could keep the scripts going before an abrupt click would curtail the game. Had our performances not been so impressive, we never would have had the audacity to audition for the middle school's drama club. Beth convinced me that without our participation, the school shows would be *très dull*. When both of our names appeared on the "accepted" list, not only could I have been knocked down with a feather but this created quite a buzz with the "them" population. Suddenly, we were receiving quite a number of additional gawks and stares in the halls. It would have been nice to have been propelled onto the in-crowd popular list as well, but our status as social pariahs didn't budge an inch.

Neither one of us was ever cast in a lead role, so I was spared the mortification of having "Sturnberger" displayed in bold print across the front cover of a playbill. Beth didn't have to worry about things like this since her last name, Cole, had already been shortened from Kolinsky by her mom for her own musical career. However, Beth and I spent a considerable amount of time conjuring up a better name for me when I made it big and it would be blasted in lit bulbs across a Broadway marquee. Like that could ever happen!

My across-the-street neighbors are into lights in a big way. They're also the kind of people who decorate their lawn with gigantic, inflatable ornaments and blinding, blinking neon-wonderlands on Halloween and Christmas. You can count on seeing large, bouncy Santa Clauses, snowmen, and ghosts shining even brighter and puffier at night. One morning at the end of October, Noah and I were kneeling by the window sill, watching out for the garbage truck. He started screaming as soon as he saw the more than scary, twelve-foot, black-robed witch with a sinister pumpkin face wavering all hideous-like in front of the stucco and wood façade of the neighbors' property. I shut the shade right away and tried to divert his attention. All day long, Noah kept pointing to that window with fear in his eyes. "That's not real. That won't hurt you," I kept trying to reassure him. "Mommy will keep you safe." I attempted to bring him outside to show him up close that the heavy-duty nylon witch, secured by stakes and ropes, was able to move solely because of a motorized fan. "She's not real. She's make-believe." Noah wasn't buying it. Two steps onto the Welcome Mat, he started bawling his head off. Since Halloween is generally celebrated for just one day, I hoped that Noah's frightening experience would be a short-lived one.

At the end of that harrowing day, Craig, with his hair slicked back with gel, arrived home dressed as a vampire from his office's come-to-work-in-a-costume day. The fake blood on his chin had bled into his white cream makeup, and when he spoke, his words came out all garbled because the set of plastic fangs kept falling from his mouth. "*Vhere ees* that kid of mine?" he demanded. "Dracula *vould like* to scare the heebie-jeebies out of him."

I tried to impress upon him that more harm than good could come of it. "Noah's a little too young for that. He's been freaking out all day. He doesn't understand the concept of Halloween."

He staggered toward me. "*Vhy* are you putting up such a *steenk*? *Vhat* concept are you talking about?"

"Just leave him be," I pleaded while backing away. "He's a small child."

"He's a small child," Craig mimicked.

I could smell the essence of peppermint gum mixed with fumes of a lime-flavored gin and tonic on his breath. He turned his sight toward the second floor, in the direction of the room where Noah was fast asleep in his crib; he had been placed there a little earlier than usual. Craig brushed past me and climbed the stairs, teetering from side to side. "*Vell,* I'm going to spook him awake. It'll be funny. It'll be a riot."

I sped upstairs ahead of him, stopping at the landing. I reached out to touch Craig's arm. "You know, I've never gotten it on with such a sexy, ghoulish Count before."

His smile was devilish. "*Vell,* here's your chance." He took a bite out of my neck.

Anyway, getting back to Beth and me: neither one of us liked to perform solo, so we always competed as a duo in the high school regional talent contests, which were held each spring right before the Passover/Easter break. One year, Beth was intensely sweet on this rap routine and insisted that we perform it for the regionals. When she played the song on a boom box for my parents, they thought it was cute. That right there was a strong warning. When older people think something is cute, it's probably a signal *not to go there under any circumstances!* I just plum refused to do it. No matter how much Beth sobbed and tossed her orange and purple dyed hair in my face, I kept telling her that I didn't want to humiliate myself by pretending to be something I was not. No way did I want to give the "thems" another opportunity to laugh at me.

Nowhere, no how, do I have any of that same courage today. If I did, I would think twice about cowering when Craig spins into one of his frightful rages. I would tell him a thing or two. I might even tell him to go fuck himself.

Our singing duos never won a prize or even an honorable mention, but we kept on performing together year after year, even to the point where Beth was driving us to the regionals instead of my parents. Beth bought her own jazzed-up Mustang by holding down three separate jobs a week, which she biked to and from every one of her freshman, sophomore, junior and senior years. Even my overly hovering mother had been impressed with Beth's independence and accomplishments. For that reason, she had no problem letting me ride with her.

"She really is something, that Beth," my mother would say. "She's a real go-getter!" Her voice would spill over with admiration the same way I douse my stacks of pancakes with dollops of maple syrup and melted butter. But then from the other side of her mouth, she would vehemently object, "How can her parents possibly know what mischief Beth is getting into? *Tsk, tsk,* shame on them." There she was, sending her confounding mixed signals, just as crazy as she is now.

Beth's stepbrother was then and still is the star of the famous rock band, Ucnbeatit, so I figured that Beth, through osmosis, had a really good ear for music. We had backstage passes to lots of her stepbrother's band's concerts and even sat on the stage during his Freedom Tour stop in Miami. We were right up front with the roadies, groupies, and drug heads. It was unbelievable. Had the "them" kids in school seen us, I knew they

85

would have thought us pretty cool; perhaps they would have even moved our popularity ranking up a notch or two.

Stephen and Nathan, as the kind of big brothers who generally stuck their noses in their little sister's affairs, didn't shut up about the bad element they presumed I was being exposed to. They used to mock me plenty but did manage to hold back from their teasing in earshot of my mother, who would drive me nuts obsessing over my whereabouts. Nathan had sternly warned, however, that I would be dead meat if he ever discovered I had experimented with drugs.

At the Ucnbeatit shows with Beth, I really felt like I was somebody. When a joint was passed around, I saw Beth take a puff of it and then she offered it to me. Seeing me hesitate, she took another puff and gave it to the guy next to her. I guess I wasn't quite yet as cool as she was then.

I hope against hope that Noah will grow up being one of the cool kids. I don't want him to be too tall, too skinny, too over-weight, too this or too that. I want him smart and well-liked. I want to crush every single hurdle that's going to arise on his path. I want him to be safe. I want him to grow up being unafraid of his father. Am I asking too much?

Chapter Thirteen

There was a brief honeymoon period in my marriage when things were not as horrible as they are now. Craig appreciated being in my company then; that's when he used to affectionately call me his "kitty Kat." I remember laughing with him and sharing some fun times together, the way many happy couples appear to do. He used to be gentle when we made love, waiting patiently for my signal to slip inside and staying long enough to see that I climaxed. The drinking was much less then too. When things were good between us, Craig and I would go out to the movies, restaurants, and even went on double dates with my brother Stephen and his wife Mara.

Stephen and Mara had chosen a brand-new name when they got married; they became Mr. and Mrs. Devin. Craig ribbed them mercilessly about this and their "bleeding heart" liberalism. "Bro, you've definitely lost your balls." "Tell Mara to loosen up on her leash; the chain marks are showing around your neck."

Invariably, several hours into the evening Craig would throw out an incendiary jab about politics or current events, trying to get a rise out of my brother. "This nation is going downhill fast with all the Commies and Muslims we have in the White House." Craig didn't really care about Stephen's point of view or about what any of us had to say; we were all eventually shouted down by his regurgitated, right-wing platitudes. "Single black women with a shit-load of babies are the only ones on welfare; they had their kids just to collect more money!" or "If everyone owned a gun, there'd be no crime anywhere!" or "Taxing the rich is what did America in."

Neither Stephen, Mara, nor I wanted to dignify any of Craig's statements with a retort; we just kept eating and intermittently offered a repudiating fact. At the end of each evening, Craig would magnanimously grab the dinner and bar tab and insist on paying. From a wad of rolled bills he pulled out of his pocket, he would throw down one or two hundred dollars on the table while proclaiming, "These people work hard; they deserve to be tipped well." No one at our table besides Craig would be impressed with this grandiose gesture. I love and respect my brother; he is an intelligent and successful lawyer. I admire that he had the self-confidence to adopt a name that was sophisticated and non-sectarian. On all of those occasions, Stephen did a good job of hiding his true feelings, never voicing a single complaint against Craig just for the sake of peace and harmony within our family. Whatever thoughts he harbored about my husband, he managed to keep to himself.

Craig was more enthusiastic then about roping in clients and carped less about not being a professional baseball player. His muscles were still toned and his stomach didn't have its beer barrel bulge. While Craig was in high school and the star of his varsity team, the local newspapers had gone to town pasting his photo on their front pages each time he whacked another home run out of the ballpark. Scouts picked up on the stories and approached him in his senior year, offering him a position with the minors, but

Craig's parents absolutely forbade him to do anything other than attend college.

They didn't believe that being an athlete was a legitimate career for a Jewish kid. Not many in sports earned the kind of money that is earned today. Craig enrolled at the local community college, but academia never proved to be his thing, so he became a life insurance agent instead. Unfortunately, he preferred the notion of moving about to being stuck in one office chair. We were introduced to each other at a networking event and started dating just after he passed his licensing exams. As soon as Nathan met Craig, he thought there was something really fishy about him. "I can't put my finger on it, but there's something not right," he had confided in me. I had told Nathan, "You're too suspicious of everything and everyone. Being sick has turned you into a cynical grouch."

With Craig's charm and high school celebrity status remaining intact, he was able to impress enough clients to make a decent wage, but even with this success, he was still generally pissed off. Craig grew to hate the insurance business and he took every opportunity to curse his parents and me for forcing him into it. "You've ruined my life!" he tells us often. I've tried reminding him that I had nothing to do with the relinquishing of his baseball bat, but he regards Noah and me as a "noose around his neck." That's a direct quote. If he didn't have us to take care of, he would have "Packed my bags and headed out west to reclaim the fame that I deserve." He's told me this more than once. With the venom spewing out of his mouth, anybody would think I'd cut off both his arms and legs.

Despite the increase in his extended absences from our home over the last few months, fewer commissions have shown up in Craig's pay stubs. Craig tells me that it is now tougher to clinch a deal and get people to part with their money, but I suspect he is doing more fooling around and less selling on these supposed business trips. Stephen keeps asking me how long I am willing to suffer the role of the unknowing, innocent housewife. He was indifferent to Craig when he first met him, but now I believe that he absolutely detests my husband. He's mentioned how friends of his have spotted Craig hobnobbing all over town, each time with a different female on his arm. In response, I typically give my brother a blank stare, thinking this will undermine the credence of his insinuations.

The truth is I'm not ready to move out on my own. Noah is still a baby, and I am holding onto the hope that Craig will one day change for the better. He certainly had no problem transforming from the nice, considerate guy I had originally thought him to be to the monster who constantly accuses me of bringing him down. This is just the way it has to be right now. I'm biding my time. I just have to stay strong and in one piece until some major force comes along—perhaps under the guise of an earthquake or a tsunami—and disrupts the situation I'm in without causing too many casualties.

Chapter Fourteen

"Mom, what's really going on with you and that box? What were you hoping to accomplish with it?" I asked in response to her phone call and inquiry about the baby's health. Noah had developed a slight cough and was running a low-grade fever. Although we hadn't communicated since another one of our quarrels, she had seen my post about Noah on Facebook. "Whatever prompted you to start writing that journal?"

"Nathan," she said, plain and simple.

"Nathan told you to do this?" I asked, trying hard not to sound like I was mocking her. "When? When he was ill?"

"No," she stated impassively. "He told me recently."

"Okay." I took a moment to mull over her response. "Sufficiently weird. How did he tell you this?"

"Through another one of his messages. He said, 'Mom, go find something you like to do, and just do it.'"

"Mom, that's not Nathan talking." I used every ounce of effort to not let my voice express just how exasperated I felt. "These are words from a Nike ad. You probably saw it on TV right before you went to bed."

"But then," she continued, dead serious, "the next day my horoscope confirmed the message for me."

"All right," I said as calm as could be. "I'll play the sucker; what did that say?"

"'Provide help to others in need; you will find the source of their comfort within yourself.' And then, the next day's horoscope told me to 'continue to create and clear away the past.' The day after that, the horoscope said to 'detach yourself from that which is weighing you down.'"

She honestly believed that out of the millions of people who read the newspaper, those horoscopes were intended just for her. She didn't get that horoscopes are written as generalities for entertainment purposes only. She continues to absolutely infuriate me! For someone so intelligent, why does she act like a total idiot sometimes?

"Messages come to me all the time," she went on so matter-of-factly you would have thought she was talking about her shopping plans for that afternoon. "You can't deny that they all point to Nathan. I really believe that he is still around and watching over us."

I wanted to say that Nathan was dead and that was that. There were no messages. No ghostly appearances. Her hanging on wasn't making it easier for the rest of us in the family. She also insists on telling me "We choose the family we are born to." How this actually takes place, I simply have no idea; it's part of her inventory of nonsensical beliefs. Even if I were to accept her premise as true, I can't for the life of me figure out why anyone would have chosen to be born to Nanny and Poppy, as she supposedly had. Furthermore, and this is the bigger question, *why in the world would I have ever chosen to be born to her?*

I guess she was starting to get her back up because she began to speak again. Her tone became aggressive and as pompous as a strutting peacock. "I take it that you are not interested in the carton I gave you. Will you kindly pack it up and have it ready for me to bring home on my next visit?"

"You messed up the first time you made that threat and didn't follow through," I pecked back at her. "I'll return it when I'm good and ready to do so."

I suppose I could have sounded nicer, but I was in a lousy mood. My anger was justified and intense, but it should have been directed at Craig. My body was still hurting from feeling like it was split in two. Craig thinks I'm a prude for favoring the missionary position. When he enters me from the rear—me on all fours—I feel like nothing more than a slab of meat. The entire time he's pumping away at my backside, I'm conjuring up the image of two orangutans copulating at the zoo that I happened upon when I was a little girl. My dad and I had been enjoying a father/daughter outing, strolling along licking our ice cream cones and appreciating a temperate May climate.

"What are those funny gorillas doing?" I asked him.

"Where?"

"Over there." I pointed to the cage diagonally across the path. One furry creature was steadily grinding his pelvis against another furry creature he had mounted, who was firmly locked in place.

"Oh, that. That's just how those animals like to play." My dad took hold of my arm. "Come on, let's hurry over to the manatee exhibit so we can catch them being fed." Picking up the pace, I had to run to keep up with him.

Being a curious eight-year-old, I had not been satisfied with my father's rushed explanation, so I made it my business to read up about those orangutans in the school library. Orangutans and gorillas are pretty much similar animals except orangutans come from Asia and gorillas come from Africa. I learned that male orangutans become extremely aggressive when it is time for them to mate. If the females are not willing and cooperative, they will be forced to be so. Strong females are sometimes able to escape the males' advances, but more often than not, the females have to endure the process even though their interests have not been aroused.

Lately, Craig has been on a new health kick and has been watching his diet. I guess it's working for him because he's dropped quite a number of pounds. His bike rides are getting longer and longer, which definitely works well for me. I've been pressing him to take Noah on these trips; it hasn't hurt for Craig to spend a little time with him, even in this minimal way. By the time Noah sits down for dinner in the evening, he has had plenty of exhausting fresh air; putting him to sleep at night has become even easier.

In addition to this brand-new regimen, Craig tells me he's now starting to do a shit-load of business. I don't know if he's managed to attract additional clients or if he's trying to worm more money out of his old ones.

"Referrals," he tells me over the phone. "I'm getting in lots of referrals. I'm swamped every day writing up new policies."

"That doesn't sound like a bad thing."

"Are you kidding me? It's great! Eventually, they will be paying off big, but I won't be eating dinner at home again tonight."

"Okay."

I hope this burgeoning referral business will turn out to be as lucrative as Craig tells me it is. I have yet to see any increase in the dollar amount of his pay stubs or bank deposits, but Craig just keeps on wining and dining a ton of clients. After his bike rides, he showers and then goes right out the door, wearing his Calvin Klein dress pants and shirts, looking more dapper and debonair than he has in a long time and leaving me with the lingering scent of lavender and sandalwood from his Drakkar Noir after shave. Not without gratitude, I've been spending my evenings in solitude and reading about my family's not so golden personal history.

For some reason, with Craig getting into his new shape, his sex drive has diminished with regard to me. He has been acting a lot less gruff as well. Although when he is home, he's still glued to the TV, watching football and other games non-stop, his beer consumption is down and his attitude isn't as belligerent. I'm not complaining about any of this one bit! I don't care what's up with him. I'm enjoying this freedom as long as I can get it.

Odd as it might seem, I can't believe I miss the old Craig that used to scream at me and treat me like dirt. His recent behavior has been more than cordial and it's starting to freak me out. If I ask him about work, I'm told everything is going fine and running smoothly. What exactly does this mean? Either he's selling more insurance or he's not. He's missed more dinners at home than usual, but brings Noah and me the leftovers from a bunch of late evening business sessions. The bike rides with Noah have continued on the weekends and Craig's even volunteered for bath duty and night time reading sessions. Something is up. I don't know how to act around him anymore. He's starting to resemble the person I fell in love with, but the romance and passion are nowhere to be found. If I walk by him wearing nothing at all, there's no reaction. No grabbing. No sexual innuendos. No fat jokes either. Nothing. We're acting like polite strangers. "Did I tell you that Dan's cousin had twins?", "Tomorrow, I'll be stopping by the cleaners on the way to work. Do you need me to take in anything of yours?"

Is it possible he's been seeking professional help? I've heard him say a million and one times that psychotherapy is for weaklings and yellow bellies. *What about a marriage counselor?* If he's seeing one on the sly, then I'm just going to have to demand my own equal time. There's no way that Craig is telling the entire truth about our relationship.

I rested my hand softly on his crotch when he slid into bed last night and started stroking the mound between his legs. Craig told me he was tired and not so sure he was up to fooling around.

"I think you're up just fine," I replied.

I kept stroking him until the shaft stiffened firmly in my grasp. I lay across his chest and placed his hands around my breasts. "Squeeze them," I whispered as I licked his earlobe. I felt my nipples harden and press into his skin. I slid further down and engulfed his penis in my mouth, licking the stem with my tongue. He came quickly and then relaxed. I curled up to be close to him, throwing my arm around his torso. He shook me off.

"I'm really tired. Kat, give me some space."

I guess something must have gotten into him all of a sudden, because as I turned to sulk in my corner of the bed he sprung around and pinned me face down on the mattress.

"Okay," he said. "If you really want it, this is how it's gotta be."

I was stuck in a senseless cycle of anger and feeling misunderstood. I couldn't help but wallow in my own pity and isolation.

After the unpleasant ordeal of feeling victimized by my own husband, I unhooked my terry robe from the back of the bathroom door, and on tippy toes descended the stairs to the living room. As quietly as I could, I flipped on the table lamp on its lowest setting and stretched myself out on the couch. Bundling up under the knitted, blanket throw was the only way I could feel safe that night. If the world would let me, I would have stayed in that spot forever.

Chapter Fifteen

Craig must not have had a good day at his office. After his car engine stopped humming and the garage door clicked shut, I heard a lot of grumbling and heavy steps heading towards the kitchen, where I was sipping tea by the counter. Noah was busily chewing on stacking blocks in his playpen, distracted further by his favorite nursery tunes ringing out from the CD player.

Loudly, Craig demanded, "And where's the proper greeting for your husband when he gets home?"

I eased myself off of the stool and grudgingly headed toward him. Craig took one step forward but stumbled and almost fell to the floor.

"I'm sick and tired of women who think they know better than me. I'm the man! I call the plays!"

I wasn't sure how to react. He was definitely angry over something and had obviously downed a few drinks already. *So much for the healthy regimen.* He lifted himself up and stood glaring at me as if I had done something terrible to him. I froze in place, not knowing what was going to come out of his mouth next. Craig, positioning himself like a defensive tackle in a Buc's game, rammed his head into mine. He was an antlered goat on attack. *Bam!* My forehead was killing me. Next, he ran to the side table in the den, ignoring Noah, who had now pulled himself into a standing position and was silently observing the havoc. With both hands, Craig picked up his iPad and sent it smashing toward my feet. The tablet hit my right foot, and my instep exploded with intense pain. Immediately, it began to swell and I collapsed on the floor. Craig ran upstairs and shut himself in the master bathroom. Noah started to wail. I wasn't sure if he was frightened by the outburst or if he just wanted to be rescued from his playpen.

"Mommy will be right there. I just have to fix Mommy's booboos." Noah watched me crawl into the kitchen to extract a plastic bag from a drawer and then hoist myself up to scoop ice cubes from the freezer. Just yesterday, I had applied an ice bag to Noah's lip when he cut it on a jagged edge from a tinfoil box. I had left the box on the table while I wrapped up half of a tuna fish sandwich, not realizing that Noah could reach that far from his high chair. Seconds before he had clamped down hard on the metal teeth, I was able to grab the box away from him, but there still was a vast amount of blood streaming from his mouth—way beyond what one would expect from a minor nick. The bleeding stopped within ten minutes of me applying pressure. Had I not learned that mouth injuries in young children typically look much worse than they really are due to the many blood vessels in the area, I would have raced with him to the emergency room of the nearest hospital. A day later, his wound had dulled and he didn't appear to be bothered by it, but Noah cried louder when he saw me with the concocted ice pack. "No, sweetheart, this is not for you. You're fine. This is for Mommy." Noah continued to whimper.

What the hell was that all about? I hoped my foot wasn't broken. If I was lucky, there'd just be a nasty bruise and I'd have to hobble about for a few days. I didn't consider the bump growing on my forehead. *What was I supposed to do about this?* Lately, things seemed to be copacetic between me and Craig. I didn't recall doing anything to set him off. We hadn't had sex as often, but he didn't seem to want it. I'd been reading a lot, but then again, he seemed to be totally detached and into his bike rides and sports shows. *Was this the sort of thing people called the police about? Should I file a violence report? No, this isn't serious enough. The police would probably call this an ordinary domestic dispute. No way was Craig willingly going to leave the house, so calling the police would only make things worse.*

Again and again, he has threatened that the townhouse was paid for by his own sweat and hard earned dollars and I wasn't entitled to any of it. I heard the bathroom door open and shut, and Craig entered our bedroom. I could hear him talking on his cell phone. I wished that he would conk out on the bed and fall into a deep sleep instead. *Tomorrow, he'll probably act as if nothing happened. It'll all be smoothed over. He'll most likely be on his very best behavior—maybe even bring me home flowers as an apology. Maybe I should fix myself up a little bit before he comes home. If I act warmer towards him, he won't get so short tempered with me.*

As best I could, I packed a bag for Noah and myself with diapers and things I could find downstairs and headed off to stay with my parents. Luckily, I had some extra bottles of pre-pumped milk to bring along.

Needless to say, my parents were upset to see the condition I was in. I told them that I had fallen down the stairs and Craig was working late. My mom grabbed Noah while my dad set up the Pack n' Play. Right away she asked about the mark on Noah's mouth. I told her it was a silly accident that had happened yesterday.

Her taut lips opened to form a square. Vertical lines separated her lowered eyebrows. "Are you certain about that?" she growled at me, a predatory wolf on attack. "Are you telling me the truth? Did Craig have anything to do with it?"

"What exactly are you getting at?"

"Just tell me what I need to know!"

Leave me alone. Leave me alone. Oh, God please make the shrew leave me alone. "Yes, yes, and no. I swear to you it was an innocent mishap. He banged his mouth. It happens all the time with little kids. Craig wasn't even at home at the time."

She moved in closer and scrutinized my eyes. My body ached inside and out. I used every effort not to blink.

The supreme interrogator then hugged Noah and smacked a wet, smushy kiss on his forehead. "My darling, sweetheart," she cooed, her face miraculously transforming into a happy-go-lucky expression. "Let's go exploring in the kitchen and get you something delicious to eat." After feeding him a bottle, some oatmeal, and who knows how many other ill-chosen, night time treats, she gave him a bath and put him to sleep. He was thrilled to be on a mini vacation.

I dragged myself over to the couch in their den and flipped the channels on the TV.

"Should a doctor be looking at your foot?" my dad asked.

"Nah, it's just swollen. It'll be fine."

I could tell that my dad was getting more and more distressed.

"How did you fall down the stairs?"

"Wearing stupid flip flops."

"You're the stupid one if you wore flip flops going down the stairs," he responded. I could tell by the tone of his voice that he was pretty upset. "I hope you don't wear them when you're holding Noah."

My mother stood in the doorway and chimed in, "She didn't fall going down the stairs. She's stupid, but not in that way."

"I'm not up to talking about anything right now." I felt weak and my words came out slowly. I paused to take a deep breath. "I'm exhausted. Do you think you could both leave me alone for a change? Mom, I'm in no condition to handle your badgering."

Well, that did it. The floodgates opened up and an entire dissertation came gushing out of my mother's mouth: "I kept prodding and pushing you. I was desperately hoping that you would pick yourself up and leave Craig. No one—no one at all—

deserves to be abused or held in a mental prison like you are. Especially not in their own home!" She sounded frantic.

"I just told you that I'm not discussing this now." *Beagle-eyes thinks she knows everything!*

"I've seen domination before. It destroys lives; it destroys peoples' spirits." My mother ranted on like a fanatic rousing up a crowd of onlookers. All she was missing was a podium and microphone. "You do not have to be subjected to this. Nothing good ever comes from it." Her head shook as her hands sliced through the air. Her face was turning red.

"You look like you're going to blow a fuse; just calm down," I told her, perturbed that she had snared me into her drama. "You're making something out of nothing. This doesn't have anything to do with Craig."

"I don't believe that for one minute." She advanced to where I was sitting and thrust her face within inches of mine. "Okay, smarty-pants. Why couldn't you call him to come home early to help take care of you then?"

"Believe what you want." I turned my face away, pretending not to listen, but her words definitely hit home.

Her voice took on a kinder tone and she took my hand in hers. "For some unknown horrible reason, there is a strong pattern of abuse that runs through our family history. None of us have to continue to be victims."

"You're taking this way too seriously, Mom. It's not worth getting all hepped up about."

"Kat, how could you be satisfied with so little? You have natural wants and rights: to be safe, to be loved. Don't give up. Don't surrender to somebody else's definition of what they think you should be."

The tears rolling down my cheeks prevented me from reading the clues on *Jeopardy* that was playing on the TV screen. I sniffed to clear my nose and throat.

My mother continued. "I love Noah with all of my heart. Of course, I want him to grow up to be a strong independent man, but I do not want you sacrificing your own life to accomplish this. What is Noah learning from his father, how to be a macho drunk? That if you're dissatisfied it's okay to bully your wife?"

All along, I had attempted to spare them the truth, but she was dead-on with her description.

Next came my father's turn. He spoke as softly and concise as always. "There are always other options. You are not alone. Kat, you have a family that is willing to support you. We'll formulate a plan together. We'll make it work."

I looked at the both of them. Their eyes were full of love and concern.

"I'm not ready to leave Craig. I believe that I can still make this marriage work, and I am willing to put the effort in to accomplish that goal."

My mother sighed, throwing her hands into the air. Disappointment was written all over her face. "When you first got married, I didn't know how to reach out to you. Nathan had just died and we were all grieving. I suggested counseling time and time again, but you told me you didn't believe in it. Then I thought that maybe you might miscarry, and that would put an end to the relationship."

You were hoping that I'd lose Noah?

"You said that you really loved Craig," she went on. "I questioned my right to interfere. In wanting you to have a caring, responsive mother, I admit that I went overboard when you were a little girl. I tried to give you a different life than I had, and I went to the opposite extreme. Now, I see scars on your face and bruises on your foot, and I know for sure there must also be bruises on the inside. Don't think for one minute that they are not there, Kat."

Overboard? That's some gross understatement. So what if I am hurting? Without Craig, I'll be alone for the rest of my life. I'm fat and I'm ugly. No one else is ever going to want me.

"You're still a beautiful, young woman, Kat," she began to plead, "with plenty of golden opportunities waiting ahead. I can't bear to think of you living with that monster anymore."

"Craig's not a monster!" *Why am I defending him?*

"Let's make an appointment to see a divorce lawyer," she continued. "You'll get through this, I promise you, and you'll be a thousand-million-times better off for it."

My father took my silence as his cue to call his friend, who was a family lawyer. He left a message saying that we wanted an appointment to meet with him as soon as possible. My mother was going to babysit Noah while my father and I attended the consultation.

My cell phone rang; the screen indicated that the call was from Craig. Neither my mother nor father wanted me to talk with him, but I decided to anyway. They immediately marched into the kitchen to afford me some privacy.

"I'm really upset," Craig said quietly. "I take it that Noah's with you at your parents…can we meet to talk?"

"I don't think so at this time."

"Then I'll say what I need to say now. Can I do this?"

I just listened. He spoke softly in a monotone, as if he was reading a script.

"It's no secret that neither of us is happy. This isn't how I want my life to be. I hate my job. You know that. You also know that I haven't exactly been faithful in our marriage. Well, I've met someone that I think I'm in love with. We've been seeing a lot of each other. She's fabulous; I'm crazy about her. We had a very big fight and it was almost over between us, but I think I've patched that up now. That's why I got so upset and angry tonight. It was wrong of me to hit you. I know that. I'm sorry. I really am. I don't want to hurt you anymore. This woman is willing to give me another chance. She's moving to Arizona and I want to go with her. We're starting a business together—a sporting goods store. Here's the thing: I want a divorce. I want to sell the townhouse for cash. In return, you get to have Noah. No more fighting. This can all be resolved cleanly. Kat, are you still there?"

I ended his call without saying a word and flung my body onto the couch. Hot bile rose to my throat. It tasted sour. Grabbing one of the corner throw pillows, I yelled, "You asshole! You detestable son of a bitch!" I took to pounding the pillow with my fist, wishing that it was his face. Who the hell did he think he was? Did he view me as garbage that he could throw away when it suited him? *Noah was only worth the price of a townhouse?* What about the good times we had? What about Noah's future? Wasn't there anything worth saving and working to fix? What about the love we had once shared together? Was any of it ever real? Had our whole life together been fake?

"He's leaving me," I announced to my parents, who came running back into the room, anxious to get the gist of Craig's message. "He wants to move to Arizona." It felt like I had just been run over by a ten-wheeler truck. I was in more agony than when Craig was attacking me physically.

"Wow, that sounds like good news," Dad said, eyeing my mother. She nodded in agreement at the same time she was rescuing the pillow to restore it to its proper place.

I sat up, burying my head in my hands. "How could he do this to me?"

My father said, "I'm not sure how to respond to that. Mom and I would prefer to celebrate his leaving. We're grateful that we have you and Noah here with us in one piece."

My mother seated herself by the end of the coffee table and my dad sat on a cushion next to me, gently encouraging me to lean in on his chest. "Kat, everything will get sorted out properly when we see the lawyer. It's better for things not to become uglier than what they already are. An amicable separation will be better for Noah and you in the long run."

"Dad, how am I ever going to manage?" I cried, my heart breaking, the fabric of his shirt dampening with my tears. "How am I going to pay my bills?"

"That's what we'll talk about with the lawyer," he told me with a most reassuring, kind voice as he slowly stroked my hair. "Trust me. It's going to work out. Mom and I will not let you down."

That night, I wished I could climb into a rocket ship and fly off to the moon. I kept hearing Craig's words over and over in my head. He hurt me. He hurt me so much. What a fucking bastard! Who was this chick? Where did he meet her? Did I know her? I wanted to run away from everything and everyone. I tossed and turned in the bed, I got up and straightened the sheets and blanket, I went to the bathroom, turned on the TV, got back in the bed, and tossed and turned some more.

I checked the time on the clock radio by the bed. It was 3 a.m. I was still wide awake. Everybody else in the world was lying with their eyes closed, off in dreamland. Their lives weren't falling apart. Only mine was. I plumped up the pillow, pulled down my nightshirt, and yanked the blanket over my head as if I was in a cocoon. No, falling asleep wasn't happening. All sorts of sounds and visions buzzed in my head, so I decided to grab the envelope containing my mother's writings that I had thrown into my backpack at the very last minute. For days, I had been engrossed in reading that kid-lit, full of suffering and heartache—only it was my mother's real-life story. Little Myra's sadness and confusion was making my mother seem a lot less of an ogre, which was a role she had worn so perfectly in the past. She had always been concealing a truckload of vulnerability. *How dare she turn the tables on me now?* Could she guess the part I was up to? Had she shared these same stories with Nathan and Stephen? *What is it that she is hoping to gain from all of this?*

I thumbed through the stack of papers until I reached what I thought to be a different genre. What else was there to do?

"Black Bubbe" by Myra Sturnberger

Bubbe Leah was my father's mother. She had spent the last seven years of her life residing in our home in Stamford Hill, when she was no longer able to take care of herself. For much of her days, she would keep to herself, and we did our best to generally ignore her. My father chose not to speak one word to her for the entire time she shared his home. There was never a "Hello" or even a "Good Morning" or "How about a cup of tea?" As far as he was concerned, she might have very well been dead already.

There were, however, set rituals that had to be performed before Bubbe would partake of any meals or retire to her bedroom in the evenings. All of her food needed to be pre-tasted to prove it had not been contaminated or laced with poison, and my mother was required to check beneath her bed to assure Bubbe no man was in hiding, planning to rape her.

"Ada, do your job," she would direct my mother each night before crawling under the many layers of woolen blankets.

Our home was not a very happy one. As my two older sisters and I were growing up, our parents subjected us to many rules and restrictions—most of them extreme and unfair. We were not allowed to ride bikes, roller-skate, whistle, chew gum, or play with toys, dolls, or stuffed animals. We were also forbidden from interacting with our neighbors.

People would often just stop, stare, and point at us whenever we ventured outside our house. It is understandable to me now why those people would have regarded us with so much

111

suspicion. At the time, however, I had been taught to view these people as the enemy.

One day, I overheard my two older sisters whispering about Bubbe Leah.

"She's ugly," ten-year-old Joan had complained.

"And smells disgusting," Esther confirmed.

"Why does she have to live with us?" Joan asked.

"You do realize," Esther had stated with the full weight and authority of her eighteen years of age, "that she's really a witch, don't you?"

"A real witch? Really? How can you be so sure?"

My eyes widened in astonishment. I took a deep breath and tried especially hard not to skip a single word of Esther's explanation.

"I know it for a fact," Esther declared. "Everyone in Stamford Hill believes it too. She's known as the 'Black Bubbe,' but don't ever let her hear you say that. No telling what she'll do to you."

I had read in my fairytale book—the only book I was allowed to possess—that witches were capable of doing terrible, hateful things, but Bubbe Leah didn't do too much besides drool and sit around. She often parked herself in the crimson armchair angled in the corner of our dining room with her walking stick resting against the tiled mantle. In the winter, she would enjoy the lit fireplace with its cackling sounds penetrating the otherwise dank silence of the room.

On rare occasions, I would join Bubbe Leah when I was feeling exceptionally lonely. Despite being afraid of this "crazy woman," I remember nestling on the floor next to her, getting as close as I could to her thick stockings and trying to ignore her musty old person smell. Wedging my face between the cushion's edge and the excess fabric of her voluminous skirt, the coarsely woven cloth would scratch my cheeks, but I didn't care.

Together, we would watch the British Broadcast programs on our little oak-encased television. The simple black and white images on the children's shows were welcomingly gentle and peaceful. The characters spoke in a sweet singsong cadence, in sharp contrast to the fear-provoking yelling that mainly filled our house at night. Since my grandmother hardly spoke English, she understood very little of what we watched.

One spring afternoon when I was six years old and the London fog and chilly weather had cleared, the opportunity had arrived for Bubbe Leah to reveal the extraordinary magical powers everyone presumed she had.

An Irish family had moved into one of the gray sandstone Victorian houses on Craven Park Road, just one street past the school building that I attended. Their daughter, Julie, bearing lots of freckles and copper hair worn in pigtails, was introduced by the teacher as the newest member of our class. Surprisingly, Julie agreed to play with me one day after school. As we traveled along the short distance together, we giggled and busily exchanged stories, but upon reaching my house, Julie had adamantly insisted upon remaining outside on the sidewalk.

I ran to find my stash of white chalk, and then Julie and I proceeded to the brick wall at the end of the street. We were busily scribbling the numbers for hopscotch on the cement when a crowd of about eight to ten children assembled on the opposite side of the street and began marching menacingly toward us.

"Better save yerself, Fenian," lanky, pimple-faced Billy Cooper had yelled out. "I'd leave now, if I was you."

A different boy with ruddy cheeks tugged at my cardigan, loosening a button and causing it to fall to the pavement. A thick-lipped girl named Marilyn Shaw shoved my chest. The others encircled me and began to poke my body from every side. Julie took advantage of that moment to escape while I suffered blows to my arms and legs. I wanted so much to burst out crying, but I could hear my father's admonitions in my head: "Crying makes you a baby" and "Crying is a sign of weakness." I took off running as fast as I could, my heart pounding.

Billy took the lead in the pursuit and lunged forward to grab me. Because he was so much larger than me, I feared him slamming my head onto the gravel or knocking my teeth out of my mouth. At that same exact moment, however, Bubbe Leah strode ferociously onto the front porch of my house, thrashing her cane vigorously into the air. She bellowed a thunderous roar, shouting in a foreign tongue, which might have been Russian, Polish, or Yiddish; I could not understand a single word of it.

114

Then in English she had yelled at the top of her lungs, "Stop what you doing! If you don't, I curse you all!"

Everyone suddenly stopped in their tracks, standing frozen in place. Bubbe Leah outstretched her free arm, extending her gnarled pointing finger, and gazed upon the motionless bullies.

"A hex on you that harm that child," she warned, making sure to make eye contact with each child present. "I count to ten. If you still here, you covered in warts and be jackass forever!"

Bubbe Leah's eyes rolled upwards, revealing just the whites beneath their eyelids as the skin on her face appeared to turn the color of alabaster, her elevated walking stick held rigid. In a very short time, the street began to empty out. Doors were opened, shut, and then bolted, one by one. I looked around in total shock. The impact she had made on the crowd was truly amazing. I realized then that Bubbe, unequivocally, was a real witch! Esther's point had definitely been well proven.

I followed my grandmother as she limped her way down the long hallway toward the dining room and seated herself once more in her favorite chair. Her weathered face revealed a lifetime of hardship and sorrow. After releasing a winded sigh, she motioned me to her side. I knelt on the floral carpeting and clung to her skirt. Its ruggedness had proven to be a temporary safe haven, shielding me from the anger and cruelty of the rest of the world.

"You be okay," she uttered while patting my head. "Ach, television not only place to act."

Chapter Sixteen

I learned at the lawyer's office that I actually have more rights than I supposed. No matter what Craig had said in the past, he wasn't entitled to all the proceeds from the townhouse. Why I had so easily believed his bullshit regarding our marital assets and how they would be distributed is beyond me. In high school and college, my grades were more than decent. There's a certificate with my name in fancy lettering shoved in the back of a drawer somewhere in recognition of an Honors Master's degree. Be that as it may, my brain must have shriveled up to the size of a pea since then. I guess if someone calls you stupid enough times, you tend to believe it's true.

The law was also distinctly clear that Craig wasn't going to be able to walk away from supporting Noah. At one of our scheduled mediation meetings, he put up such a stink about his required financial obligations that even his own lawyer had to take him aside to educate him and calm him down. It saddens me that Noah has to have such a lout for a father. The Separation Agreement stipulated that Craig be the one to move out of our home before the divorce became final, and Craig readily complied by moving in with his girlfriend. That's something he made no fuss about.

I told him to take whatever furniture he wanted, but he was only interested in his sports' paraphernalia and the new giant television. Noah watched Craig put his things together and waved bye-bye to him as if it was a regular workday. It broke my heart to know that Noah had no idea of the changes that were occurring in his life. Craig headed to the garage and called out, "See ya, kid."

That's it? You're leaving your child and that's all you have to say and do?

The plan was for me and Noah to move in with my parents until I figured out exactly how I needed to proceed, but first I had to sell the townhouse. That meant doing a major clean up job. Mom suggested detonating the place and having a realtor do a staging with fitting rental furniture and specialized knickknacks. Goaded on by her not-so-subtle attempt at reverse psychology, I picked up a broom, a can of Pledge, and a spray bottle of Lysol and went to work. It was amazing how much stuff I had previously shoved behind closed doors, into cabinets and crevices, and onto the garage floor that could now be trashed. I even enlisted Noah in the task of tidying up. We made a game of it: who can toss the bear, doll, or dinosaur in the correct carton? While our family's structure was being totally demolished, I kept the boxes with his toys unsealed so he wouldn't feel too cut off from his own personal little world.

To our surprise, the townhouse sold fairly quickly; a single guy from Canada bought it for a winter refuge. He even bought a lot of the furniture too. We agreed on a mid-December moving date. My father was pretty insistent that my share of the money go straight into my own bank account; he also kept stressing that I was not to dip into my savings for anything until I secured a job and was managing better. The Child Abuse center where I had been working before told me to come back as soon as I was ready, so I decided on a part-time schedule, my mom taking care of Noah on the days I was away.

I packed up Noah's crib, infant gear, and other gizmos and had them transported to my folks' home with my clothes and more meaningful mementos. Noah was already there when the moving truck and three guys arrived. As the truck filled up, I became more unsettled—hollower inside. I didn't feel like I belonged anywhere anymore. It was as if I was suspended mid-air, my legs and feet dangling above the ground.

Initially, I was consulted as to which piles of boxes and objects were going and which ones were being left behind, but after a while, my presence at the townhouse was no longer required. The moving men collaborated at a rhythmic pace, getting the job done methodically. How quickly the townhouse that was once my home assumed an air of indifference. It must have been angry that I was abandoning it, but it ought to have known that I enjoyed very few hopeful or happy day while I resided there. It had borne witness to the pain and humiliation inflicted upon me by Craig at his very worst, keeping my secrets as a good friend would, but now I regarded its lifeless, evacuated spaces with distaste. Before the truck and I drove away, I took a walk-through and one last look at the matured ficus hedge in the backyard, sadly acknowledging that Noah's growth would no longer be matched against its height.

It didn't take long at all for Noah and me to acclimate to our new living arrangements. Truth be told, it was a good feeling not having to watch how I walked or talked because Craig was no longer around to constantly criticize me. I had been on the defense for so long that I had forgotten what it was like to just be me, acting naturally without the worry and apprehension that it was forever going to piss somebody off. With mom and dad on call most of the evenings for babysitting duty, my time has been freed up to pursue the activities that appeal mostly to me. No more Sunday night, Monday night, every night football, basketball, and baseball games buzzing loudly in my head, forcing me to seek out a quiet corner to escape the noise and Craig's unwanted attention. The creepy thing is that I now choose to remain in my room watching the television, reading more of Mom's crap, or just staring into space.

Chapter Seventeen

The Christmas season was soon upon us. Good Christian children everywhere were getting ready to receive all the toys happily scribbled on their wish-lists plus barrels of candy canes, new clothes, video games, and the latest electronic devices. Noah, in his first observance of Hanukah at my parents' home, was about to be introduced to dreidel spinning, eight days of burning oil, and the consumption of greasy food. Knowing my son's preferred tastes, he probably would forgo the potato latkes and sour cream, even if they were laced with applesauce.

"This holiday is not about gift giving," my mother used to preach to Nathan, Stephen, and me when we were much younger in regard to Hanukah. "The world is becoming too materialistic. It is about the rededication to our faith. We don't do things just because everybody else does."

In commemoration of this holiday, the three of us would be allowed to stay up until the wee hours of the morning with a spinning top and a bag of M&M's. Did we sorely resent not being Christian at those times? You bet we did!

In spite of her past sermonizing, my mother was currently going crazy looking for just the right Hanukah present for her grandson. She settled on a Thomas the Train riding toy. "Look over here, Kat. When Noah presses this red button, he'll be able to hear Thomas speak!"

"He'll love that," I told her.

"And look at these things I bought him too." She excitedly pulled out wooden puzzles from one of four shopping bags.

My father, who was reading the TV Section of the newspaper nearby, raised his eyes in our direction.

Mom kept taking items out of the shopping bags as if they were bottomless. Out came books, stuffed animals, bath tub playthings, shape sorters, push toys, and walkers.

"Going a little overboard, aren't you?" Dad asked, shaking his head.

"These are all educational," Mom defended. "I didn't buy anything beyond what he needs. I hardly spent much at all."

Lowering his gaze, Dad uttered, "It's not the money, Myra. I'm not an ogre. I just don't want Noah to lose sight of what this holiday is supposed to represent."

"He'll have time for that when he's grown up a little more," she exclaimed, yanking out an engineer's cap with the caption "Thomas' Lil Helper" on the visor.

"Oh, that's so cute," I gushed. I didn't say what else was on my tongue. I could have called her a hypocrite. I could have said that when I was a child I would have preferred to receive all sorts of goodies too, especially at this time of year. But it was my child who was now at the end of the receiving line. Why should I be the one to screw up his winning the Hanukah jackpot or put a dent in him riding whole hog on Thomas the Train?

My girlfriend Sheila, whom Craig disliked intensely and thought was a whore, invited me to a speed dating event held at a martini bar close to the mall. She said it was a good thing to do if we ever wanted to have dates for New Year's Eve. I tried telling her that the only member of the opposite sex I was interested in was Noah. She wouldn't take "No" for an answer and reminded me that Noah's bedtime was hours ahead of the Times Square ball drop. As a compromise, she suggested that we could skip out early if we both were having a miserable time. I put on my silver chandelier earrings, black, fringed sheath and patent leather pumps, dolled up enough to stir a comment from each of my parents. "You look attractive in that dress," said my dad. "She looks like she's asking for it," said my mother.

The restaurant was dimly lit and crowded with men hoping to look cool in their button-down shirts with most of the buttons opened and women who seemed overly anxious in tight short dresses and ultra-high sandals. I felt older, fatter, and less attractive than all of the competition except for Sheila, whom Craig often referred to as "horse face" behind her back.

Sheila and I sat next to each other during the series of short "dates", which were set to last 3 minutes. When the bartender blew his whistle, the guys shifted to move on to the next females in the row. At the end of the evening, we were supposed to provide the bartender with a list of names with whom we wanted our contact information shared. After the bell had been rung five times, my list was still empty. Candidate number six, wearing black trousers and a D&G type dress shirt, parked his ass opposite me. His looks were so-so, not too irritating. I guessed he was somewhere in his early 40's. Leaning over the table, he lowered his voice and asked, "You want to skip this crap?"

"And go where?"

"Somewhere…less noisy."

I gave Sheila the heads up as I followed number six to his car. He brought me to his apartment in Delray Beach, we smoked some weed, he donned a condom, he came, I came, we got dressed, and he drove me home. It wouldn't piss me off if he never calls.

Chapter Eighteen

During our alone-time together, I took Noah for a ride through our old neighborhood. As I passed by some of the children playing on the sidewalk with their scooters and bikes, I felt a little nostalgic for the life I had hoped to have. Everything appeared to be greener. The lawns had been freshly mowed and edged, their borders looking clean and sharp. The meandering rows of hibiscus hedges were neatly clipped, and the pink, purple, and magenta bougainvillea vines, soaking in the plenteous sunshine, were toppling over from the weight of their blooms. As we headed toward what used to be our townhouse, we drove under a crowning canopy of live oak trees, all of which were far taller than what I remembered them to be. Noah squealed, "Home! Let's go home!"

Outside the garage, it looked like the Canadian—I couldn't tell exactly because he partially had his back to me—was talking with my prior neighbor Sam, the hunk who had planted our ficus fence. Both men were wearing Nike gym shorts and wife-beater shirts. The Canadian was resting one of his high-top sneakers on a basketball and kept wiping his forehead with the corner of his shirt. I think I heard him say, "I won. You lost. Lunch is on you." I waved to them from the street. There was so much sex appeal radiating from Sam's body that I couldn't stop gawking at him. If he was a model in a magazine ad, I would have run to the store— right there and then—and bought whatever product he was pitching. At first, I could tell it didn't register who I was, but then

Sam approached my car with an easy-going swagger and that open, amiable smile of his. The sight of two heavenly dimples indenting his cheeks made me feel even more lightheaded than I already was.

He squatted down by my driver's seat. "Hey, how are you doing? How's my buddy back there?"

"Fine," I announced, lowering my window as Noah pushed at his seatbelt, anxious to get out.

"Can I hold him?"

Sam took my nodding as a cue to free Noah and gave him an enormous hug. "How are things since the divorce? Noah certainly doesn't look any worse for it."

I walked over to where Sam was standing and gave him some cursory details about my job prospects and where I was living. He listened while swinging Noah in the air. Noah cried, "More!"

Sam said that he would have invited me in, but he needed to shower and clean up after his game. He called over the Canadian, who then recognized me. We exchanged pleasantries, although it felt awkward. He was living in what used to be my home, eating at my kitchen table, and sleeping in my bed. I didn't need to hear what appliance had broken down or which toilet was leaking. Our exchange turned out to be at a minimum, so I presumed everything must have been working as promised. I quickly returned my gaze upon Sam's luscious hairy chest that now had my kid pinned against it. Lucky him; I would have liked that to be me.

The Canadian said, "I've got to get going. Don't forget one o'clock at Duffy's," and Sam answered, "Yes, I'll be there."

I unplugged Noah from Sam's protective arms and belted him into his car seat. Like mother, like son, he was not willing to let go of Sam so soon. While my displeased child sniveled, I handed him two toy trucks—one for each hand—and shoved a red-shirted Curious George stuffed monkey under his arm.

"Why not come for dinner next time you drive through?" Sam asked as he gave Noah a peck on his cheek.

Not wanting to sound too overly anxious, I replied, "That's a nice idea. Thank you," and settled in behind the steering wheel. Without any prompting from me, Noah waved bye-bye and blew him a kiss. "Mwah, mwah," he vocalized, a silly lesson learned indubitably from my mother.

I put the car into drive and sat watching Sam retrieve the ball and dribble it into his garage. For the first time in a long while, I was feeling buoyant. I turned on the car radio and listened to Mariah Carey sing "Touch My Body." I sang along with her: *"Put me on the floor, wrestle me around, play with me some more, touch my body."* I checked the rear-view mirror and saw that Noah was slumped over the chest restraint and fast asleep.

This is so silly. I am getting all excited over nothing. He's being neighborly, nothing more. What's the matter with me?

That night, I got into bed and started fantasizing about

getting together with Sam. *Did he mean for me to bring Noah as well? I just assumed not. What an idiot I am. I'll have to ask him when I call. I'm not calling him. He was just being friendly—that's all. I don't need any pity dates! What's his story anyway? Good-looking guy divorced for five years and not married again so far. That's it; he's gay. Why didn't I ever realize that before?*

Strictly on my own accord and not because of my mother's hammering, I have lately been choosing to exercise most nights instead of watching TV, which has cut down on my salt-sugar-fat snacking. My newer skirts and pants are actually beginning to fit me with a lot of room to spare. This looks promising; I'm a long way away from where I need to be, but I'm thinking I might even be able to get my old figure back someday after all.

Chapter Nineteen

Noah's second birthday is approaching and Mom has been in a dither trying to plan the best way to celebrate. She suggested I bake cupcakes for the pre-school where Noah is enrolled for a three-time-a-week class. I don't understand why she can't bake them herself—she's been cooking up a storm every night since Noah and I have arrived. Although there hasn't been a trace of starch or sugary dessert on any of her menus, they have not been disappointing in the least. During the day, her vegetarian, healthy-living cookbooks are spread open by the range and kitchen table, and each night an impressive banquet has been served. We've been treated to delicious butternut squash soups, casseroles, quinoa salads, and fiber packed fruit concoctions. I've taught Noah to say, "Yummy in my tummy," and the both of us have been repeating the phrase often.

While Noah has been enjoying these meals and extra attention that comes with them as much as I do, his personality has gone through major alterations. He has become temperamental and stubborn, furiously shaking his head, stomping his feet, and throwing anything not nailed down. He's acting like the kind of kid in a restaurant that you wish the parents had left home. Just looking at him the wrong way could turn him into Godzilla, King Kong, and the Hulk all rolled into one, making me feel absolutely powerless to control his outbursts. If I capitulate to his demands and try bribing him with his adored organic mashups in the squeezable pouches, splotches of spinach, peas, or apple puree end up on the walls, me, and all over his clothes. Even my mother has not been able to tame the wild beast with her larger than life treats and bribes.

Noah's walking has picked up speed, and his high energy is now running circles around all of us. Mom is forever exhausted from trying to keep pace with him as well as trying to restore order to her home. My little guy, who used to be an angel, is quickly turning into quite the devil with his raging outbursts and erratic screams. Along with the baby fat, his sweetness has been diminishing at an alarming rate. "No!" comes out of his mouth a million times a day, boxes full of diapers or detergent get dumped, and toys get smashed, jumped upon, or abandoned. He stubbornly refuses to go near the potty, let alone use it, and he exhibits no remorse whatsoever for the things he's broken or misplaced, which results in frequent visits to the dining room corner for "time-out."

Noah's mischievous behavior has made it impossible for me to bring him to work, as I had been doing from time to time. Friends in the office conferred that he was right dab in the middle of a horrible stage.

"You start to question why you have them in the first place."

"My parents tell me all the time that a good smack on the bottom never did their kids any harm. I know we frown upon that now, but you can see where they were coming from."

"Try giving him away until he turns nice again, but you'll have to wait forever for that to happen!"

It was my bad luck, as usual, that Noah seemed to be approaching his terrible twos way ahead of the game. After I had told my parents how much Noah's first year's tuition was going to be, they wasted no time in handing me a check for the full amount, saying, "It'll be worth every penny!" I enrolled him at the start of the January term.

At my parents' prodding, I've started searching for a suitable apartment—one that's not too far from where my folks live. Some of my co-workers live in pretty decent, affordable buildings, so I might consider these as possible options. Truth be told, I'm not very anxious to leave the setup I have; all the cooking and cleaning for Noah and myself so far has been provided gratis. This is a lifestyle to which I have well-adjusted and one which could suit me just fine in the long run.

Stephen and Mara were definitely on my mother's guest list for Noah's birthday party. Mom was still undecided, though, about including Craig's parents, who had made the effort now and again to stay in touch. She suggested that I also invite Sam.

"No way."

"It would be a good way to continue the relationship, Kat."

"No way, Mother. Just forget about it."

Although I was attracted to Sam and thought about him a lot, I didn't think, despite the loss of twenty pounds, I was in such good shape and ready to date him.

The next morning, however, my mom announced, "I called him."

"Please tell me that by saying 'him' you are not referring to Sam." Her reddened cheeks immediately confessed her guilt and saved her the trouble of verbally doing so. "You called Sam to invite him? Oh my God. I can't believe you did that! There you go again, meddling in my affairs. When will you ever learn? When are you ever going to stop interfering and let me live my own life?"

She shrugged and made some sort of goofy smile as if to say, *Oh well, what's done is done.* I was not amused.

"You know," I said as my blood pressure went zooming sky-high, "you could write down another twenty more volumes in your journal and you still wouldn't be cured!"

"What do you mean by that?"

"Mom, have you ever heard of borderline personality disorder? If not, you should look it up because it describes you perfectly: impulsive actions and chaotic relationships with other people. Adult codependents are forever getting involved in other people's lives. I highly recommend you seek the appropriate help and treatment so you can once and for all concentrate on your own maladies and stop sticking yourself in matters where you don't belong. Goddammit!"

Her mouth shut tight and she backed away. *Good. Now she's getting a taste of her own medicine!* I quickly left before she had a chance to respond. Every stinking spare moment, I've been reading her stupid stories and look what that superficial, holier-than-thou imbecile of a person goes and does.

She's asked for the box back time and time again since Noah and I have been living with her. I don't get it. *Forget about Bubbe Leah having been a witch; what kind of weird sorceress is my mother that she has this crazy power over me?* Just to spite her, I should throw all her papers in the box and chuck it in a faraway garbage can, skirt and all.

Chapter Twenty

Sam had begged off coming to the birthday party, but promised to call me at a later date, possibly for a dinner at his home. Kept afloat by the festive atmosphere, guests, balloons, abundant presents, and whipped cream cake, Noah managed to survive the entire celebration without having to be chastised or being sent into the dining room for a time-out.

I did receive my call from Sam a few days later, and I hastily agreed to join him the following Friday evening. All week long, whether I was at work or playing with Noah, a romanticized scenario of Sam and me worthy of a daytime soap opera kept playing in my mind. I envisioned us groping as we climbed the stairs to his bedroom, his tongue piercing deep inside my mouth. Maybe we wouldn't make it that far. If we were naked by then, we could jump on the couch or down onto the rug. I imagined him thrusting into me, my legs about his hips and maybe my back against the banister. My curiosity about the dinner and what would transpire that upcoming evening was surely piqued.

That Friday afternoon, it took forever to choose what I wanted to wear for my date with Sam. Avoiding peplums, flounces, and horizontal stripes, I was hoping to camouflage much of my undesirable flab and cellulite to achieve a fairly slenderizing silhouette, and so, my better judgment led me to the dark, stretchy pieces hanging in the closet. With discarded articles of clothing strewn all over the floor, I stood in front of the mirror for a midstream assessment. The combination of a push-up bra and the plunging neckline on my halter top made me look like a woman with a purpose, definitely not a shy or bashful babe in the woods. There was no way that Sam could avoid taking a peak at what I deemed to be my one and only best feature. The Lycra, skin-tight pants I had on were doing a semi-passable job of containing the damage from my expansive butt. *Not so great, but not too bad either. I just have to remember to squeeze it in.*

Once fully dressed and made up, however, whatever little self-assuredness I had quickly disappeared. I paced inside my bedroom counting, "One, Mississippi, two, Mississippi…." By the time I reached "Fifteen, Mississippi," I had substantially calmed down and believed my nervousness to be in check. Grabbing the Coach wristlet sitting on the side table, pre-packed with the house keys, a few tissues, lipstick gloss, and a couple of condoms— never having bothered to renew my birth control prescription, I proceeded to leave.

On the way to the front door, I passed by the kitchen. Mom was feeding Noah a combination of Cheerios, bowtie pasta, little pieces of boiled chicken, and grapes, which he appeared to be guzzling up. They both heard me say a rushed goodbye and "I love you sweetheart," which were intended exclusively for Noah. When she turned her head quickly in my direction, my mother had that look of disdain on her face again: the one that said, "Why does my daughter look like a hooker?" *I don't need her to tell me how to dress. I don't care what she thinks. Why should I care what she thinks?*

I turned around and ran straight back to my bedroom. Off came the ensemble dripping in blackness and sex appeal, and I stepped into the new, lemon, cotton, eyelet shirtwaist dress I had originally bought for the occasion and the two-tone beige sandals that went with it.

The drive to Sam's house should have taken hardly any time, but there was more traffic on the roads than I had anticipated. With my level of stress being on a par with the seeming impatience of the other commuters, I had no compunctions about contributing to the discord of tooting horns. I honked out my frustrations along with everyone else. *It's a green light you idiot. Move! You're cutting me off ? Oh, what am I doing sitting in this parking lot? Maybe, it's a sign I should turn around and go home? No. I can do this. I can do this. I'll have fun tonight. Sam's a decent guy.*

As I steered my car through the entrance of the townhouse community that Noah and I had left, I again felt a longing for the life we might have shared had we stayed with Craig. *Maybe we both needed to try a little harder to make it work better.* A gift-wrapped merlot jiggling next to my skirt rolled on the passenger seat and threatened to fall to the floor. I reached over to secure it again by my side. *I can't keep dwelling on the past.* I forced my mind instead to focus on the fantasies I had been conjuring up all week long, and my craving for Sam intensified. I felt wet and ready. *Take a deep breath. I'm just pulling into his driveway.* I pictured Sam opening the bottle of wine and pouring us each a glass while soft jazz played in the background. If things went smoothly, maybe I'd get a taste of Sam that night as well.

The door opened and I threw my arms about Sam after giving him a peck on his cheek. He smelled so good. He must have been wearing *Male* cologne. I had bought it for Craig one birthday, but he complained it smelled too sweet for him. The color of Sam's button-down shirt matched the aqua blue of his eyes. I just melted looking into them. His thick wavy hair was tousled to make it look deliberately messy. God, could he have been any sexier? He squeezed me gently and then pulled away faster than I would have liked. I recovered by telling him how wonderful it felt to be off by myself in a social setting. He smiled and said he understood then led me into his kitchen. There was a huge pot simmering on the stove with something delicious brewing inside. I noticed that the table was set for three.

"I invited my girlfriend over for dinner as well. I thought it would be good for you to meet Shari."

"Oh—er…great idea."

"She's recently divorced too, and I thought you would have a lot in common."

"That was so considerate of you."

No matter how well cooked that dinner might have been, it

still tasted sour in my mouth. Shari, Sam's girlfriend, was saccharine sweet, and not the kind of girl I'd be interested in paling around with. Besides being a size two, her streaked blond hair was pulled back into a ponytail without a strand out of place. She was wearing a cute mini dress and an obvious boob job. I imagined myself looking like a gargantuan, yellow elephant sitting next to her.

My phone rang just as I reached the driveway of my parents' home; I was feeling empty and letdown. The security light caught the movement of my car, but then went dark after twenty seconds, leaving me alone and undetectable in the moonless and starless night.

"Hi babe, it's me."

"What do you want, Craig?"

"Just calling to see how you and Noah are doing." He sounded like he had been drinking. "I was remembering some of the good times. You know, when things worked well between us."

"And?"

"I could so lick your puss right now. You wanna suck my dick? Do you want to?"

I didn't respond.

"I'm really hard. So hard. I want to fuck you really hard!"

I turned off my phone. I placed my hand under my panties and rubbed until a wave of exhaustion radiated down my body.

Chapter Twenty-one

At Noah's party, Stephen had taken me aside and suggested meeting for breakfast one morning, just the two of us. He wanted to spend some time catching up on my status since my divorce. I appreciated this effort, as I know that both Stephen and Mara usually like to spend their weekends with just each other. We had settled on a coffee shop in a strip center not too far from the beach in Hollywood and not too far from where Nathan used to live.

My brother put down the *Sunday Times* he was reading as soon as he saw me approach. I leaned in for him to tap my cheek with a kiss and then slid into the wrought iron chair at the curbside table he had chosen, planting two piping hot mochachinos on the tabletop. A moist breeze rattled the top page of the newspaper. Stephen pulled his coffee closer and jump started the conversation by asking me whether I had heard from Craig.

I didn't mention to him that Craig had made several more calls to my cell, which I let go right to voicemail. Craig's message is always the same: he's drunk and he wants to fuck me. I would never tell Stephen that I was actually tempted to take Craig up on his offer. Part of me thought it would be fun; kind of like having "forbidden sex." Maybe he's changed. Maybe he's gotten the fabulous girlfriend out of his system by now. Maybe, in a fit of desperation, I'll consider obliging him some day

"Aside from the money he sends regularly for Noah, no, I do not hear from him," I lied.

Stephen often sides with my mother in thinking that I am holding on to a lot of anger. I hoped to sway him to believe otherwise by coming across as levelheaded and in control. Nonetheless, he squinted at me with half-closed eyes under wrinkled brows, his chin jutting forward. "Don't you think you should be seeing a therapist with all this turmoil going on in your life?"

A paper bag holding my bran muffin and his cheese Danish was still tucked under my arm. I would have preferred eating my pastry while savoring the atmosphere before having to engage in a dispute with my brother. It was a warm day and we were shaded by a canvas umbrella. Most of the tables were occupied by people reading newspapers, skimming iPads, or interacting with their leashed dogs.

"What is our family's obsession with therapy?" I snapped. "You've morphed into Mom, haven't you?"

"You're living in a protective bubble. You can't stay with Mom and Dad forever. And if you believe there's nothing wrong with this, you need to seek professional help."

"I'm not discussing this with you."

I pointed out the brown Labrador retriever a short distance away. Stephen smiled and mentioned how much the dog resembled Zeke, Nathan's dog, who was loved and adored by everyone. Zeke had the kindest soul. He was smarter and a lot more caring than many people I know. Nathan had lost all his faith in God when he was ill and doubted that any goodness could be found in humankind. Zeke became the one and only true dependable relationship in his life. The dog catered to Nathan's moods and depressions and protected his master with unconditional allegiance. Zeke went everywhere that Nathan went—even to the weekly poker game, where he drank beer just like all the other guys.

"Kat, what about writing your feelings down then?" Stephen suggested. I could tell he was being careful and deliberate in the phrasing of his words.

I shoved back my chair so hard it caused a grating sound. "Are you kidding me? Are you giving me an assignment as if I'm still in Junior High School?"

"Kat, I love you," he said, eying the patrons at the other tables as if to see if anyone had been disturbed by my outburst. "You don't realize how angry you sound sometimes. You've got to do something about this!"

I told him that I was really okay and that things were starting to work out.

"Your social life is non-existent. It's time for you to start meeting new people instead of shutting yourself off from the world. I hear you're mostly reading in your spare time."

"What, are Mom and Dad spying on me for you?" I pushed myself away from the table and jumped to a standing position. "Are they keeping a log of how much toilet paper I use as well?

You think it's not shitty for me having to live with them all this time?"

Stephen leaned in. In a hushed tone, he cajoled me to sit down again. "Please relax. I didn't mean to offend you, but this is an example of just how uptight you are. Take a sip of your drink. Take it easy. It's the two of us having a friendly conversation."

"If you are going to continue in this vein, then I wouldn't qualify the conversation as being friendly. To me, it sounds all one-sided."

"I get it," he said. "I won't pry any further into your mental or emotional state, but I am going to make one last ditch effort to try to convince you to seriously address this issue. If you are not going to see a therapist, at the very least you should try writing some of your thoughts down on paper. Put everything in a letter and send it to me as proof."

Again, I questioned if he was serious. "What are you going to do, grade it? Give me a gold star if you like reading it?"

Stephen exhaled and rested against the back of his chair. I stared at the little Lacoste alligator emblem on his chest while he dislodged his collar away from under his neck. I think I saw his bottom lip quiver. "I was very close to Nathan too. You're not the only one who is still grieving. Maybe this is an exercise we can each do. It will help us both."

I placed the Danish on a paper napkin. "Do you want to split these or should we each eat our own?"

"I don't care," he said, peering at the Danish.

141

I peeled the decorative paper off my muffin and took a bite. "What's new with Mara's side of the family? What has she been up to lately?"

He looked up at me, and our eyes locked. "I thought you were watching your weight. How come you're eating that?" The words to *The Itsy-Bitsy Spider* swam through my brain as I maintained a steady, forced smile. After a short while, he turned away and uttered, "She's busy at work. Her folks are fine."

As I took another bite, this one much larger than the first, I nodded. "Is she still happy with her job?"

"Yes, she is happy with her job." He began to tap his fingers on the newspaper.

I shoved the balance of the uneaten muffin into my mouth. "Will she be taking time off any time soon?" My words came out so distorted I wasn't sure if he understood me.

"I don't know." His tone was brusque. "Why don't you call her and ask her yourself?"

I guess he heard what I said. I continued to chew. "So, is this the way this is going down then?"

"What do you mean?" He still sounded mega-disgruntled and his finger tapping turned into knuckle tapping.

"You're just going to be all uppity and noncommunicative?"

"How do you expect me to act, Kat? I was hoping to talk some sense into you this morning, but now, I understand that's impossible."

142

I folded the napkin to contain the scattered crumbs and took a drink. "How about we call a truce? I love you. You love me. Let's just finish our breakfast and enjoy each other's company. Can we do that?"

He clasped his hands and brought them to rest on the table. "In silence?"

"No. Um...we can talk about TV. Um...did you see last week's *Amazing Race*? Would you have eaten the bull's testicles?"

A chuckle escaped from his mouth. "I would consider doing it for a million dollars."

I shook my head vigorously. "No way. You would never do it."

"For a million dollars, I might."

"Never," I announced, raising my voice. "You don't even eat watermelon or matzoh balls."

His shoulders popped up and down. "That's different."

"No; it isn't. They're easier to swallow."

I'm sure that Stephen and I were sharing an identical thought at that moment. There is no doubt that Nathan would have eaten a dozen bulls' testicles in a heartbeat if he had to.

Chapter Twenty-two

I could have sent Stephen an email, but instead I did it the old-fashioned way by taking pen to paper. It seemed it would be better for my "letting go" if I had something tangible, more solid to let go of. After I finished writing, I licked a stamp and stuck it on the addressed sealed envelope, into which my folded letter had been inserted before I gave it to Noah to hold. He and I walked along the sidewalk together to drop the letter in the mailbox. I scooped Noah up in my arms to plant some extra kisses on his cheeks and allowed him to lift the flag, indicating a letter awaited the mailman's pickup. I didn't believe Stephen when he said this exercise was meant to heal each of us. I'm not checking up to see if he carries through on his end of the bargain.

I made a conscious effort to write that letter in my room one night. It was a little slow going at the start, like the first time you use a new ketchup bottle. The initial squirts are always the trickiest to pry loose, but eventually much of my locked-in emotions connected with Nathan's illness and death came tumbling out. I think I'm feeling better already for having done the exercise.

Nathan was in his late twenties when he first became ill. He had started to gain a lot of weight, which was not commensurate with the amount of food he was eating. At his heaviest, he had gained an additional 120 pounds. I didn't tell him to his face, but my brother looked absolutely gigantic. His shoes and clothing no longer fit; he was lethargic, angry, and in a bad mood most of the time. Of course, he had to be feeling so uncomfortable in a body he wasn't used to. I now know that feeling well, but naturally, for other reasons.

Despite a battery of tests, the doctors could not ascertain the origin of his illness. They were aware that his kidneys were not filtering as properly as they should, but no one could pinpoint what had caused his disease. One doctor suggested removing some of the excess fluid that was filling his body.

After several attempts were made to reduce the swelling and fluid retention, Nathan underwent hemodialysis. While on the machine, both of his kidneys stopped working. It was now necessary for him to be on dialysis for the rest of his life. He did not fare well with this procedure. For a year and a half, he suffered from cramping, vomiting, fainting, nausea, staph infections, surgery, repositioning of the stents and ports, ulcers, inflammations, sleepless nights, and a debilitated, low functioning life. Not one of us in his immediate family was cleared by the hospital to donate a kidney. You can bet we would have—each one of us was ready, willing, and more than eager to step up to the plate to do it. The doctors offered logical explanations for each denial and wouldn't budge from their decisions. It was such a sinking, awful feeling not being able to help Nathan in that way. It was hard not to feel guilty too as we still had the option of going about our everyday lives while his life was growing shorter and frailer with each minute.

Several people came forward to be tested; some did not match his blood type, others were not a close enough genetic match, some people sadistically pretended to continue with the process knowing they would pull out before the transplant surgery would ever take place. Nathan was on the national transplant list, but the possibility of receiving a cadaver's kidney was years away. His condition worsened.

The doctors suggested that he switch to peritoneal dialysis. For approximately thirteen hours a day, special fluids entered his abdominal cavity to enable his intestinal walls to filter the blood stream. Adding in sleep, there were very few hours left in the day for Nathan to enjoy any quality time. After fourteen months of adhering to this cumbersome procedure, he had become much weaker and the bags of liquid were becoming almost too heavy for him to handle. To say that he was despondent is an understatement. He no longer wished to continue living his life this way. Neither would I. Most people wouldn't.

A kind, selfless woman named Jo whom we had never met before responded to one of my mom's urgent pleas sent out to several civic and religious organizations. Jo, who is six-foot and one inch tall, skinny, with a petite triangular nose and naturally blond hair, agreed to be tested as soon as possible. The genetic match and blood types between Jo and Nathan turned out to be perfect, which was pretty amazing because Jo was born Catholic and looked nothing like any of us; we being of the short, wide-nosed, thickset tribe.

The transplant surgery took seven and one-half hours. After three and a half, the surgeons informed us the kidney had been lifted out of the donor's body and placed into Nathan. It was as if Jo had given birth to my brother all over again.

When Jo was recovering in her room and Nathan was out of surgery, she insisted on seeing him. She wore just her hospital gown and slippers and dragged the morphine drip alongside her as she walked. We crossed the hospital floor, rode the elevator up, and traveled down another building wing until all of us reached the post-op area. There was a breathing tube taped to Nathan's face.

"Look," my mom had said to Jo. "Your kidney is working inside Nathan. It's keeping him alive."

"No," Jo had answered. "It was always Nathan's kidney. I was just holding onto it all this time for when he needed it." Well, I don't think there was one person in earshot of Jo's statement that wasn't balling their eyes out. What a wonderful sacrifice this person had made, and she was being so humble about it. Her words and deeds restored my faith in the potential goodness of the human race.

Nathan was placed on ultra-expensive anti-rejection medication and was being closely monitored by a skilled clinical staff. While he was still recuperating in the hospital, four days later in another hospital just forty miles away, my mother's mother Ada, aka Nanny, died from pneumonia. Drama and trauma were hitting my family from all angles. It was like being bombarded with giant emotional cannonballs. Only my mom appeared to be stalwart and unbending from the strain. Like I've mentioned before, I never saw her cry or complain once.

Within a few months, almost half of the excess fluid had been drained from Nathan's body and he regained some strength and mobility. The new kidney was functioning properly, and Nathan was keeping himself hydrated and well nourished. He was starting to rebuild his life; he was talking about renewing his career and dating again. Six months later, he was playing softball and racquetball and living independently. Nathan and Jo became very, very close. Although a former non-believer, he began to speak about the miracle God had brought into his life. Jo kept repeating that the decision to give Nathan her kidney was the easiest one she had ever made. It had just been something that was meant to be.

As the scar tissue from the transplant had not healed well, Nathan had opted to have corrective surgery. Four months later, that surgery was successfully carried out, and after two days of bed rest, Nathan was ready to be discharged. The day my mom was supposed to pick him up from the hospital, she received the call telling her not to make the trip. Nathan had died. Gone. Like the snap of fingers. Buried. Evaporated.

In all honesty, I could never stand being in any of the hospital rooms with those lingering, putrid smells. One time, Craig and I went out into the hallway and I started to puke. Those odors are what I remember most about Nathan's hospitalizations, besides the times he would embarrass me and pee into the urine receptacle right in front of me. I hate everything about those times: the elevator rides up to the floor where Nathan had been waiting to see us, mingling with strangers, each of whom had their own heartaches to bear and were wondering who in the elevator had it worse; practicing the smiles to greet my brother so I appeared rosy and optimistic; hating to say goodbye at the end of the day while wishing to be anywhere else but there; keeping him focused with small talk about really inconsequential matters while we waited with him in the pre-op; talking about sports and world events while we waited for him to wake up in the post-op; telling him how much better he looked when we knew we were lying; coaxing him to eat when we knew he might vomit everything that he had just eaten; trying to ignore the screams from the crazies and the shouts from the armed police in the emergency rooms; keeping Nathan company in the dialysis room and wanting to run out of that disgusting place as quickly as we could.

I thought the homeless people on the dialysis machines were disgusting. Their clothes were ragged. Their hair was matted and unclean. Their bodies reeked. Why did Nathan have to end up lying next to them? He didn't belong in that place! How did something so terrible ever happen? What was the point of going through all of that pain? He had suffered so much and then—*and then*—all of it ended up being for nothing. A total waste. What was the stinking point? He had to go and die anyway.

He should have never ever gotten sick! Why didn't he take better care of himself? Other people go into hospitals. Other people die. This is what movies and television dramas are about, but these things should never have happened to us! If Nathan hadn't died, I would never have been married to Craig because Nathan's intuition about Craig had been right all along.

And what guarantee is there that what Nathan had hasn't been passed down to the rest of us? What if Noah gets it? The thought scares me so; my heart might break in two from having to live with so much fear.

I didn't call Nathan a lot when he was ill because I kept hoping it was all a bad dream; a horrible, horrible nightmare. If I didn't speak with him, then I could make believe none of the crap was really happening. I was angry at him. Mom had told me that I was making a big mistake and warned me to get over it. She had said that I would be sorry if something happened to Nathan and I hadn't called him. Well, the big ugly something happened. I don't want to feel guilty and be angry at myself forever, but I am. Unfortunately, all of this remorse and all of Mom's messages will not bring Nathan back. Nothing will.

Chapter Twenty-three
MYRA'S JOURNAL

Trips to Downtown London:

I can recall, at five years of age, seeing piles of rubble and broken-down buildings in the city of London where grand structures had once stood. The visions of these ravaged areas appearing inexplicably among vast expanses of new construction crawled into view as I rode on the lower level of a 653 double-decker bus. Sitting with my head pressed against the window, I could hear and feel the grind of the bus's massive gears each time the pneumatic tires would start to roll, causing the vehicle to lurch heavily forward.

In my hand, I would clutch the ticket printed by the conductor, who would count out the pennies and then accordingly adjust the wheels on his Gibson ticket machine. In those days, if our bus stop had arrived before the conductor collected his fare, we would have to leave the coins in the care of another rider, never suspecting that the money would be pocketed instead. Those coins were much heavier than the ones used nowadays. They used to leave a musty, metallic odor in the palm of my hand.

Infrequently, my mother and I would head toward the West End on this bus route, supposedly to buy something unique that could not be purchased from the grocer, chemist, fishmonger, or butcher on Old Hill Street, which were all a short walk from our house. Our family's meals were cooked fresh daily, and since the refrigerator in our kitchen was just a small box, it was necessary to make regular shopping trips for our basic staples. So when we headed off to the West End, I would assume that something much larger or more unusual was being sought. Now I have come to realize that the city bound trips were just abbreviated attempts at my mother's running away.

The mammoth London double-decker busses were painted bright cadmium red and looked like red dinosaurs to me, dwarfing the ubiquitous black taxicabs, lorries, and other such vehicles that always seemed to clog the roads. At each stop, a new set of dreary clothed characters would step up to get on board. Some of the elderly needed help rising to the height of the platform. Some had to shake out their wet umbrellas before sitting down. Some read newspapers to occupy their time; others sat mesmerized by the scurrying shoppers, street signs, and tree trunks that went dashing by outside.

I could tell that the people who had dozed off quickly, whose heads bobbed up and down while their mouths hung open, emitting a medley of grunts and snores, were heading home after long shifts at work. They appeared bushed and drained, but my mother, sitting anxiously by my side and lost in a world of her own, seemed to be the most worn out of all.

In my opinion, the busses were the only objects to shine in those dismal settings. I recall seeing a lot of rain, a lot of fog, a lot of grey, a lot of drenched feet and stubbed out cigarette butts, and a lot of dripping umbrellas. There were few smiles and little laughter, as most people concentrated on the narrowness of themselves while trying to figure out how best to set their affairs in order after the lengthy battles of war—both worldly and personal. With regard to my mother, she was incapable of ever putting her affairs in order. The resistance she came across in trying to do so was far too powerful for her to ever overcome.

Chapter Twenty-four

On Getting Lost:

My mother, Ada Kaufman, didn't exist in a vacuum. She had a history, and those who came before her had a history as well. I would like to write more about her, but I'm afraid that I would be jumping the gun by not picking up first on my story in the West End of London

As it was, she would lose me more often than not after we disembarked from those bus trips. Roaming about the busy streets alone, I would eventually be deposited at the Lost and Found bureaus of certain department stores—D.H. Evans and Selfridges to name a few—by kind, concerned strangers who had passed me by, disturbed at seeing a young girl of six, seven, or eight years old looking as dazed and bewildered as I was and seemingly detached from any grownup's supervision.

Watching a myriad of shoppers going about their business of buying stockings, lipsticks, and handbags, I would constantly wonder if my mother had even noticed my disappearance or would care enough to search for me. I visualized her engaged in discussions with salesgirls choosing just the right color Cutex nail polish or the perfect silk blouse to go with her Jersey knit suits and presumed her to be too engrossed in that process to become distracted by my absence. After what seemed like hours—but were probably closer to minutes—she would appear wearing her camel-hair, winter coat, one of her many felt hats, and a flustered face, tapping her ruby red polished fingernails vigorously on the counter, behind which I typically sat eating biscuits and kicking my legs. The lady in charge would return me to her as if I were someone's missing item of clothing she had plucked from a shelf or dug up from a Lost Items box. "Come along then," my mother would say as if I had been dawdling all along. "We have to catch a bus."

If there was a lesson to be learned about holding on to a child with a firmer grip or maintaining one's child's presence within view, it evaded my mother's mind, as disintegrated as it may have been. I can remember staring down from the top of the steep escalators that led to the London Underground system or wandering through countless, tiled corridors connecting to the noisy train platforms with my mother nowhere in sight. There were plenty of grocery stores, medical clinics, parks, and neighborhoods where I was similarly abandoned. How I would make it home on these occasions still baffles me.

Chapter Twenty-five

Tracing my roots as best I can:

To fully understand what made my mother the way she was, I need to tell you about Shlomo, Leah, Zvi, Miriam, and Hod. The most logical starting point will be with the recounting of Shlomo's journey out of Russia. As with a dominoes setup, this I believe is where the first dotted piece gets toppled, precipitating the erosion of whatever decent behavioral traits my ancestors might possibly have exhibited prior to that moment in time.

***

Shlomo had just come to learn that his wife, Raisa, was carrying their first child. Neither one of them needed to say "Oi, another mouth to feed! How will we ever manage?" for they both knew, without a doubt and as impossible as it was to imagine, their lives were about to become even more grueling than they already were. With so little money in Shlomo's pockets, his makeshift family was fighting to stay afloat in an existence best characterized by constant battles in an antagonistic, stormy sea. The sea, however, was more of a wasteland. Where they lived in the Pale of Settlement, there was hardly any expansive view of water. The closest Raisa and he came to seeing it was what they managed to pump out of a well.

The young couple was forever struggling to make ends meet, living with constant hunger pangs in their bellies and now with a baby on the way, things could only become that much worse. "Raisa," he would caution his wife, "more than ever we must shepherd our resources wisely, otherwise there will be three pitifully starving Jews in our household instead of just two."

Despite his fervent belief in the Almighty and a strong commitment to living a pious life, Shlomo would worry constantly about being thrown out onto the streets. Such a fate had befallen Schmulavitch's son, Yitzhak the tailor, down on his luck and brought down even further by drunken thugs, stripped, kicked, and left as a pile of manure as a bull would leave a dumping on a field. Yitzhak's head was so bashed in on the side that he walked about muttering like a deformed child who had gone soft in the brain. Schmulavitch and his wife were hard-pushed to support themselves and Yitzhak's wife and five children. Eventually, they packed up the daughter-in-law with her *kinder* and sent them to live in the neighboring village where the *machatonim* lived.

The home in which Shlomo and Raisa dwelled, with its meager furnishings and hay-covered flooring, closely resembled the shack from which it had been originally converted. "God," he used to pray, "you have given me this hay to prevent me from going completely crazy. I am glad for this gift, but is it too much to ask for just a little more comfort in my life?"

Whenever he would become anxious about the state of their lives and his inability to provide for their future, he would rearrange the hay into multiple piles, creating designs, intricate and complex, that only he could see with his mind's eye. It was as if he were a masterful musician composing a grand symphony or concerto out of stems of straw instead of musical notes.

Raisa would complain, "You should be making better use of your time and imagination. Perhaps there is furniture or clothing that you could be constructing instead? At least those items could be sold."

Mostly, Shlomo would try to ignore his wife's grumbling. "Did you forget that I am the man of this house? What audacity you have to challenge my authority!" Sometimes, he would counter, "You are too quick to judge me; unintelligent as you are, devoid of any *sechel*. How in the world am I supposed to pay for the materials or wood?"

"Take your axe and go chop down your own wood from the forest," she would offer, not masking her discontent. "You can go under cover of the dark so you will be less likely to be seen."

Shlomo would shrug and tell her that he was too tired at the end of each day. "You should be grateful that I have the hay to toss around instead of you."

Their home was divided into two areas: one for sleeping and one for eating. Raisa's candlesticks—her only decorative possession—had been respectfully placed on a rickety, wooden table in the center of the eating room. She had wanted to sell the candlesticks to help pay for food, but Shlomo refused to allow her to do so. They were the only objects she had retained from her childhood home and he insisted upon having them lit each Friday evening with the arrival of the Sabbath. Raisa had clung to these candlesticks as she had hidden in a pantry while her parents were beaten to death; they no longer bore any religious significance for her. Despite Shlomo's best efforts to correct what he considered her sinful ways, she had relinquished her belief in both her faith and the chosen destiny of her people. "So be it," she had conceded. "I will keep them for now because they can be used as effective weapons when the assaults begin anew."

Living in that part of Russia, it was true that the safety of Shlomo and Raisa was in constant jeopardy. Here it was thirty plus years after the assassination of the Czar Alexander II in 1881 and wanton attacks upon the Jews were still commonplace. Every once in a while, the "Blood Libel" lies would resurface, accusing Jews of killing non-Jewish children to obtain blood for religious rituals and the making of matzohs. Those falsehoods would spur on the gullible, ignorant gentiles into randomly striking out, raping, torturing, and killing Jews while destroying their homes. Innocent Jewish babies, stolen from their mothers' arms, would be mercilessly slaughtered before their parents' eyes. Shlomo's own parents had been beaten to death and his sister, Rachel, had been viciously raped before her throat had been slashed.

It was while he had been wandering aimlessly alone in the aftermath of such bloodshed, misery, and loss, he first came across Raisa, who was in the same sorry, desolate state. They drew upon what little strength they had to carry on together. However, the threats of that ruthless, unjust brutality forever hung over them.

Trying to be pragmatic and resourceful in an atmosphere of such barbarism, Raisa and Shlomo had agreed to marry and live together as man and wife. They found a farmer willing to let them take up residence in a shack in the far corner of his property. He was not outwardly kind or sympathetic by any means; the price he demanded for rent was exorbitant and grossly unfair because he was well aware of the laws prohibiting Jews from owning land or from living in certain regions of the village.

"Fittingly, you may live among the vermin as long as you continue to make your payments on time," he told them.

They had bowed their heads, relishing the promise of safety after the long grievous onslaught, and rushed into their new abode before the farmer changed his mind.

The very next day, Shlomo had been fortunate to secure a position with a baker, whose former apprentice's body lay amongst those slaughtered and amassed in a pile waiting to be set on fire, not even affording it a proper burial. Shlomo was quick to learn that the baker parsimoniously guarded his stock, insuring against free access to the supply of baked goods.

"We sell these," the baker instructed grimly. "We do not and will not ever give them away. Take what does not belong to you—even so little as a bite—and you will be facing a military squad."

Absent the opportunity for free handouts, if Shlomo had wanted more food to eat then he had to work even longer hours for it. With the paltry wages the baker paid him, he found it almost impossible to keep his and Raisa's bellies full and satisfied, although plenty of their friends and their relatives had been starving as well. They had sought aid from others in their community, but had found none. What they did discover, however, were Jews cowering in fear and readying themselves to meet their Maker. Insecurity was the only certainty by which Shlomo and Raisa could live their lives.

Besides the lack of food and other grave concerns, the couple now had the future of their yet unborn child to worry about as well, and so they decided that Shlomo should travel—perhaps as far west as England and especially before the new immigration quotas would make it more difficult for him to do so. Many of the young men they had known had similarly chosen to make this journey. Some had even gone farther on to America. News had been shared by their relatives who had stayed behind, telling of secured jobs, economic growth, and newfound freedom from persecution. Packages had been sent home filled with money and unusual items the likes of which had never before been seen in their shtetl. As a learned man, Shlomo had been well versed in the teachings of the *Torah* and the *Talmud*. As such, he deeply believed that making this trip was the right decision for his family.

Chapter Twenty-six

This is how I started off being British:

After Shlomo packed up his *yarmulke* and *teffillin*, which he had always dutifully bound to his arm and forehead in the mornings, and with the knotted *tzitzit* fringes of his *tallis* extending from under his vest, he bid his goodbyes to Raisa and set out on his journey in search of plentiful food and an honest paying job. "I will send for you and the baby, who will have emerged from your womb by then, God-willing, as soon as I am settled in the new land and have accumulated some wealth," he told her with conviction. "In the meantime, until I have arranged for your transportation and our permanent living accommodations, I will forward you money and supplies as often as I can."

"Travel safely," Raisa replied. "I will count the days until we are together again."

When Shlomo had safely reached the City of London, however, he was not overjoyed by what he saw. There were already many Jews living in the East End, the area where he had intended to establish his new home. The competition for bakers' assistants was very stiff, and there were many émigrés from Poland and Russia already in line for the few open positions with considerably more experience than him. He decided instead to continue on with his journey and go to yet another town where there would be less able men for him to compete against. He made his way to Nottingham, the home of Sherwood Forest and the mythical hero Robin Hood. This was where very few Jews had chosen to reside and where he had hoped he could finally succeed in his quest to earn a decent living.

The first item on Shlomo's agenda was to find a suitable, safe place to reside. He stepped through the dilapidated entrance indicated by an overhead sign of a horse with outstretched wings into a local inn and pub in the section of town called The Poultry. Despite the early hour of the morning, he was surprised to see how crowded it was.

The room was full of nightshift workers from the bicycle and hosiery factories speaking in languages not at all familiar to him. The building in which he stood seemed to be hardly fit for human habitation. Its broken-down condition made Shlomo too afraid to chance spending the night there. Utilizing hand gestures and roughly drawn sketches, Shlomo was able to ask the bartender, who happened to be of German descent, about the availability of an alternative sleeping arrangement.

With frothing pints of murky brown, stout beer in each of his hands, the bartender somehow managed to inform Shlomo of a room to rent that was situated not too far away in the home of one of the overseers from the German Lace Factory. Shlomo wasted no time in following the bartender's directions. Before long, he was standing face to face with the overseer's wife and handing her money for a full week's lodging and extra cash for the use of her oven during the off hours. He then went on to purchase a variety of flours, seeds, yeasts, nuts, onions, and fruits from the nearby village store, all of which he stored beneath his bed.

(It boggles my mind to think how difficult it must have been for Shlomo and all the other immigrants to dive into a completely new world, new culture, and new customs without being able to converse in the local vernacular.)

A studious and observant man, Shlomo had taken all the advice that the baker in the old country had reluctantly shared about his trade. Following the baker's procedures without so much as a scintilla of deviation, Shlomo set about mixing, kneading, and baking a multitude of baked goods in a variety of shapes, textures, and sizes. He became quite adept at producing rich, thick crusted breads and buns, all of which gained the favorable attention of the entire overseer's household.

After receiving their encouraging praise and requests for plenty of free samples upon which they layered ample servings of butter and fruit preserves, Shlomo was ready to present his baked goods to the local marketplace in Nottingham.

To his way of thinking, pushcarts were pushcarts and the same the whole world over—nothing elaborate—just the means to transport one's wares from one place to the next. He had been familiar with the pushcarts of the artisans, shopkeepers, and peddlers in the land he came from, but in Nottingham's market, his eyes exploded with the multitude of fabrics, colors, and produce being offered for sale on the pushcarts lining the alleys and crisscrossing the public square. Yes, there was *tref* there as well—pigs' snouts and pigs' feet—but Shlomo made sure to park his cart the farthest away, lest his wares be tainted and be rendered non-kosher.

The aromas emanating from his products, some of which had come straight from the oven, lured his customers in like bees drawn to pollen. In the early morning hours, lines would form in anticipation of his arrival with those dense, heavy loaves which differed from the sweet, milk-white, pasty versions the townsfolk were used to.

The customers would often make jokes about his *tzitzit* protruding from his waist. They would ask, "Why do you insist on wearing a tattered tea cloth below your belt?" Others would refer to him as the "Yid", "the Jew who traveled from afar", or "the funny man with the side curls", but many times people would fight over who could purchase his last remaining bialys or *beigels.* His ryes and pumpernickels, some with raisins and some without, smothered in caraway seeds or spotted with fried onions, were scooped up the minute he unloaded his cart.

Within months, Shlomo's success earned him enough money to establish his own shop. He proudly and appropriately titled it Kaufman's Bakery, which had a more modern ring to it than Kopferberg's Bakery. Despite pleas from the overseer and his family for Shlomo to remain in their home, he elected to move into the vacant room above the bakery, which he leased for a few shillings more than his current rent. Now, there was no longer any reason for him to trudge to the marketplace with his pushcart. The people came to his store in droves seeking his delicious baked goods, and they treated him with admiration and respect, affectionally referring to him as Solly The Wonder Baker.

(Not for nothing, but I am an excellent baker. I make a great zucchini loaf, a store-bought-looking challah from scratch, a variety of delicious cookies, and sumptuous quiches and pies. I guess I have a fair share of good old Solly's genes. Kat, if and when you read this, you will come to realize this about yourself too!)

It was easy for Shlomo to get caught up in this new life and the prosperity it offered. Without realizing it, he had shed his prior history like a snake sheds a layer of its old useless skin. It had peeled off of him without him feeling any remorse for it whatsoever. Accordingly, he had not given another moment's thought to his wife, Raisa, who was still living in the Pale, where each and every day had most surely continued to be a hardship.

One wintry day, travelers from London had stepped into the bakery. Both men were wearing long winter coats and fur hats. As Shlomo rushed about filling their orders, he listened to the banter between them. It seemed that they had come from the same area of Russia from where he had once ventured forth.

"And what say you about Schmulavitch?" he had asked

them nonchalantly. His intent was to throw them a few names before finding out about the fate of Raisa, not wanting to give them any indication that the two had been related.

"He's doing the same as always," the ginger-headed man named Mordecai had replied.

"And what of his son Yitzhak?"

"The soldiers came in the middle of the night and pulled him into the street, where he was forced to dance for them in his nightshirt," Mordecai had continued. "Every time he fell, they laughed in his face and poured vodka on him. At the end of his jig, they tossed the remnants of the bottle at him and then set him on fire."

The other man named Chaim added, "Some say it was a blessing in disguise, though no one could guess who the next village scapegoat would be."

"What about Miriam the grain trader, Moshe the peddler, or Avrum the newspaper printer?"

The travelers reported all the ups and downs, births and deaths, blessings and sorrows that had befallen these people in question.

"And what about that young woman with the black hair turned prematurely grey? Raisa, I seem to recall her name was."

"Oh, her," Mordecai acknowledged. "Yes, it is an interesting story, but one which we do not have time to tell. We are on our way back to London and hope to reach the shul before sundown." He took out his handkerchief from his coat pocket and sneezed repeatedly into it. "Ugh, the dampness of this country is seeping into my bones."

"While he's blowing out his brains, I will tell you quickly," Chaim announced. "Raisa would regularly visit the post office. Do you remember the one on the main street? Don't bother answering me—I am such a fool. There was and still is only one post office. Anyway, the postmaster informed her each time that there were no unclaimed packages addressed to her. Fearing that someone else had interceded and taken what was rightfully hers, she made sure to visit the post office during the wee hours of the mornings—so early, in fact, the postmaster hadn't finished saying his morning prayers. Alas, no money or news had ever come to her through the mail."

Mordecai's nose had been rubbed red and sore. "Chaim, are we to stand here all day? Please skip the generalities and get to the specifics of the story." He sneezed and fumbled around in his pocket to retrieve another, cleaner handkerchief. "I could recite the entire *Torah* while standing on one foot in the time you are telling the baker about that woman Raisa."

Shlomo cut two slices of a warm pumpernickel-raisin loaf. "Eat this," he said, handing each of them a portion. "It'll do you both good."

"Thank you, but what I need more than anything right now," Mordecai responded, "is to be davening in shul so I can get back to my wife Shoni and lap up her chicken soup with giblets and kreplach."

168

Mordecai seated himself on a chair by the door. He sneezed again and tidbits of raisin and bread speckled his beard. While Mordecai picked at his hair to clear up the mess, Chaim finished telling Shlomo about Raisa.

"She had checked with other wives who had similarly been left home, but no one had any information about her husband. His name was Shlomo Kopferberg. Have you come across him in your own journeys? No?"

Shlomo lowered his head, busying his hands by rearranging the platters of rolls and biscuits. "No; not in these parts."

"Well, truth be told, she didn't hear from that Shlomo ever again. After months of continued disappointment, Raisa and everyone else had assumed that her husband had met with a disastrous fate, believing that he had probably been killed by a band of thieves or a drunken mob. Not so rare for those parts. After all, it happened all the time."

"That's too bad," Shlomo commiserated.

Mordecai arose. "Chaim, your tongue always has a habit of running away from you. Finish your story and let's be off!" Turning to Shlomo, he requested, "Add a dozen *kichel* and a chocolate *babka* to our order please."

Chaim continued. "In keeping with custom, Raisa had torn her clothes and reluctantly observed the mourning rituals, sitting Shiva for the full seven days. At the end of the period and now a grieving widow, she had thrown the fate of her young son and herself onto the mercy of the *Kahal*, hoping they would show *rachmones* and provide her with *tzedakah* from the community council. If matters weren't bad enough, she next became ill from a festered appendix. Such misfortune. *Az och un vai*. May God shine his light down upon her and grant her peace and the strength to carry on."

After hearing this latest news, Shlomo placed the wrapped items into one large, brown paper bag for the travelers and they soon departed. With regard to Raisa and her child, he had decided it was best not to instigate trouble by disturbing her situation any further.

Chapter Twenty-seven

How my father's parents met:

For a period of two years, Solly had been benefiting from a safe, comfortable lifestyle in what was known as "Merrie Olde England", albeit after having obliterated the memory of his former home and family in Russia from his mind as if they never were.

To Solly's way of thinking, Raisa had been far too delicate a creature to have survived that arduous journey to Nottingham. In the long run, the way he saw it, he had done her a favor. *She's probably remarried by now, but if she has been mutilated or fallen dead from some wretched disease, it really is not my concern anymore. Too much water has flowed under the bridge.*

With regard to his own state of affairs, Solly was far more sanguine in his assessment. *My clothes no longer fall off my spine from always being hungry, my girth has substantially broadened, and I have money saved and deposited in a Nottingham bank that is protected by thick steel doors and British policemen who drink more tea than they do vodka.*

In this wonderful country, he now had money to spare, not as much as the Rothschild's fortune, by any means, but enough for him to go to sleep each night without worrying about where his next meal was coming from, which band of drunken hooligans were going to steal his belongings out from under him, or who was going to slit his throat for their mere amusement.

As a well-respected, upstanding citizen of the community, Solly Kaufman walked about believing he was a prosperous man. He only had to bring to mind the shack he had shared with Raisa to acknowledge just how far he had come economically. When the residential property situated above his bakery came on the market for sale, Solly didn't have to think twice about purchasing it. He literally ran to the bank to withdraw the exact amount of the asking price and a few hours later held the deed to the property.

From this space, he carved out two flats: one served as his own living area and the other provided him with an additional source of income. It had been an easy property to rent, and he had many good tenants who paid him on time, mostly keeping to themselves. Such was the life he now enjoyed, reaping rewards as a free, affluent businessman. Without a doubt, it beat scampering about from hand to mouth, praying frantically to live yet another miserable day among brutish savages.

One day, a pregnant woman came to inquire about the rental flat. From the short conversation Solly had with her, he learned she was a widow who had fled her native land immediately after her dead husband's body had been placed in the ground—yet another victim of a pogrom— and had tenaciously set out to create a safer, better life for her to-be-born child.

Her name was Leah, and although he found her face to be extremely unappealing, after she did move into the rental flat, he invited her to share his company and evening meals from time to time. It just so happened that Solly had grown tired of having to constantly fend for himself. Confined by her condition and her own reclusive nature, Leah would seldom venture outside her new home, but she did welcome and accept Solly's invitations.

(What a convenient, easily-made substitution: one pregnant woman for another!)

By supreme coincidence, Leah had also turned out to be a talented baker. One evening after a day's work, Solly was inserting his key in the slot of his front door when he was overcome by the delicious scents emanating from the rented room. He assumed those scents related to baked goods being produced in Leah's oven, so he went over and rapped on her door.

"What are you making tonight?" he had asked as soon as her face appeared. A full-sized apron, bulging at Leah's midriff, covered the printed floral dress she wore. Specks of flour dotted her brown frizzy hair, which was pulled back away from her face. He was surprised and a little put-off to see her real hair and not a *sheitel*.

"Nothing special. Nothing special at all," she had answered, appearing hesitant and guarded.

"Well, whatever it is, I think it must be special because I am an expert in these matters. Please, tell me what treats you have made. The aroma is so enticing."

Leah waved both her hands into the air as if she was shooing Solly away. "They're just ordinary strudels."

"No, my dear. There cannot be anything ordinary about your strudel. I have yet to see them and I am already tantalized. May I be so bold as to ask to sample one?"

She shuffled off, leaving him by the landing with the door still ajar, and came back with a folded dishtowel encasing a small portion of apple strudel. After saying the appropriate blessing, he immediately took a bite. It melted in his mouth too soon, for he would have loved to savor the richness of that treat as long as he could. The texture of the layered pastry was light and delectably sweet and the filling contained ingredients that delighted his tongue.

"I would very much like to sell this strudel in my store," he anxiously told her. In his mind, he could hear the neighborhood yentas raving about them already. "Would you be willing to give me the recipe?"

Leah took an abrupt step backwards. "I can't give you the recipe. It has been kept as a family secret for decades."

"Then perhaps you will consider making them yourself. I will certainly compensate you fairly for the ingredients, time, and effort."

Solly could tell that Leah was struggling with the notion he had proposed.

"Think of the child you are carrying, Leah," he urged. "The extra money will surely make things easier when you bring that new soul into the world."

Solly's unrelenting perseverance successfully broke down Leah's resistance. Her strudels, all made fresh from a variety of seasonal fruits, eventually became the number one best seller in Kaufman's bakery. No one could recall having tasted anything like them before. As the profits rose higher, Solly was happy to delight in the increase to his wealth. Funnily enough, he also found himself enjoying Leah's company more and more.

Chapter Twenty-eight

I was always told my grandmother was an ugly woman:

Even though she was several years older than him and not a particularly attractive woman, Solly would still thank God for the blessing of bringing Leah into his life. The bakery now produced large batches of strudel daily, requiring Leah to use the larger ovens in the store instead of the smaller one in her home. Because she had never indicated any desire or willingness to become married again, he had tried to refrain from bringing up the subject, but he often wondered if that all would change once the new child was born. In this vein, their relationship continued along the lines of a most congenial one.

Leah gave birth to a son and named him Jack. Solly's intentions were to act as best he could as a father figure to that child, doing what was right by all the parties involved. The child had not turned out to be as great an intrusion in their day to day lives as he had initially feared, but it occurred to Solly that he needed to maintain stricter control over him as he was growing up.

From Solly's perspective there were a few matters regarding the child that perturbed him from the very beginning. *What decent, respectful Jewish woman names their son Jack?* he would question. *After which ancestor of blessed memory was he named? What had been his father's Hebrew name? What about Leah's father's name? How could Leah not have remembered either one?* Solly was not shy about asking Leah to help him resolve these uncertainties.

Leah had claimed that period of her life had been filled with so much fear and suffering she had totally blocked it out. She could not, therefore, give him a rational explanation for why she had chosen the name that she did. Upon hearing this account, Solly chose to halt his probing and not bother Leah any further about that particular subject, but he found himself sitting up in his bed at night with these same concerns going around and around in his head. *But how do you derive a Hebraic name from such an Anglican one as Jack? When I offered Leah such ideal substitutes as Abraham, Moses, or Jacob even, she held her ground, not budging one inch. 'It's such a distasteful, goyishe name,' I told her, but she wouldn't retreat from her asinine positon.*

Yes, our differences in our approach to child rearing seemed slight at first, but there are certain customs that are of great importance to me and matter little to her. Leah would have Jack's hair cut the minute his curls fall over his forehead, temporarily blotting out his vision. I, however, will insist on observing the Upsherin ritual and force her to wait until Jack turns three years old. That first snip of his locks will mark the beginning of his formal education as well as his obligation to keep the commandments and perform good deeds. On this, I will be unyielding. This young lad must be molded in a proper fashion. He needs to be strictly educated as a Talmudic scholar, but his mother stubbornly keeps fighting me whenever she can on this course, which irks me to no end. She is after all just a woman and very limited in terms of her knowledge and responsibilities with regard to the Jewish faith.

One evening after the "Closed" sign had been displayed on the bakery door, Solly, speaking matter-of-factly, suggested the idea of marriage to Leah. To him, it was the obvious means to a desired end—one in which he could have the final say in all matters concerning Jack. He had been bending over the till, pretending to be engrossed in counting the cash as she swept up crumbs.

"I believe this is as good a time as any for us to be wed," he mentioned. "What do you say?"

Without any display of surprise—feigned or real—Leah had slowly turned her head in his direction. Her smile and subtle nod indicated her acquiescence to his proposal, but then she edged her way toward the cash register. If she had been expecting a kiss or embrace to acknowledge their newly confirmed arrangement, she had no real understanding of the man she had just agreed to marry.

"We're in a public place. Touching in such a way would be highly inappropriate," he had stated with haste, sidestepping her advance and hoping to avoid any impropriety.

"Forgive me," Leah uttered, stopping short to lower her face.

They were married the following week and continued to run the bakery together as routinely as they had before until Leah had begun to suffer from indigestion, nightly sweats, and disorientation. She had surmised that because of her age she was probably going through "her womanly changes." In reality, Leah was pregnant with another child and she was about to become a mother to yet another boy whom they would call Hod, a name that indicated splendor, glory, and majesty. Solly's aspirations for forging a righteous path for Jack then became secondary to his duty and life's mission to ensure that his own son—that special, most divine one—would live up to the highest attributes of his name.

Solly and Leah lived side by side in a loveless marriage, acting more like business companions than doting, enthusiastic spouses. They performed their perfunctory roles so the outside world perceived them as a wholesome unit, in which they cared for their two sons with patience, diligence, respect, and an abundance of love—all with the strictest adherence to the rules and customs of the Jewish religion. In actuality, Leah and Jack were miserable within this structure that they believed to be far too constraining and they bitterly resented Solly for imposing it. Solly's actions with regard to his younger son, however, became even more extreme. He persisted in demonstrating shocking disregard for Hod's welfare, dignity, and comfort, almost to the point of being utterly vicious and sadistic, despite Leah's futile attempts to deter him.

179

Chapter Twenty-nine

Karma does exist. Everybody gets theirs in the end:

It was Solly's custom to store sacks of flour in a loft next to the bakery. In the very early hours of each morning, he would climb up to the loft using an old, wobbly, wooden ladder to retrieve the supplies needed for that day's baking. One day, when Jack was ten and Hod was seven, just as Solly was about to begin his descent, he lost his footing and fell off the ladder, severely injuring his spine. His pain must have been extremely intense, almost too much to humanly bear, for he shrieked and screamed and carried on uttering nonsense between his bellowing and tears.

When Leah ran to him after hearing the calamity, he cursed at her using the vilest words she had ever heard, which she did her best to ignore. She stayed by his side until he was taken to the hospital, where the doctors did what they could to keep him alive. They could not, however, put him back into one piece.

(Try as I might, I could not feel sorry for him when I heard about his accident. What he did to Raisa was downright cruel. Although I have heard similar stories about abandonment and desertion among other immigrant families.)

For the rest of his life, Solly was bound to a wheelchair and doomed to a horrid, agonizing existence. As such, he was forever subject to Leah's care-giving and mercy. It was not her nature, however, to be a sensitive, compassionate woman.

"Leah, I need a spoon!"

"Yes, I heard you. I said, 'Just a minute'."

"Leah, my soup is getting cold!"

"It won't kill you not to drink it piping hot."

"Leah, you gave me the spoon, but I now have *lokshen* stuck to my chin!"

"Like a baby, I should feed you with a bib tied around your neck? The noodles on your face won't do you any harm."

"Leah, fetch me my *siddur*. It is time for me to recite the blessings for after the meal. Leah? Leah, can you hear me? Leah, turn to face me so I know you're listening to me!"

After all was said and done, Solly had married whom he had married.

Without having Solly's extra set of hands to lend assistance, Leah had not been able to keep the bakery fully stocked and functioning to the same extent as before. She simply couldn't devote enough time to run it as a profitable business. Many hours of each day had to be spent nursing her husband, who had become cantankerous and was constantly expressing his anger and frustration about his imposed immobility. In addition, Leah was now singularly responsible for managing the daily activities of her two sons. Therefore, she took it upon herself to sell the bakery and rid herself of one extra chore. Solly was already mad at her. What difference did it make if she stoked an existing fire?

The reserves of money that Solly had accumulated could only last so long with withdrawals being taken out on a constant basis and the absence of any deposits being made. After a period of five years, the funds began to perilously dwindle down, necessitating Leah to take action to stem the negative flow. In a desperate attempt to bolster her family's income, she took it upon herself to design jewelry, which she had hoped to sell.

She would sit at the kitchen table until the early hours of the morning cutting and twisting wires, pasting colored fragments of glass, and threading beads to form decorative brooches, earrings and necklaces. When she had a fair amount made, she would load them onto an old pushcart—the very one Solly had used when he first came to England—to traverse the many dirt roads across town and hawk her creations.

Leah was well aware that the local commoners would mock her as she passed them by, but because her day-to-day responsibilities were great and her options for earning a living were meager, she did her best to ignore their taunts. *Keep staring at your feet*, she would tell herself. *A few more paces to the market square and my load will become lighter. If I spit in their faces, there'll still be no bread and cheese on the dinner table.* It had been hard physical labor, and Leah became grumpy and irritable for having to do it.

Solly's demands for her attention seemed to be infinite, and her days on the road were challenging and draining. Although Jack was then away at school, Leah had little patience to address Hod's needs. She would find herself looking at her younger son and asking, "Who ever needed another mouth to feed and someone else to worry about? I would have been better off with the hot flashes instead of having you."

(One would think that loving one's own child is the most natural and compelling virtue of all human behavior; evidently not so with our family.)

Leah had never been the doting type, and her younger son was becoming more self-centered and difficult than she cared for him to be. At the end of her long days, she began to resent having to tend to him; after all, had he not been an unintentional addition to their family?

"Why can't you behave more like your brother Jack?" she would ask Hod. "He is a wonderful son, providing me with such *nachas*. Jack will surely make something of himself. And what do you do? You spend your days getting into all sorts of mischief, adding to my sorrow. The char lady tells me she has her hands full with you. You think she doesn't see you pinching an extra biscuit or taking pennies out of the savings jar, but she does. Spare me your excuses. I'll take the char lady's word over yours every time. She says you're a liar and a cheat. What good are you?"

Solly, on the other hand, continued to be obsessed with all of Hod's comings and goings. It became Hod's responsibility to account for every minute of his day to his father. To Solly's consternation, Leah had succeeded in preventing him from molding Jack into what Solly considered appropriate for a young Jewish male. Solly's entire focus had then centered on Hod and ensuring that he became observant and erudite in all of the Jewish scriptures and texts. Under his guidance and instruction, Solly hoped for Hod to be the rabbi of all rabbis. *What do I care about that?* Leah would ask herself. *To speak the truth, I am glad of it. It gives me less to worry about and more time for myself.*

During his confinement in his wheelchair, Solly would pray, seeking forgiveness from God for all of his prior misdeeds and promising zealously to tutor his son and make him the most pious of all Jews.

To Leah, it seemed as if he was reenacting Abraham's sacrifice of Isaac to prove his unyielding loyalty. She heard him muttering words and phrases that indicated he was being plagued by guilty thoughts and brooding about his own mortality. If Leah asked what he had to be guilty of, he would raise his hand and brush her away. When she hid in the kitchen with the door ajar, she would overhear him confessing deeds of bigamy and abandonment, but she never confronted him on this; he would surely have punished her for eavesdropping. Leah would ask herself, *Does he think all this praying will give him back the use of his legs and his manhood? In a way, I hope not.*

Chapter Thirty

Who were Nanny's parents and where did they come from?

I want to deviate a little and now introduce you to Zvi and Miriam, who were my grandparents on my mother's side. I never had the opportunity to meet Miriam, as I was born after she died. Zvi hardly spoke any English and his interaction with me in my younger years was limited to a friendly smile and a pat on my head. The little I know about him was garnered from conversations shared between my aunts and uncles and from anecdotes that have trickled down through the generations.

As a part of the mass migration of Jews from the Baltic region in the early twentieth century, Zvi Grossman came with his parents, seven siblings, and as many of their personal belongings they could possibly carry to England in the summer of 1905.

His family had paid large sums of money, most of which had been in the form of bribes, to various schemers and travel expediters along the way, but their accommodations and conditions had been nothing more than inferior and squalid. Huddling together, they tried to maintain dignity and decorum where delirium and panic had often run amok in the wagons and second-class compartments of the trans-continental trains and steamship. After they had crossed the Channel into the British Isles, they expressed a collective sigh of relief despite their ultimate objective to meet up with cousins in New York.

At the docks, where they were all supposed to have boarded the ocean liner to America, Zvi was denied embarkation privileges. He was seventeen years old and was prevented from stepping on to the ship because an infection was detected in his right eye. His parents decided that it was unwarranted for everyone to be held back. "Once your medical problem has been resolved, Zvi," they tried to reassure him, "you will be able to seek passage on the very next ship heading west."

Reluctantly, Zvi had said his farewells to his parents, brothers, and sisters and set out to London to pass away the time until he could receive a good medical report and then, likewise, be cleared for sailing. Although he did not speak the native language, his trip to the capital city was eased by the massive flow of fellow trans-migrants.

They traipsed along, crossing pastures and small towns, following the routes of the newly developed bus system conveniently set in place throughout southern England. They learned to drink tea with milk the British way and developed affinities for strawberry jam covered crumpets and all things chocolate, which included Cadbury's Bournville Cocoa and Fry's chocolate bars.

He carried his one suitcase and a slip of paper containing his destination, which his mother had slipped into his hand while saying, "Zvi, you are a very sweet boy but not among the cleverest of my brood. I am hoping your tailoring skills will help you get by. I expect you to remain obedient and as mild-mannered with your superiors as you have been with us." She wrote the name and address of their *Lansmen* in large letters as neatly as possible because Zvi's eyesight was poor—even more so with an eye infection.

"A friendly stranger, if need be, might be able to decipher this information and steer you in the right direction," she suggested while stuffing bank notes into his hands. "Hide this money beneath the layers of your clothing. Remember, you must always be on guard against thieves and dangerous pickpockets. I pray it will not be too long before we will see each other again in New York."

(Some of our relatives still live in Brooklyn to this very day.)

As he conversed with fellow travelers in Yiddish—the prevalent language of the Ashkenazi Jews, of which he was one—he learned that there were Jews who had assumed prominent roles not only in financial affairs but also in political positions throughout the British Empire. He came to realize that England was a great nation of justice, kindness, and mercy where Jewish principles and culture had been allowed to thrive.

Guided by the address his mother provided, he passed by areas with funny sounding names like Maiden Lane, Plumbers Row, and Prescott Street until he arrived in Whitechapel and was able to secure affordable lodging with his parents' contacts. They gave him a job in their family's clothing shop, where he befriended their cousin Miriam Rosenstein, a seamstress who was neither outstandingly beautiful nor unpleasantly ugly and a few years older than Zvi.

Everything about Miriam appeared to be broad, which included her Slavic forehead, bosom, buttocks, and shoulders. As a child, her father would tease her about being capable of hauling a wagon by herself if the need ever arose. She had been gifted with a good head on her shoulders, which enabled her to be focused and pragmatic. Taken as a whole, she imparted a feeling of dependability and trustworthiness. The sharp, angular features of her face hinted at her inner strength, masking any signs of softness, but Zvi had been strongly drawn to her nevertheless. Her almond shaped, cat-like eyes made it seem like she was piercing right through him whenever she would peer his way.

(Kat: Your Aunt Joan has eyes like these.)

Chapter Thirty-one

We do come from a stock of brave, talented women:

While Miriam was still living in Poland, not fortunate enough to have already met her *bashert* and despite her parents and younger siblings begging her to stay, she jumped at the chance to accompany her cousins out of Lodz as a governess to their small children. Unlike her brilliant sister Bertha—who played Vivaldi's *The Four Seasons* on her violin with dexterity and precision—and her angelic sister, Yetta—prodigious at mastering all of Chopin's piano sonatas—she had no special talents to develop other than darning and mending the holey socks and torn elbows of her family's clothing. Why then wouldn't she grab the opportunity of free passage to the west?

Not one to shy away from adventure, there was no question in her mind that it was more dangerous to stay in a land fraught with violence than to accept her cousins' kind offer.

"Allow Bertha and Yetta to come with me," she had tearfully implored her parents, but the girls had sterling prospects at the Academy of Music.

"Why would you rob them of their destined success?" her mother had questioned. "They are delicate, refined young women with respectful careers ahead of them."

Years later, Miriam would lament, "If only the others had that same tenacity and foresight as I had, then they would still be alive." At the close of World War II, she would sadly learn that no one within her circle of family and friends had managed to survive the death camps. Such would surely have been her fate had she stayed with them.

Two years after the journey to England, she sat sewing buttons on a double-breasted, grey serge suit in her cousin's menswear shop, when a young man named Zvi Grossman, still smelling like the streets of the homeland but with the purple wrapper of a Cadbury's milk chocolate bar sticking out of his breast pocket, stepped through the door. Breaking off a square of the bar for himself, he then offered a piece to the others in the room. She detected right away that he possessed the potential to be a loyal and generous provider.

"You should see his full head of dark brown hair," she had boasted to Deborah, a transplant from Lviv, who sat next to her as she made the horizontal slots for the buttons. "He has a thick, bushy moustache and such eyebrows that make him seem worldly, just like the furry bears we see in the London Zoo. He might be younger than me but his countenance makes him appear so much older."

Deborah placed her arms around the growing mound perched on her lap. "Don't waste your time with him, Miriam," she had advised. "You are still aging even as we speak and need to be courted by someone more marriage worthy. Someone as strong and handsome as my Joseph."

"No, you are wrong," Miriam had disagreed, smug with an abundance of self-confidence. "This one seems as right as your catch. I shall not let him slip through my fingers."

It did not take long for lonely Zvi to become totally enamored by all the attention that Miriam had showered upon him. She laughed at his jokes and held his hands when he spoke about his family, expressing just the right amount of solace for his predicament. As she had intended, he easily became putty in her hands. Within months, she convinced him that it was not necessary to look elsewhere, let alone cross the Atlantic Ocean, to achieve the semblance of a family. She alone could provide all the family that he could ever need.

All of her maneuvering eventually paid off and Zvi longed to marry her, forgetting about his trip to America and intending instead to remain in London forever. A telegram tersely providing information about the upcoming union was sent to the rest of the Grossmans, who were then settled in their Brooklyn home.

Before a small gathering of family and friends, they were married by the rabbi on a Thursday night in the local shul, which was a narrow, rectangular, three-story brick building with paneled interior walls. The couple stood under the *chuppah*, midway between the mahogany *Aron Chodesh* and the raised *bimah*, wearing clothing designed and sewn by their own hands.

For his part, Zvi wore a black three-piece suit, white, stiffly starched, collared shirt, and a white bow tie. Deborah had taken great pains to make sure the four button holes on Zvi's vest lined up perfectly. Miriam's mauve, silk gown was styled with a bodice of vertical frills and gigot sleeves, which were puffed at the upper arms and then tapered from the elbows to the wrists. Ribbons had been appliqued around the hem, waist, and three quarters of the way down the skirt. She did not carry a bouquet, but she did have a floral crown of orange blossoms at the peak of her veil.

Seeing Miriam lead her new husband away from the *bimah*, Miriam's cousin, who was seated in the upper-floor woman's gallery, commented to her sister-in-law in a hushed tone, "Zvi might tailor pants for a living, but Miriam is the one who will *wear them* in that family."

Together, Miriam and Zvi raised six children—five boys and one girl—in a home where the rituals and Jewish commandments, observed for centuries by their ancestors, were celebrated and upheld. They rejoiced in the freedom and liberties provided by their adopted country, happy to have escaped the repression and pogroms of their past. No longer would they or their children be subjected to spontaneous angry rioting fueled by drunken lunacy and inflammatory accusations such as "Christ killer" and "blood suckers". They established a comfortable home in the East End, and Zvi gained the reputation as a fine, skilled tailor among the men in the community.

Miriam was responsible for daily care of the children and ran a well-synchronized tight ship. As an excellent cook, she filled her home with the tantalizing aromas from the likes of cholent, gefilte fish, *kishkeh*, and tzimmes. Each week, dough for the Shabbos challah was braided in her tiny kitchen, and one of the boys' chores would be to bring it to the bakery, where it would be baked in time for Friday night meals.

Not having strayed from his religious roots, Zvi attended the daily *shacharit* and *ma'ariv* services at the synagogue, bringing his sons with him when they were not in school. The parents had respect for each other and their children, and the children understood this; not once did Miriam or Zvi have to raise an angry voice. Their home was a peaceful one where *shalom* flowed from corner to corner.

Back in Lodz, Miriam had witnessed many crimes perpetrated against innocent girls and women. Each day sitting alongside her own mother, she would wind and unwind spools of thread, worrying constantly until Bertha and Yetta had returned home safely from their studies or rehearsals.

Sweet Dora Michnik, not yet twelve years old—who lived two floors up in the same apartment building—had been accosted by a group of troublemakers on her way home from the butcher shop one day. She was later found in the stairwell, bleeding and in a state of shock. Not only had they taken the Vienna sausages and lambchops she was bringing home for dinner, but they had brutally robbed Dora of her innocence.

Miriam and her mother had rushed to the upstairs flat to

lend their assistance to the distraught young girl and her family. Turned away at the door by Mrs. Michnik, they were told, "There is nothing to be done. Only time will heal." When the two women returned home, they collapsed into each other's arms on the settee.

"We need to be more vigilant than ever," Miriam had cried.

Although Miriam now lived safely in London, she was still wary of possible hidden dangers lurking behind the tall buildings and dark alleyways. Her daughter Ada had beautiful shiny blond curls, making her an attractive target for lecherous evildoers and mischief-makers. Fear of Ada's safety hounded Miriam morning, noon, and night, and so she assigned one of her sons the task of accompanying his sister as she travelled home from school.

"She's not to be left out of your sight! I want to see two heads, four arms, and four legs coming through the door. Is that understood?"

Unfortunately for Ada, not only had she inherited Zvi's compliant nature, but she'd also inherited his limited brain capacity. Her performance in her academic studies had been uninspiring and sub-standard. When she began to work full-time at the age of fourteen, Miriam assigned her oldest son, Morris, the responsibility of greeting Ada at the bus stop at the end of the day.

"You are to be at the corner bus stop before the bus comes into view," she would instruct Morris.

"But why?"

"Your sister must make sure to keep her hat on her head.

Her hair must always be concealed. She'll be unsteady. I don't want her falling off the platform when she readies herself to jump off."

"But mother, I've never seen anyone fall off a bus platform."

"On this subject, Morris, there will be no debate. In the old country, children never questioned their parents. Please do as I say."

None of the many paying jobs that Ada undertook lasted too long. At each of her positions, a major mishap would occur, wreaking havoc on the goods she was meant to sell or upon those unlucky enough to be standing near her post. Fragile glass bottles were accidentally dropped or smashed. Expensive perfumes were inadvertently spilled. When her sales receipts were tallied, they never added up correctly, which resulted in her customers being short-changed or overly compensated.

One day, she came home and withdrew to the solitude of her bedroom, brooding miserably, to avoid being seen by anyone in her family. Oh, how pitifully she had cried, not singing or dancing about the house as was her usual custom. Miriam had immediately marched into Ada's room, demanding an explanation.

"I think I am pregnant. I don't understand how it happened," Ada had sobbed.

"You don't know how it happened? I think you very well know how it happened," Miriam had yelled back. "Pregnant?

Trugedik? Oi! Gevalt!" she wailed.

"How can I carry on? What will become of me?" Ada had beseeched, pulling on her mother's arms as buckets of tears rolled down her face.

"I am shocked," Miriam had responded. "My heart is breaking into pieces. I needed this like a *loch im koph.* A hole in my head you have given me! Who is the scoundrel? I need to know. We will force him to marry you."

"It was Arthur." Ada's teeth chattered as her limbs trembled. "He brought me to the cinema yesterday. He placed his hand on my knee."

"Yesterday? You're telling me this occurred yesterday?" Miriam had shrieked.

Ada nodded.

Finally, Miriam was able to take in a long breath and calm down. "He placed his hand on your knee? That's all that happened?"

"Yes." Ada's voice cracked.

"You promise me this is all he did? You promise me this on your life?"

Ada nodded again.

Miriam embraced her daughter. "Ada, my *mamelah, nebekh,* you are not pregnant. That is not how babies are made." She stroked Ada's hair and kissed her head. "Such a beautiful *punim*, but with so little brains."

Chapter Thirty-two

Talk about child abuse:

Turning my attention back to Hod, the younger of Leah's sons, I want to share with you how miserable that boy's life must have been. There were not many Jews living in Nottingham in the early 1900s, so he was very much a loner in his community and an outcast in the public school he attended. With a disabled father and a mother who was a traveling peddler, he became an easy target for the other boys to ridicule.

Beginning at a very early age, Hod was required to memorize extensive passages from Solly's collection of holy books, which he would then be quizzed about for hours on end. He was expected to know all about the kings, prophets, the history of the Israelites, and the famous rabbis as well as their commentaries. When Solly announced a specific book and segment number, Hod had to recite the Torah portion by heart and render details of the many interpretations. This imbecilic drilling went on for a number of years.

Hod was not permitted to engage in any other activities at the end of the school day except for studying Hebrew and the biblical narratives. Yes, there were times that Leah tried to intervene on Hod's behalf, but she was told in no uncertain terms by Solly to shut up and mind her own business. Considering Hod to be *his child alone,* Solly treated her with extreme contempt—a form of repugnant behavior that Hod unfortunately had learned to imitate.

It didn't matter that as Hod grew older, he became the captain of his cricket team or the lead singer in the school choir. Solly had no concerns about how well his son conducted himself in the classroom, performed on tests, or completed his homework. There was nothing Hod could have done to soften his father's temperament or lighten his own load other than to chant a prayer as perfectly as a Chazan on *Kol Nidre*.

When Hod was nine years old, he had been late for one of his father's lessons because he had been attacked by a gang of anti-Semitic boys who had called his mother "an ugly whore" and left him bruised and smarting on the side of the road. Leah had heard of this incident from the gossiping fishmongers in the village. Hod's school cap had been thrown down the drain, and the boys had peed across his shirt and pants. Somehow, though, he had managed to limp home.

Absent any pity in his heart for the torture Hod had already endured, Solly proceeded to beat his son mercilessly with a stick for not reporting to him on time. Welts erupted on the boy's arms and legs, from which rivers of blood streamed down and soaked into his already soiled shoes and socks. That day, Hod was required to stand erect and recite a litany of sacred prayers codified in the language that had been passed down *L'Dor v'Dor* (from generation to generation).

It is no wonder that Hod grew to abhor his father as well as his religion; this hatred had been whipped into him.

Chapter Thirty-three

My father's emancipation—quite a gutsy move:

After countless recitations, repetitive lessons, and around-the-clock interrogations by his father, the day of Hod's becoming a Bar Mitzvah was finally approaching. It was the day he was to read and chant from the Torah at his Synagogue, proclaiming his manhood before the isolated, Jewish community in Nottingham. On that auspicious day, Hod would finally earn his ticket to freedom from his dreary, unhappy home and bid adieu to his father's maniacal, uncompromising, and heartless demands. He made a solemn pledge to answer to no one else but himself for the rest of his life the moment the service had ended and the congregation had completed their version of *Adon Olam*.

Shortly after his thirteenth birthday in 1927, fully-clothed, Hod surreptitiously crept out of bed. He tip-toed about his room, taking care not to wake the full-of-himself Jack, who was stretched out on a pile of blankets in the center of the floor. Jack had grudgingly taken leave from his advanced studies to be present at his brother's Bar Mitzvah ceremony.

"Solly expects you to be here," Leah had warned Jack in a costly, long-distance phone call with Hod nearby.

"It's a meaningless ritual that I care nothing about," Jack had responded.

"Please make it your business to be here, Jack. He'll take it out on me and make things worse if you don't."

Hod proceeded to empty the coins from his father's pockets and his mother's purse, adding these to the remains of the loaves of bread uneaten from the evening meal already stuffed into his pockets. Without any misgivings, he shut the door on their snores and ill-tempers, hoping never to see any of them again.

Journeying southward past Leicester and Oxford, Hod had passed through moorlands, national parks, and across green rolling hills until he managed to find himself at the southern coast of the country. After two weeks of using his wits to keep himself fed and sheltered, he came to stand among the salmon fishermen, mud flats, and salt marshes where the rivers and the English Channel converged, although he still had yet to find the spot where he could feel safe and gain some sense of belonging.

Hod's sturdy legs and curiosity led him all the way to the city of Southampton. As a strong breeze blew across his face, he heard the powerful blasts from a funnel not too far away, and he made the decision to head toward where he thought a ship might be docked. As he drew closer to the port, he knew, deep down, that he was going to board a ship regardless of its destination. The lure of the open sea and the adventures it promised buoyed his spirits and kept him steadfast on his tracks.

The S.S. Cameronia, with its single funnel and two masts sitting majestically by the pier, came into view as Hod neared the water's edge and duly impressed him with her splendor. She was surrounded by rows of luggage and crates marked with insignias of cotton, tobacco, cloth, and spices, which were stacked curbside and waiting to be transported to cities and towns in the British Isles; and there were crates containing olive oil and tea being readied to be loaded on for cargo.

Slipping past the various areas where eager first, second, and third-class passengers were awaiting the signal to board, he had nonchalantly picked up a crate designated as cargo and followed closely on the tails of one of the crew. It might have been because of his more than average height and fake cockney accent but he managed to make his way up the gangway without opposition. He was totally shocked and pleased at how well he blended in with the other shipmates.

Chapter Thirty-four

The swashbuckling stunt was anything but adventuresome:

After Hod unloaded his crate in the holding platform, he attempted to seek out a sufficient hiding place in the crew's quarters until the anchor was pulled and the ship set sail. A few hours into crouching on the floor under a heap of blankets, he heard the voices of two men approach. One man was wincing in pain while his companion was trying to calm him down. Hod deduced from their conversation that they were coal stokers. One of the men had suffered a serious burn coming into close contact with scorching hot metal and had been given permission by the ship's doctor to take a break from the boiler room's blistering heat. Without warning, the blankets came flying off of Hod and a soot-blackened face pounced within inches of his nose.

"What have we here?"

"Please, please don't turn me in. I beg of you," Hod had pleaded.

After seeing that his injured mate was resting comfortably on his bunk, the unharmed stoker grabbed the back of Hod's collar and marched him up a series of narrow flights of stairs all the way to the bridge, where he received permission to approach the Captain with his captive. The Captain, framed by a white-topped hat, handlebar mustache and full beard above the neck and by an impressive grouping of polished brass below, stood firmly before

Hod indicating he wasn't going to take any nonsense from a stowed-away ragamuffin. "You did the right thing," he told the stoker, and to Hod he said, "Looking for a free ride, are you? Let's see how well you swab the decks and clean the heads to pay for your fare." The squalor and predominant filth on the ship in the lower quarters made Hod's nasty job almost impossible to accomplish. Despite the young lad's grunting and cursing, no one seemed to have any sympathy for his plight, which from his viewpoint was bitterly unfair.

The ship was making its reverse crossing to America and, once she had reached the city of New York—passing first by the grand lady of Liberty that Hod managed to catch sight of and which had somehow caused him to become misty-eyed—he was immediately turned over to the Immigration Services, where he was detained for three weeks and kept behind bars.

Throughout his imprisonment, he had the advantage of observing the merchants, immigrants, dockworkers, and vendors busily going about their days in the cavernous, wharfside structure of the pier. It reminded Hod of the Nottingham Victoria station, a far posher edifice with its glass roofs and central pillars but with the same level of frenzy and pandemonium taking place inside.

From his limited perch, he witnessed all kinds of people rushing by as they negotiated the terms of business deals, trafficking in both essential and exceptional goods. He couldn't help but inhale the excitement and exhilaration of that amazing place. It seemed that every which way he turned his head there were riches to be gained, and he promised himself that he would definitely return to claim his own fortune in that golden-paved city one day.

When the S.S. Cameronia was once again eastward bound, filled with its exports for the European market, Hod was delivered back to the same stern Captain, who assigned him the very same tedious cleaning duties as before. "This should teach you not to pull a fast one ever again." The crossing had turned out to be just as wretched as the one before it.

Four and a half days later—which were four days too long for Hod's liking—the ship came into dock once more on British soil in Southampton, and a member of the crew was directed to throw Hod off the plank—the same man forced to surrender a box of home-made toffees to Hod's pair of kings in one of the many onboard, nightly poker games. "Nothing personal, kid," the ordinary seaman shouted, grabbing hold of Hod's britches and hurling him ashore.

Finding himself right back where he started and none the worse for his nautical adventure, Hod decided he needed to acquire money and lodgings. On the *Camey*, as the crew lovingly referred to their vessel, he had picked up some noteworthy gambling skills—cigarettes, oranges, and chocolates had comprised many an ante—and so he immediately went about searching for gaming opportunities. It had seemed like the most logical thing for him to do. With his lucky dice in tow and wearing a cocksure, winning attitude, he travelled from street corner to street corner, wagering and betting, cursing and shouting like the best of them until he had a tidy sum tucked away in his pockets.

In his wanderings, he came across some petty thieves who would frequent the open markets prowling for unsecured wallets and accessible merchandise, always staying just slightly ahead of the law. These rogues had recently purchased a second-hand delivery van to make early morning runs from the fish markets to the restaurants, providing a legitimate cover for the group's black-market dealings. They invited Hod to join them.

Under the tutelage of Frankie, Giuseppe, and Mario, he became quite adept at refurbishing stolen jewelry and distributing it to unknowing retailers, accomplishing the same with antique furniture, fine art, and silverware mysteriously brought across the Channel from Italy. There seemed to be a steady stream of valuable goods ready to be remarketed.

Once they were able to eliminate the stench of fish from the more valuable wares, they would reap large profits from these shipments. The more daring their deeds were, the greater the thrills and the manlier Hod believed he had become. For five years, the group stayed together, smuggling booty from the Continent to vendors reaching as far north as Scotland and as far west as Wales.

Where are your holy ethical principles now? Hod would imagine chastising his father, picturing him falling out of his wheelchair and groveling at his knees. *Where is your famous Pirkei Avos? In the toilet, most likely! Don't bother pleading for mercy. I shall never forgive you! I will not lift a finger to help you, old man. You deserve to be treated with the same cruelty that you dished out to me. Not even your prayers will be able to save you now.*

If the strenuous, mental exercises inflicted upon the young Hod had reaped any benefit at all, it would have to be said that the older Hod had developed a sharper, more absorbent mind in response to all that relentless drilling, enabling him to soak up an encyclopedic volume of knowledge with ease. He prided himself, therefore, in being proficient in a lot of different subjects.

Before an audience of his less educated comrades, he could recite facts and dates without a moment's hesitation, conveying that he was also an expert in areas about which he actually knew nothing. Given his presumed superior intellect, it was natural for Hod to become the mastermind behind many of the gang's larger, more complicated undertakings, which he plotted, outlined, and explained in detail to the others. At these times, they would have followed his lead unquestioningly had Hod not insisted the violence be kept to a minimum. For this he was often called a "pussy" and a "mummy's boy" by Frankie and Giuseppe, who had been willing to take on greater risks and strike at richer patsies. Their grumbling did not let up.

"He's never really been one of us," complained Frankie.

"He's a Jew boy at heart," claimed Giuseppe.

"Harold," Mario told him, for by then he had ditched the name Hod for a more modern, less Jewish-sounding one, "it's time for a parting of the ways. We'll divvy up what we've made so far, but then that's it. We don't know each other after that."

Harold, having grown tired of the group's past escapades and wary of the more dangerous capers it was about to undertake, did not put up a fuss. He managed to leave with a sizable share of the spoils, prompting him to conclude that *whoever says, "Crime doesn't pay," is wrong*, as he went about charting a new, less villainous path for himself.

One morning, Harold was eating eggs, sausage, and bacon at a corner tea house while reading the *Daily Mirror*. He noticed an advertisement in the newspaper offering a beauty shop and its upstairs flat for sale that just so happened to be a few miles away from the house he was renting. Harold took a sip of his strong Earl Grey tea and smiled. He fancied himself being the proprietor of something substantial and honest and found the idea of finally putting down roots to be appealing.

Gobbling up the rest of his meal, he drained his teacup until it was bone dry and left a sizeable tip for the waitress. Three hours later, he cemented the deal by presenting a caseload of cash in exchange for the deed and went about purchasing a fair supply of brushes, combs, shampoos, and peroxide to practice dying strands on the heads of his willing girlfriends, of which there were many.

Now a tall and handsome eighteen-year-old, Harold appeared to have quite a way with the opposite sex.

Harold visited several W H Smith newsagent stores to buy all the fashion and trade magazines he could find, which he read intently. Understanding that bobs and shingle cuts had run their course, he learned how to form multi-colored spit curls, finger waves, and sculpted coifs in accordance with the trends of the Hollywood beauties. He approached each wetted head as if he were creating a new piece of art. He combed, shaped, twisted, and dabbed, weaving the elements of form, function and motion with such an intensity that his models sat silently in awe. If the final hairdo failed to achieve what Harold had hoped for, he would shampoo the model's hair and begin restyling all over again.

Whenever his models bearing his work came into the public view, people would stand up and take notice. Many other women wanted to have their hair styled by Harold too. Clients from the ritzy as well as from the lesser upscale neighborhoods of London began to strut into his salon, each one wishing to be a leading lady's look-alike— "I prefer the *Greta Garbo*.", "Give me the *Jean Harlow*.", "Did you see Bette Davis in *Hell's House?* That's how I hope to look, only I want to appear sexier than she did."

At the end of their appointments, the clients would sashay out, their chins held high, feeling as sophisticated and elegant as the glamorous movie stars they idolized. It did not take long for Harold's appointment books to fill to the brim and for him to be regarded as an overnight sensation. Articles containing his photograph began to appear in all of the trade journals, newspapers, and magazines.

Invited to attend high society events from flower shows to balls, Harold became astutely knowledgeable in the rules of etiquette, sipping his champagne and sherry on befitting occasions but wisely choosing to drink only Pimm's liqueur in the viewing stands at the Season's polo matches. Outfitted in his requisite blazer and white trousers, his dashing appearance elicited flirtatious glances from many a debutante.

While he rubbed shoulders with the elite, money flowed through his fingers like water in a kitchen sink. He was wealthy enough to buy luxurious clothing, fancy cars, vacations on the Riviera, and entrance into the most exclusive gambling clubs, where the doormen appreciated his reputation for being a generous tipper and alluring starlets and voluptuous showgirls strode arm in arm by his side. But then suddenly, Harold came across something that his money could not easily buy and his bigwig, carefree lifestyle came to a shattering halt.

A spirited mustang of a woman surrounded by a crowd of young men and women was sitting opposite Harold at a tea dance one Sunday afternoon, talking and laughing in a world of her own. As if a spell had been cast upon him, Harold could not stop staring at her. He eyed her clothing; although it seemed well-tailored, he thought it ordinary and unimpressive. The moss green, checkered fabric was of the long-wearing, durable kind. Encircling the neckline was an embroidered collar, too intricate to be anything but handcrafted.

He studied her hair and the manner in which it had been provincially combed; he was mildly amused. A lemon ribbon, possibly once threaded through the rim of a wicker, shopping basket, had been tied neatly in a bow at the crown of her head. The brunette sitting at his side tugged at his arm to reclaim his attention, but Harold shoved her away with the flick of his wrist.

"Here's a ten-pound note," he told her. "Go get yourself a taxicab ride home." His date protested, but Harold maintained his focus on the young, energetic woman. He observed her skip over to a man with wired spectacles fitting snugly on the bridge of his nose, whose face bore a slight resemblance to hers in the way of rounded cheeks and forehead. She cupped her hand to his ear and whispered something that triggered a robust laugh. All of her muscles seemed to participate in the exchange. Harold's voice took on an ominous tone. "Leave now or you'll regret it."

The date in her low-cut, shimmering, satin gown threw her stole over her shoulders and pouted. "I came here to have fun. Why do I have to leave now?"

Harold ordered her to shut up. "Because I'm telling you to, and you don't like it when I get angry. Do you?" As his date departed, he did not turn to say his goodbye. He had become too entranced by the vision of the woman across the dance floor, outwardly a vulnerable ingenue wanting to be tamed.

An apparent interchange of witticisms took place between the man and woman Harold was keeping tabs on, causing them to guffaw. They giggled and winked, their arms gently touching, comfortably invading each other's personal space. Scowling with displeasure, Harold shifted in his seat but then noticed another lad in the group; he too wore eyeglasses and his facial features were not unlike the twosome's he had been studying. He signaled for a waiter.

"Do you see that blond over there, the one with the bow in her hair?" he asked. "Does she come here often?"

"Uh huh," the waiter responded. "Her name is Ada Grossman. She comes with her brothers every week."

"Which of those men are her brothers?"

The waiter eyed Ada and her cohorts. "All five of them."

"That's good to know," Harold told the waiter, slipping ten shillings into his hand. His mouth stretched to produce a *Hey, I've just won the Irish Sweepstake* smile, but his eyes retained the coldness of a voracious leopard about to ensnare its prey.

Harold leaned back in his chair, spreading his legs apart. He took out a toothpick from his pocket, peeled off the paper casing, and poked at the peanut pieces stuck in the grooves of his teeth. He observed the ease with which Ada and her friends communicated with the brothers. They appeared to share an affection that was so painfully blatant it produced an immediate longing in the pit of his stomach. He became intensely envious of them. A sharp jab of the toothpick against his gums made it crack in half. He threw the wooden splinters in the ashtray. All of his emotions churned into knots, making him feel restless and off-kilter, as if he had tripped over an invisible stumbling block. The one thing he felt sure of, however, was that he desperately wanted to experience that same kind of love and devotion for himself.

Harold tugged at the cord belonging to the phone on his table, bringing the candlestick base closer to his chest. He picked up the heavy receiver with his left hand and inserted his right pointer finger into the fifth top circle on the rotary dial, turning the dial toward a fixed stopping position before releasing it. The phone rang at the table where Ada and her brothers sat. As soon as she answered his call, he spoke into the mouthpiece and asked her to dance.

As Ada and Harold danced their first dance together, he hoped that the band would never stop playing so he could hold onto that girl forever. Her fervor for the music flowed from her body into his arms like an electric current. Without his realizing, the puzzling sensation he had initially experienced that day festered from a benign seed into a disturbing, gnawing, uncontrollable, malignant growth. More than anything else, he had wanted to totally possess Ada, and he had no intention whatsoever of sharing her with anyone else—least of all her brothers.

Chapter Thirty-five

When we're young, we see the world as being perfect:

Ada knew the words to all of the tunes the popular bands used to play. That included the latest waltzes, foxtrots, and tangos. At seventeen years old, her secret wish was to be the lead singer with one of these bands one day, but she dared not share this dream with anyone else.

After the evening meal's dishes had been stored away on weekday nights, she used to practice the latest dance steps with her brothers to songs that were played on the family's Pye model radio. Each of the brothers would take a turn leading Ada around the parlor and dining room. Sometimes, Miriam would join in the merriment, but Zvi, complaining of his two clumsy left feet, never did; he was partial to the BBC programs that aired classical music.

"You should listen better," he would instruct his children, but they would laugh and call his symphonies and concertos "fuddy-duddy" music. "My *zeyde* master violinist. *A groys klezmer. Muzik fun di mlhakim.* Of the angels." Zvi's face would beam with pride as he recollected the music of his grandfather, but his sons and daughter had no patience for his reminiscing.

"My sisters are accomplished musicians too," Miriam would declare, laughing as she was whirled or dipped by one son or other, "but we Rosenstein girls love to dance to any kind of music."

Ada much preferred to hear the bands in person at the Sunday afternoon tea dances, being that there were no static interruptions and the sound was less tinny. All the slick musicians, wearing stylish, matching suits and ties, would be seated behind their stands bearing the band's motif. She had memorized the names of each and every one of them and all but held her breath until the female singer came on stage so she could discover what dreamy chiffon or silk formal gown she would be wearing.

Saturdays in the Grossman home were always too dull and insufferable for Ada as her parents had been strict about observing the Sabbath. While her brothers and father would be busily praying in shul, Ada would be counting down the hours and minutes until she could reconnect with her friends, savoring the festive atmosphere and excitement of the dancehall.

She loved getting dressed up for these tea dances, and because of her mother's sewing skills, she had lots of beautiful dresses to wear. On that ill-fated day when she met Harold in May of 1934, she wore a green and white, padded shouldered, mid-calf length frock and four-inch platform shoes. A yellow ribbon was tied through her hair, and she believed she looked just like a movie star.

The five brothers, Ada, and a few of their female friends sat around a table, on which had been placed a pink satin cloth, a black Bakelite telephone with a rotary dial, and a stand supporting a six-inch card with the number five printed in bold ink. From the look on the young man sitting diagonally across from her, Ada could tell he had been eying her up and down. She noticed the older woman he was with had left abruptly. Ada guessed the woman might have been his sister in a hurry to remove an unattended kettle from a heated stove. She was not surprised when the telephone on her table started to ring, so she anxiously picked up the receiver to answer his call.

Despite Harold's voice sounding friendly and overly confident, Ada attempted to act kittenish and coy because that was considered the proper thing to do. He had called her a "blond bombshell," which was both naughty and fresh, but it put a smile on her face and made her feel all mushy inside.

Harold's good looks and overall appearance compelled her to accept his offer to dance right away. His grey double-breasted suit, white starched shirt, and silk striped tie, which were immaculate and chic, were definitely impressive and she had gone absolutely gaga over his debonair, pencil-thin moustache and smooth combed-back hairstyle made slick with just the right amount of Brylcreem.

As he gracefully steered them around the dance floor to the tune of *I Only Have Eyes For You*, Ada felt giddy to be so close to a man so tall and so sure of his own moves. His right hand, resting just above her waist, applied a minimal amount of pressure each time they were to change directions or she was about to be twirled. Ada imagined herself as a princess and her partner as a prince in the center of a royal ball.

When the music stopped, Harold had continued to hold her until the band began to play again. This time it was a waltz. For much of the time, the gap between Harold and Ada remained an acceptable distance, but Harold kept trying to pull her much closer to his chest. When he escorted her back to the table at the end of the number, he asked if he could see her again, and she eagerly agreed.

Over a period of the next three months, he escorted her to fine restaurants, the theater, films, and horse tracks. Throughout these dates, he had acted courteous and polite like a proper gentleman, bringing flowers to Miriam, pipe tobacco to Zvi, and boxes of chocolates for her five brothers.

One evening after a night in the West End, Harold proposed marriage and Ada accepted. As soon as she arrived home, she went running to share the news with her parents, who expressed nothing but pure joy. As was customary, Ada's parents were anxious to meet her betrothed's family as soon as possible.

"They are very busy, hardworking people. It's not so easy for them to take time off from their hectic schedules," Harold confided in Ada. "Nottingham is almost 130 miles away from London, and my parents are terrible travelers. I'm sure your parents won't mind waiting until the day of the wedding to actually meet, considering the difficulty involved."

"That's too bad," Ada said, taking note of the downward turn of Harold's eyebrows and his fluttering eyes. "What if they could talk over the phone? Is that a possibility?"

"No. Not at all. They're old-fashioned and rarely speak on the phone. It would embarrass them to have to communicate this way. I know it sounds odd, but that's the way they are. If you were familiar with the people of Nottingham, then you would understand."

"I'm trying to understand, Harold," Ada said.

"Well, don't try too hard. I don't want your precious brain working itself into knots over this. Yes, it's not a perfect arrangement, but it can't be helped."

Miriam and Zvi were disappointed when Ada told them there was not going to be a coming together with Harold's parents to acknowledge and celebrate the *shidduch*.

"A little unusual for Jewish parents not to gather over *schnapps* and *babke* to discuss the nuptials," Miriam acknowledged. "Regardless, you tell your young man not to worry. By all means, we shall wait."

Chapter Thirty-six

The warning signs reared their ugly heads:

Sometimes, when Ada was indecisive over a show or movie she and Harold were about to see, Harold would lose his patience. "Just pick one already! Christ, it doesn't really matter if it's a Western or a comedy; the tickets will probably be sold out by the time we get there." If he had to wait too long for Ada to be ready for a date, he would seem tense and on edge when she finally arrived. "After all this time, I'm ready to call it quits for the evening and leave you home."

On several occasions, Harold simply stopped seeking Ada's input or opinions on what they were about to do or with whom.

"We'll be going to the Victoria Club with Gloria and Dave after dining in the West End. The reservations have been made."

"We're driving to Brighton for the day. Hurry up in the car before I take off."

"No, we're not going to the kosher restaurant; I feel like having shrimp tonight; it wouldn't kill you to try it."

Whenever Ada would inquire about their honeymoon plans, he would inform her she could find out everything she needed to know when they got there.

"But where is it that we're actually going? How will I know how to pack? How long will we be there?" she had asked one day.

"No need to worry your pretty little head," Harold had said, planting a kiss on her forehead. "Let me take care of this for you, darling. It will be one wonderful surprise. I've even chosen all of the clothes you'll be wearing. I've already bought you some smashing outfits, so you won't have to bother bringing any of those nasty little homemade dresses you've had to wear in the past."

"Oh, I see," she had responded, her head tilting as she bit her bottom lip. "But how will you know the size? The colors I want? Which shoes I have to go with them?"

"Hush," he had said, raising his finger to his mouth. "Like I said before, it will all be taken care of for you. You will be decked out from head to toe in nothing but the finest garments. I've already bought you a full array of fully-fashioned stockings and garter belts to match." This last comment had elicited a giggle from Ada as she covered her face with the palm of her hand and a pink glow spread across her cheeks. Harold kissed the back of her hand. "Trust me on this. You must learn to trust me."

"When will I meet your brother Jack? Does he look like you? I hope he likes me. What color do you think your mother will wear to our wedding? It would be nice to talk to her about the plans so she can feel a part of them. Will I like your father? He's a baker you said. Hmm. Perhaps he can bake some cakes for the dessert. What do you think, Harold? Harold? You look like you're miles away, you silly boy!"

"That's it; I'm up to my neck with all of your pestering," Harold had said in a huff. "We're going there right now. Let's get this over with once and for all so you can stop your girlish nagging. You're bound to find out what they're like sooner or later, so let it be sooner."

Later that evening, Ada had recounted the details to Miriam about her meeting with Harold's mother in the lobby of a hotel in Nottingham. She and Harold had driven there nonstop; he wouldn't even take a break midway in the trip for Ada to grab a sandwich and a cup of tea.

"I had to go to the loo so badly, but Harold told me to keep it in because there'd be cleaner toilets in the hotel where we were heading. That's where and when his mother told us his father had died," Ada reported. "What an unusual, most peculiar woman she was. Not to be nasty, but she looked at least twice your age. She hardly said two words to me and looked at Harold as if she were being introduced to him for the very first time as well."

"You will treat her with kindness and respect nevertheless," Miriam had advised. "And we will do our utmost to make sure she is made to feel welcome at the wedding."

Ada did not let her confusion about Harold's mother, the honeymoon, and Harold's escalating jumpiness unnerve her. All she wanted to think about was being the future Mrs. Kaufman. If she began to feel slighted, then she would gaze at the beautiful platinum ring with its huge diamond solitaire sitting on her left hand. *It's true that Harold has been acting bossier toward me,* she would tell herself, *but this must be his way of making sure all our plans run smoothly. I still can't get it out of my head, though, that he didn't know his own father had died. How unusual! He didn't shed a tear when we found out. It even looked like Harold was laughing on the inside, but that must have been from the shock of it all. I would have simply fallen apart if I was finding out the same about my own father. God forbid!*

Oh, I can't wait until we move into our very own flat above his store. It's going to be so romantic. I'll have a beautiful home, darling children running around to care for, and a generous, handsome husband to call my own.

One evening as the engaged couple exited a theater in the Soho district of London, Harold's temper suddenly erupted and he unleashed an offensive stream of profanity which shocked and embarrassed Ada to no end.

"Please stop," she begged. "Do lower your voice. We're in a public place."

"What the bloody hell do I care if anyone can hear me? Let them hear me. It'll be good for them to hear me. That's what they get for hanging around and sticking their noses in my business. They deserve to hear me! Bloody hell!" Harold had screamed back.

Ada was terrified, and in a knee-jerk reaction she

immediately pulled off her engagement ring and handed it to Harold, which he kept in his clenched fist. "I do not believe anything is worth suffering this kind of humiliation for," Ada added before stomping off in the direction of where Harold's car had been parked.

Harold lit a cigarette and then threw it on the pavement, grinding it to a pulp with the sole of his shoe while muttering and cursing to himself. He then lit another cigarette. After taking a few puffs, he threw this second cigarette into the gutter. "Goddammit!" he had yelled, and then thought better of it, rushing to catch up with Ada.

"Please forgive me," Harold begged before breaking down into a sob, but she had adamantly refused to change her mind.

When they were seated in his car, Harold tried sweet-talking and cajoling Ada out of her decision, but she clenched her teeth, folded her arms, and stared straight ahead.

"Ada, so help me God, I will jump off the London Bridge if you do not take my ring back. I mean it! Don't be a silly girl. Stop acting like a baby. People raise their voices all the time when they get angry. Everyone does. You're just not used to it in your sheltered home. It's time for you to grow up and see life as it really is."

Ada didn't utter a sound.

Harold slammed the steering wheel. "Ada, I love you. I need you. This whole thing will just pass over."

"I'm not so sure about that, Harold," she whimpered, although she was trying with all her might to remain strong and convincing.

"I will kill myself if you don't take me back!" Harold had cried out, his voice tight and desperate. "I promise you I will. I really mean it! I am definitely going to throw myself over one of those bridges crossing the Thames. You have to marry me. Don't think for one minute that I won't do it." Harold's tone became angrier and louder still. "You'll take the ring back if you know what's good for you!"

Ada inched closer to the passenger door and placed her gloved hands and bag in her lap. "I want to go home now," she said softly, not removing her focus from the window. "Perhaps I should take the bus."

Chapter Thirty-seven

One should always trust one's instincts:

Harold placed Ada's engagement ring in his pocket and insisted on driving her home. It just so happened that she did not have enough money in her purse for a taxi and the trains and busses had stopped running that late at night, so Ada had no other choice but to allow him to do so.

All along the different neighborhoods they passed, she sat fuming in her seat. Harold kept whistling the same tune over and over again, which Ada found to be most annoying, but she would not violate her vow of silence to tell him to stop. When he parked his car by the curb in Whitechapel, she adamantly refused to give him a parting kiss and rushed ahead so she could intentionally shut the door in his face.

As soon as she could, Ada ran about the house trying to locate Miriam and Zvi so she could tell them about the quarrel.

"If such a tragedy occurs, God forbid," her mother moaned, "it could cause a stigma to befall upon our entire Jewish community."

Next was her father's turn to speak while her mother groaned and beat her chest. "Suicide, *aveyre*. Very big sin. Cannot bury near loved ones in holy cemetery."

"When we lived in Poland, our lives were in constant jeopardy," Miriam continued between gasps. "We had to avoid confrontation at all costs. Therefore, Ada, I am now asking you to try and make peace with Harold." She approached her daughter, pinched her cheeks, and patted her on the back. "Be a good girl and don't bring unwanted attention to yourself. He's such a good man. Perhaps you over-reacted? Perhaps he became overcome with grief after unexpectedly learning about his father? After all, for him there was no *Shiva* period. He didn't know enough to say *Kaddish* for his own father. Ada, you've got plenty of years ahead of you. During that time, he'll change for the better; you'll see. Take back that gorgeous ring and let's proceed with the wedding."

"*Bubbeleh,*" her father said, "he's a good man."

"The man adores you," Miriam pleaded. "He got a little angry; some men do that. He didn't mean anything by it. It's harmless. You'll learn how to deal with it better when you're married. Don't forget about the prior *mishegas* you concocted out of nothing at all." Miriam clasped her hands together. "Good, it's settled."

"I'm not so sure it's settled," Ada replied with hesitation.

"Ach. If I have to beat sense into you I will. He's such a scholar and has a thorough knowledge and understanding of Judaism. Your father sees him as a *bal toyreh,* a knowledgeable man, always showing the highest respect before our very own eyes."

Miriam, shaking her head, grabbed Ada by the shoulders. "How could he possibly be half the monster that you claim him to be? My little *dummkopf,* you must learn to exhibit a little more compassion."

"So much money already spent on the *farkakteh* wedding plans," Zvi grumbled.

Miriam jumped in again. "It will be a crime to let that money go to waste. It doesn't matter if Harold kills himself or goes elsewhere; the consequences will still be the same for you. It will be a *shanda* for our family, and you might end up being a spinster, God forbid."

Zvi's head dropped to his chest as he declared, "I have to sit down." He walked over to his favorite armchair, his face contorted with pain and fear. "Ada, it is true you are good looking *meydl,* but poor in school." He looked at Miriam, giving her license to carry on.

"You had trouble keeping a job, yes? You may have a pretty singing voice and a friendly disposition, but these are not skills that can bring you security. A life in the theater is unthinkable for a decent Jewish girl."

Miriam walked over to be by Zvi's side. "Ada, do you comprehend how tortured we will be if Harold actually goes ahead with his threat? We could never forgive ourselves. Such pain, such disaster, such a terrible ending for such a fine young man with so much potential. Oi, oi, oi!"

Ada was beside herself with indecision. Why shouldn't she listen to the advice of her parents? They had always been her strongest support. Any time she had lost her job or returned home from school with a bad report, they were the ones to encourage her, telling her of other golden opportunities waiting up ahead. She would flounder about in disappointment and bleakness, but her mother and father, being older and wiser, would help pull her together and guide her on a new path in a better direction. All things considered, wasn't that what parents were for?

She knew of young girls whose marriages had been arranged. Love was something that was supposed to develop in the years those couples lived together. Some of the husbands had been Yeshiva students who now did nothing but study the Torah all day long. What fun was there in that? Some turned out to be hideously ugly, and this is what those girls had to face waking up each morning if they so happened to share the same bed. Some of those men could not earn a living even if they tried.

That, however, was not the case with Harold. He had said he loved her. He certainly was comfortably rich. He was more than good looking and far more intelligent than her. It was true that Harold would make an excellent provider. Of all the girls in London, she was the only one he wanted. Didn't that mean something?

Ada had not been trained to be anything other than an industrious mother and a deferential wife. Her job was to create a Jewish home patterned after the one in which she had grown. What if she had misspoken? What if she was incorrect in the way she had perceived or recalled the events of that night? Watching her mother sob and pull out her hair in frustration, Ada realized she had no other choice but to acquiesce to her parents' wishes.

Chapter Thirty-eight

Like a trapped animal, she entered the cage, unaware there would be no exit:

Harold and Ada exchanged their wedding vows in a double ceremony with Ada's brother Harry and his fiancée Rebecca in the same *shul* where Miriam and Zvi had wed. Rebecca's father had imported fabric for most of the tailors in the Jewish community, and Harry had accidentally bumped into her when she was delivering worsted wool to Zvi's factory. Actually, he had almost tripped over her because she was so petite and he had not seen her coming through the doorway when he was rushing out. Their romancing and wooing took place over three short weeks, but Harry was absolutely certain that he wanted no other bride for himself but Rebecca. What she lacked in size, she more than made up for with fearlessness and gumption.

Zvi was the one who came up with the idea of the double ceremony. "The rabbi and the *chazan* have been booked already. It makes good sense money-wise." Later he would confide in Miriam, "Just in case Ada changes her mind last minute, we won't be out of pocket."

When Miriam offered to Rebecca's parents, "The guest list will be the same with just a few exceptions. Your side will hardly have to contribute much at all," they and Rebecca readily agreed to Zvi's proposition.

Because she was so small, an empty orange crate had been placed under the *chuppah* upon which Rebecca was to stand at the end of the procession. Harry, Harold, and Ada were assigned the responsibility of ensuring that Rebecca climbed onto the crate and remained there steadily throughout the prayers and other formalities.

Ada wore a gown of ivory *peau de soie* with a floor length veil trimmed with clusters of lily of the valley, which was far more expensive than the gown Rebecca wore. Contributing a substantial amount of money toward the cost, Harold had instructed Ada on the day she went shopping with Miriam, "I want your wedding gown to wow me away. You'll be getting married only once in your life, so make sure the gown is everything I want it to be."

The eight bridesmaids, wearing pale pink and baby blue taffeta dresses with matching headbands and followed by two flower girls, marched in slowly as a violinist stationed in the corner began to play. As the two pairs of brides and grooms walked down the aisle, a buzz could be heard arising from the audience, which was separated into male and female sections. The *kvelling* and non-stop babbling of "Oohs" and "Ahs" all but drowned out the music. Some even said that the grooms, donned in top hats and tails, could have been understudies for Fred Astaire and Franchot Tone—they were that handsome!

The guests, all relatively new residents of London's East End, had mostly known each other in the villages they had left behind. They arrived at the wedding dressed in their finest garments, beaded, pleated, or feathered, all expertly measured and sewn together by their own hands. Absent from this group, however, were members of Harold's family. According to Harold, they had met with an unforeseen problem just as they were setting out from Nottingham. Speaking solely with Harold over the phone, his mother had supposedly extended her apologies and regrets.

At the reception hall, there was a healthy selection of soups, both hot and cold, salted beefs, smoked salmon, pickled fish, *stuffed kishka*, and many kinds of kugels, both savory and sweet. Differing from past tradition, the men and women dared to dance with their arms around each other until the early morning hours while a string orchestra played the most popular ballads of the day. For everyone attending the wedding, this was a new world with new ways of doing things, and for the most part, the guests were eager and happy to make that adjustment.

The only hiccup in the festivities arose after the last invited guests (Aunt Gerte and Uncle Hymie, who couldn't stop raving about the affair), had left the banquet hall and it was time to divvy the gifts between the two newly-married couples. Ada had been previously taken aside by her husband and had been warned ahead of time not to intervene with the decisions he would make. She sat watching in her chair, her hair falling away from the clips and her chin resting on her chest, trying not to look too glum while Harold, acting outwardly gracious and genuinely big-hearted, insisted that Harry and Rebecca keep practically all of the presents. It had not gone unnoticed by Ada that Harold had snubbed his nose at several of the unwrapped boxes before making his pronouncements.

When it was time to allocate an expensive Waterford crystal pitcher and six matching long stem glasses, however, Harold had deviated from his course, putting his foot down in no uncertain way.

"I'll keep that crystal," he stated clearly, placing the box with its glittering contents by Ada's feet that were no longer in her shoes. "We'll buy the other six glasses ourselves to complete the set."

Unfortunately, Rebecca had adamantly refused to cede that particular gift to Harold, which caused his jaw muscles to constrict and his eyes to become little slanted slits. His breathing became as agitated as a bull's about to charge at a matador's cape.

"I believe it was my cousin who gave us that," Rebecca piped up, "and I want it!"

"Gorblimey," Harold howled. "What difference does it make who gave what? So far, you've made out like bandits. Would it hurt you to let Ada have the one little thing her heart desires?"

"But Ada didn't say a word about it, did she?" Rebecca questioned.

"Well, she's saying it now." Harold turned to Ada. "Why don't you tell Rebecca and Harry how much you want that crystal?"

"Ada can have whatever she wants," Harry volunteered before Rebecca's elbow made a sharp indent into his ribs.

Ada took a deep breath and swallowed. "Yes," she uttered meekly.

"Speak up," Harold urged. "Has the cat got your tongue? No one can hear you."

Ada stammered, "Harold, if Rebecca feels so strongly about the crystal, I really don't mind if—"

Harold's hand rose as if about to strike Ada in the face, but he abruptly halted this movement by straightening his hair behind his ears. "You're such a shy, considerate girl. That's why I feel compelled in times like these to speak up for you. What Ada means to say is that she very much wants the crystal!"

Hastily, Miriam stepped forward in Solomonic wisdom and reclaimed the box. "Let's be fair about this," she announced while Zvi went about paying what was owed to the caterer. "How about we split the gift so Harold and Ada will take home the pitcher and Harry and Rebecca will keep the wine glasses?" She lifted the pitcher to hand to Harold and then departed to catch up with Zvi.

"You stupid midget!" Harold chided Rebecca. "You're nothing but a cheap, selfish, spoiled rotten slut." He threw the pitcher at her but purposefully aimed it at the floor, prompting Harry to dive in to grab the handle and rescue the sought-after object from crashing into a million pieces. "Take the whole damn thing if it means so much to you." Next, he roughly grabbed Ada's hand and yanked her towards him. "We're leaving right this minute."

Ada didn't have time to put on her shoes, but as she was running to keep up with Harold, she turned to Rebecca and whispered, "Please give the pitcher to my mother for my safe keeping, but do not ever let Harold know."

No matter how joyous the wedding celebration had been and how optimistic Miriam and Zvi had felt about their children's futures, there was no guaranty that Harold and Ada Kaufman would live "happily ever after" in marital bliss. Harold's bizarre and often contentious behavior grew to be much worse on a daily basis, causing Ada to go tentatively and miserably about her chores.

Harry, on the other hand, had continued to adore his wife and treat her as a goddess, fulfilling her every wish. In contrast to the worshipped, pintsized Rebecca, Ada became a woman robbed of her own will, always and forever looking back with regret at the potent time of Harold's suicidal threat when no one had been audacious enough to call his bluff. Despite her parents' hopes and contention for a different outcome, the emotional blackmailing and abuse that had been initially foisted upon Ada persisted throughout her marriage.

Chapter Thirty-nine

Life with the mad man:

As a newlywed, there was very little that Ada could do to make Harold content with the woman he had married. Each day she would try out a different recipe, hoping to create an enticing meal to earn his approval, but none of her efforts succeeded to the level of Harold's exacting standards. She was berated for not setting the dinner table the way he liked, ignored for days for over-seasoning the soup, penalized for preparing roast beef instead of leg of lamb, and struck for burning the salmon croquettes.

Seemingly at random, Harold would cancel their social engagements. Sometimes, Ada had been allowed to keep her plans without him; at other times, she would be forced to stay home to keep him company.

"But Harold, it's my best friend's wedding and you bought me that beautiful peach, brocade gown to wear. It will go to waste! What will I tell people when they ask why we didn't attend?"

"I don't care."

"But they are bound to ask questions."

"Tell them you had a nasty cold."

There was never any excuse offered to explain his behavior. If he was punishing her, she was at a loss to understand why or what terrible act she must have committed.

In public settings, Harold would call her "stupid," "idiot," and other such names, eroding any self-esteem that she may have ever possessed. Overhearing her partake in an ongoing conversation, he would loudly say, "Sound the trumpets, look who thinks she knows it all!"

"For God's sake, stop that cat-calling," he would yell if Ada ever began to sing. "You're screeching! I can't stand it. You're giving me a headache and driving me mad." Within time, Ada had stopped singing altogether, even when she was by herself.

Harold eventually found fault with all of her friends and with each of her sisters-in-law, ordering her to stay away from those "low-lives." If anyone committed an act that Harold perceived to cross him, the culprit would be banned from their home and Ada was forbidden to see them. He formulated rules, some of which were truly bizarre, by which Ada needed to conduct herself.

"You don't go out without your hair set and makeup on your face."

"Never wear stockings with snags, holes, or crooked seams."

"The silverware is to be polished and the tablecloths and serviettes are to be ironed each day before using them."

"My shirts are to be washed, ironed stiff, neatly folded, and stored in my wardrobe in immaculate order."

"I want full bottles of HP sauce and Coleman's mustard on the supper table every night without fail. Don't ever let me see them be half-full!"

At the tail end of Ada's first pregnancy, which correlated with nine months past the date of her honeymoon, she had nervously approached Harold while he was engrossed in his weekly poker game in the living room of their home. The room was noisy and filled with cigarette and pipe smoke.

"Harold, please excuse me. I'm terribly sorry to have to interrupt you in the middle of your game, but I think my water just broke and the baby's coming. I would like to go to the hospital now."

Harold had kept his head buried in his cards.

"Harold, as I said before, I believe it's time to deliver the baby. I know that this is an inconvenient time for you, but I am in pain and I want a doctor to see me."

Harold had refused to acknowledge Ada's presence or respond to her pleas.

"Harold, I need someone to drive me!"

The other card players knew enough to keep themselves out of the family matter. Harold was the head of his household and it wasn't anyone else's place to interfere, despite the severity of the situation or possibly feeling sorry for Ada, especially in her vulnerable condition.

"You are being unacceptably rude," he had said, surrounded by his cohorts. "Can't you see we have a game going here? I've been dealt a very nice hand and I intend to play it out."

"But it's not my fault my water broke."

"Bloody hell, would you just shut up and move to another room? You're making a fool of yourself. You'd think you're the only woman in the world ever to have a baby. I'm in the middle of a game and I'm not moving one inch until it's over."

As the contractions intensified, Ada made a desperate call to her oldest brother, Morris, who hurriedly drove her to the hospital so she could receive the appropriate medical care and her baby's progress could be monitored. Throughout the car ride, not a single word between the brother and sister were exchanged. They had both come to realize that Ada's situation could never be improved upon as long as Harold was alive.

Chapter Forty

War came to England:

Harold's bullying continued from the time of Ada's first baby's delivery through most of that baby's child rearing years. Esther was a beautiful girl with large blue eyes and rich, curly brown hair, but she suffered from her father's scorn and derision just as equally as Ada. She too was called "stupid", "idiot", and "fatso", and was made to believe she was inferior to everyone else on earth. There wasn't anything that the child could say or do to endear herself to her father.

When the Second World War broke out, Harold learned he was being transported many miles away to the Saharan desert. There, he would have to contend with Rommel's Afrika Korps, Yellow Fever, unbearable tropical heat, and venomous creatures indigenous to the region.

"It'll be okay for you two," he carped to Ada in a fit of self-pity. "You and Esther will continue to live your pampered, la-di-dah lives surrounded by modern conveniences and without having to make much sacrifice. I, conversely, will have no feathered pillows or mattress to rest upon while I'm out on the battlefields."

"We'll all be contributing in some way to the war effort," Ada replied.

"Bloody hell, Ada. What big fat contribution do you think you're capable of making? It's *my* business that has to be sold, *my* job to go marching off into who knows where, and *my* life that has to be placed on the line to go fight the filthy Nazis. Sod those Gerries! Sod them all for messing up *my* life."

When his conscription papers first arrived in 1940, Harold tried to turn the beauty salon's operation over to Ada, which would keep the lion's share of the profits within his family's immediate circle. Her arithmetic, bookkeeping, and managerial skills, however, were pathetic.

"Keep your columns straight: the pounds go with the pounds and the shillings go under the shillings. For God's sake girl, you've erased all the pennies!"

Harold shared all that he knew about the dying process with his uncomprehending wife, imparting a minimal amount of business sense into her head, but it was all for naught. Try as she might, Ada managed to burn the scalps of everyone unlucky enough to be a guinea pig. Some women looked like they had bales of hay sitting on their heads and went running out into the street, screaming in anguish after Ada had finished with them. Harold's patience waned with every lesson they embarked upon.

Harold would shout, "You make a dunce look smart, Ada. You've got to be the most stupid woman in the world! How are you ever going to keep our business afloat?" If an object was sitting close by, he would pick it up and fling it. Royal Doulton figurines were smashed as well as Ada's favorite china teacups and saucers. "You're destroying everything I've built. The appointments will disappear and all our profits will hit rock-bottom because you're a stupid nincompoop! It's all your fault our lives are falling apart."

Finding himself in a bind, Harold sold their living quarters and the salon below it to a distant relative. The new family moved in, and Harold, Esther, and Ada moved temporarily into Miriam and Zvi's home. In one of the first bombing raids to hit the country, the shop and upstairs flat took a direct hit. Dead bodies, debris, and wreckage filled the scene that used to be bustling with activity. All those inhabiting the flat and its surrounding environment were killed instantly.

When the time arrived for Harold to join the other soldiers assembled at the Victoria train station, Ada acted the role of a dutiful wife, masking her relief as she stood proudly saluting the British flag and waving her husband goodbye. Truth be told, she had been reveling in the newly found independence Harold's departure was going to afford her. No longer would she be forced to submit to his nightly sexual advances or his perpetual taunts and putdowns. As preposterous as it seemed, the bombs falling on London seemed less threatening than the hostile environment in which Harold had forced Esther and Ada to live.

"Please God, grant me some peace, so I don't have to be so afraid all the time," she prayed, standing on the station platform jam-packed with soldiers suited up in their olive-drab uniforms and combat boots. A landscape of marching bands, families embracing as they uttered their tearful goodbyes, smoky, steam puffing from the train engines, and a plentiful, patriotic display of Union Jacks surrounded her.

Amidst a cacophony of screeching whistles, barking orders, incomprehensible announcements made over the public speakers, and the chug-chug-chugging of the trains oozing their way out of the station, Harold and Ada parted. She could barely hear what he had to say. It was something to do with a plan he had schemed up. "Don't mess it up," he kept repeating. "The letter will say you've been fooling around like a harlot while I'm away. I'm hoping that will get me at least one furlough." Harold was now seated by a window, glaring at Ada, who forced a faint smile to her lips.

"We caught a lucky break," Ada continued praying, "when we were saved from that first bombing. Perhaps God, that luck can be extended a few more years; that's all I'm asking for. I'm hoping Esther can have at least some time to be a happy little girl—not that that's so easy at a time of war, but we'll grab any happiness we can get while the ogre's away. I'm not saying he has to die, but if he could just get lost finding his way home, I would be very grateful."

Chapter Forty-one

Remaining on the home front was no picnic:

For the seven years that Harold fought in Africa, Ada and Esther's lives were not quite as comfortable and lush as Harold had supposed them to be. Sirens went off every other minute, bombs continuously fell from enemy fighter planes, and rations were forever sparse. Furthermore, all of Ada's five brothers were spread out across the globe serving in the army, air force, ambulance, and fire brigades.

During the Blitz of 1940, fierce, raging, unstoppable fires spread across the East End of London as bombs exploded day and night, leaving charred, broken, and lifeless bodies littering the rubble-lined streets.

As soon as the sirens began to sound, Miriam would lead Zvi, Ada, and Esther around the debris and through the darkened night, sporadically illuminated by the intermittent flashing from the hostile guns of German aircraft, to the school across from the park.

Each adult would be carrying their own clunky gas mask, but Zvi also carried the cumbersome baby helmet that would be used to engulf Esther in case chemical weapons were used in the attacks. Pointing to the ominous orange and red flames attacking the city, she would sadly announce to Zvi, "Fireman Morris will be kept busy again tonight." (*Later in the year, when that same schoolhouse was sheltering almost 700 people, it took a direct hit and collapsed, forming a crater in which most of the people were buried and killed.*)

When Miriam, Zvi, Ada, and Esther emerged from the school during one break in the shelling, they discovered that Miriam and Zvi's home had been burned to the ground along with all the other buildings in that section of the city. Everyone then needed to scramble around to find other workable living arrangements. Ada's parents managed to secure a small closet of a room in a cousin's home, but there wasn't space enough for Ada and the baby.

Ada and Esther were, therefore, forced to live in the underground shelters where bunk beds and toilets were supplied by the government. Her preferred residence was the light and airy Bethnal Green station, substantial enough to maintain a library and provide well-stocked urns to distribute cups of tea. Its construction begun before the onset of war had not been completed, so the absence of a track allowed for a large, more open living space. At times, there were up to 2,000 people accommodated in this shelter.

In March 1943, busloads of returning movie goers were heading to the shelter when a woman had fallen down a flight of steps that led to the platform. This first fall had triggered other people to trip and fall until a large pile-up of struggling human beings had formed at the base of the stairs. As this was happening, an anti-aircraft rocket was being tested nearby but was misinterpreted by some as a new kind of incoming bomb, thus instigating an outbreak of hysteria which caused many more to run to the shelter. Those scurrying were unaware that access to the underground shelter, made even more unsafe by slippery steps due to the rain and the absence of a handrail, had become dangerously blocked. 300 people became wedged in. 173 men, women, and children were crushed to death and 60 others needed hospital treatment. After this incident, Ada decided the underground shelter was no longer a safe option for her and her baby.

She took to roaming the countryside and surrounding vicinities, wheeling a pram that seated Esther and also carried their one suitcase. However, not all the people in the outskirts would be friendly and welcoming. Plenty did pitch in to serve a warm meal and offer an empty bed or blankets cozy enough on which to sleep, but there were still those who refrained from providing lodging to any displaced persons.

Mother and child, travelling in groups with other women, that sometimes included Rebecca and her own baby daughter, were often turned away and forced to sleep in the open fields.

"Look for the pet owners," Ada would instruct Rebecca. "Try to see if the window sills on the houses contain budgerigar cages."

"Why is that?" Rebecca would ask.

"Someone kind to pets should also be kind to us Londoners." But oftentimes when the homeowner would come to the door and see Ada standing with Rebecca and two babies, they would complain they were short on room and shut the door in their faces.

"They think we look too much like foreigners," Rebecca would bemoan. "Either that or they just don't like Jews."

Chapter Forty-two

No, he didn't get lost:

Harold was his own worst enemy. Or to put it more accurately, his pride and ego were what got the worst of him, and that would've been just fine, had he not taken Ada and her child down with him. Ada's five brothers, just like many other soldiers returning from the war, had found it challenging to adjust to peaceful, normal lives, but they eventually did. In Harold's case, however, nothing was ever going to be normal again.

After his final, safe return to British soil, Harold became greatly incensed over the paltry benefits offered to the veterans of war, and so he refused to accept any compensation from his government. "I had given too much to receive so little," he had proclaimed with full bravado. He returned his pension in the same exact envelope in which it was originally sent with a notation written in his purposeful handwriting: "You can stick this where the sun don't shine."

Ada was not impressed with Harold's self-dignifying act of sending back the money, no matter how small the amount. Despite having to contend with his verbal assaults all over again, she had been struggling daily to make ends meet and was looking to him to be the savior and breadwinner for the family. She would have welcomed any additional pennies and made sure they were well spent. Harold, however, could never tolerate being regarded as a person in need.

"I'd sooner take arsenic than take one farthing from those measly buggars; better that we should all starve to death!" Ada shuddered to think of Esther, hungry and suffering because her father had declined a handout or a hand up. Now pregnant with her second child, she worried constantly about receiving proper nutrition and having a decent place to call home.

Ada's brother Harry had stumbled across a goldmine when he connected with Egyptian cotton suppliers during the war. This forged business relationship had expanded into a healthy trading enterprise that paid Harry extremely well. Now back from the war, he used these proceeds to invest in a chain of menswear shops and invited his brothers to join him. However, not one of the brothers wanted Harold to be a part of this new venture; Ada didn't blame them one bit.

"He'll try to rip our heads off no matter what."

"He'll scream and carry on like a thunderstorm in front of the customers."

"I've survived enough battles to last me a lifetime. I don't need any more."

"The man's a walking time bomb."

"Rebecca gave me strict orders not to include him."

As you can imagine, Harold did not anticipate this exclusion. He waited a few months for the brothers to approach him with a business offer, but they never did. The rejection was tantamount to a slap in the face that sliced a deep, humiliating scar.

"Bloody hell, I'm the only one of the lot that's not color blind," he told Ada, pacing around the kitchen as she unwrapped fillets of carp and pike at the table. "I've got a brain that works, not them."

Ada grated the fish and went to gather carrots, parsnips, and onions from the pantry, which was located in the corner of the dining room.

He raised his voice. "I'm talking to you. Don't you realize it's rude to ignore someone who's talking to you?"

"I needed the vegetables for the gefilte fish," she said upon her return as she unloaded the produce into the sink.

"And that couldn't wait? From now on, you'll stay listening to me until I'm finished." He dragged a chair across the floor and straddled it. The breath exiting his nose became faster, deeper, and more irregular.

"Yes, Harold."

"And who told you to buy fresh fish? Did you use the money from your *pushka*?"

She washed and peeled the roots, placing them in a large wooden bowl. With a chopping blade, she systematically pounded the vegetables until they were minced into miniscule pieces. "My mother gave us the fish. She said she had ordered more than what she needed."

"She couldn't just make it for you as well? After all, she's a much better cook than you." He fumbled around his shirt pocket to extract a packet of Player's Navy Cut.

"It's her recipe I'm using. The food will taste just as good."

Harold lit a cigarette and blew the smoke in Ada's direction. "As I was saying, how are those *schmendricks* ever going to distinguish shirt colors? They don't even know the meaning of style! They don't know how to hustle like I can." He lifted his arms to crisscross them around the chair back, allowing some ashes to drift to the vinyl floor. "They'll fall flat on their arses in no time; mark my words."

Ada added the vegetables to the fish mash and reached for the container of matzoh meal.

"Don't put too much seasoning in that mix. Last *yom tov*, I couldn't eat anything you made because it was too salty. I was kept up all night long having to drink water and then piss; drink water and piss."

"I will do my best to make it just as you like it." She added eggs into the mixture, formed balls, and placed them into a large simmering pot which contained the fish head, bones, onions, peppercorns, sugar, and water.

"Am I not ten million times more intelligent than all of those schmucks combined, Ada? Ada, I asked you a question!"

Ada placed the lid on the pot and lowered the flame. Using the corner of her apron, she wiped her brow. Her face was wet and red from the heat rising from the stove. "Yes, you are, Harold."

251

"Yes, I am what, Ada?"

"You are ten million times more intelligent than my brothers."

He took a lengthy drag on his cigarette. "That's right. And don't you ever forget it! Arse hole morons. The lot of you!"

Whenever the entire Grossman family gathered together, whether it was to welcome the Sabbath, the New Year, or to sit down at the Seder table during Passover, Harold would take the opportunity to express his resentment over and over again. The house of *shalom,* built by Miriam and Zvi out of love and mutual respect, had become corrupted by spiteful altercations, outward distrust, and intense animosity.

Out of uniform and close to being penniless, Harold needed to find a job. The beauty shop had long been sold—fortunate for the sellers, Harold and Ada Kaufman, but horribly unfortunate for the buyers—and all the earnings had been nearly depleted. One day, Harold announced his intent to Ada to become a dressmaker, about which he had no prior experience.

"Are you going to a special school?" she asked.

"I will teach myself," he declared.

"How are you going to figure out what you need to learn?" she asked with trepidation.

"Some of us were born with brains, Ada. You're not one of them, but I am. I'll teach myself pattern making, fabric cutting, and construction. You'll see; my garments will fit perfectly and they'll become all the rage."

"I hope so."

"'I hope so'? That's the most you can say? Oh, why do I even bother to have a conversation with you? I'd get more out of a dog."

Ada swallowed and just stared in Harold's direction, afraid to set him off by saying the wrong thing.

"Let's see who comes begging and to whom!" Harold continued. "Your brothers' eyes will fall out with envy, and you'll be there to see it happen! Our home will be a palace. I'll have you draped in furs and dripping in diamonds. Oh, I can't wait to see the look on their ugly mugs. You're not saying anything. Why aren't you saying anything? You should be jumping up and down with joy, but instead you have that moping look on your face again; it's like it's glued on."

"I'm listening to you," Ada responded.

"Well, see if you can stop sulking for a second. Where was I? Oh yes. I will out-do them all. I became famous once; I can do it all over again! You mark my words. Did you hear what I said, Ada?"

"Yes. You'll be famous again," she answered.

Chapter Forty-three

Feeling powerless and enslaved:

For twelve years of marriage, Ada continued to be subjected to Harold's bullying. She had absolutely no idea how to combat him or defend herself. Each day, he decided what clothes she wore, how she styled her hair, and the food they were going to eat. If she dared not comply with his wishes, he became more belligerent.

Each evening, Ada would slip beneath the bed covers with resignation, hoping to fulfill her wifely duties as quickly as possible. Oh, how she detested having to be intimate with her husband, having been emptied of any passion or respect she might have once held for him. If she tried to thwart his sexual advances, he responded with force. There was no limit to his wrath and condemnation. Running away from time to time was her only recourse.

Exhausted from his insults and having suffered from the immensely humiliating scenes he loved to create, she found herself withdrawing more and more. To outside observers, it might have seemed as if she had been in permanent shock or had had her tongue pulled out of her mouth.

When Miriam died of a heart attack in 1949, Ada could not shed a single tear and sank further into a bottomless depression. She lost interest in her household chores and tending to her two daughters' needs. Simple deeds like squeezing the toothpaste or washing her face in the morning became too much of an effort. Joan, who was four years old, was mostly cared for by Esther, who at the age of twelve was more interested in boys than being a babysitter. Ada's brothers became concerned with her weight loss and deteriorating condition. They approached Harold, daring to extend beyond the hostile division that existed between them, and requested that he bring her to be seen by a doctor. Harold reluctantly did so, but not without a lot of hemming and hawing and a display of irksome magnanimity.

The family doctor referred Ada to a specialist. When the specialist referred her to a hypnotist, Harold put his foot down and refused to go any further in the process.

"You're a little melancholy; what's the big deal? All this running around is a waste of my time. You don't need to be seen by a hypnotist. That's just a fancy name for witch doctor. If you ask me, hypnotism is a load of claptrap. You're just feeling sorry for yourself, Ada. I'm on to you. You think this is going to get you lots of extra attention. I'm no fool. Stop with the dramatics. Stop with the pretending. It's not going to do you any good at all."

In the past, Zvi had professed a policy of not meddling in his married children's affairs. When Miriam would grouse about her daughters-in-law— "I don't think this one is buying kosher meat" or "They were talking in the chemist about that one looking too much like a show girl with feathers in her hat and bright red nail polish" or "She made him buy a new car. What was wrong with the old one?" —Zvi would respond, "It's none of our business anymore. They're grown up and have to solve their own problems now." When the five brothers consulted with him about their sister's poor health, however, the widower agreed to intercede on Ada's behalf. He asked to meet Harold for lunch at Bloom's Kosher Restaurant on Old Montague Street. The two men sat over plates of thick corned beef sandwiches.

Zvi was dressed in a black suit. A ragged slit had been cut across his lapel. "I not made requests of you in past. Is not my nature to do so, but circumstances require me do so now. I would like you bring Ada to see hypnotist. Please Harold. Do for sake of Miriam; in memory of such great woman all of us lost, *alav Ha-shalom*. May she rest in peace."

Without saying a word, Harold removed the top layer of bread and schmeared the meat with mustard. Replacing the slice of seeded rye, he took a mammoth bite and chewed.

"We are in *Shloshim* period of mourning," Zvi continued, his sandwich remaining untouched. "I asking you do what is right. I asking you do no more no less what written in Ten Commandments. This what Miriam, God bless her soul, such woman of valor, would want. I mean no disrespect on your own parents, but Harold, Miriam treated you same way she treated own sons. I ask you honor her memory now."

Harold took a chunk out of his pickled cucumber, wiped his hands on his cloth napkin, and then took a swig of his Coca Cola. Zvi bowed his head, waiting for Harold to say something. In lieu of words, Harold let out a belch. He laughed. "Pardon me. My shoes must be too tight."

Zvi sighed, placing his hands in his lap.

"All right. All right. I'll do it because *Ani Yahoodeʒ Tov."*

Harold's words elicited a broad smile to stretch across Zvi's cheeks. "Yes. Yes you are. A good Jew!"

(Such a contradiction my father was when it came to the subject of religion.)

The hypnotist pricked Ada's finger with a sewing needle and made her cry for hours. He advised her to go home and make another baby to "fill the void created by your mother's death" as if this was the only detectable cause for Ada's malaise.

The notion of having a third child had never before entered Ada's mind. It was the last thing she wanted—or needed, for that matter. Furthermore, Harold and Ada's finances were such that they couldn't really afford another mouth to feed. Had Harold not been such a gambler, willing to take too many risks at the race track and in poker games, the family could have been living well on the proceeds from his thriving garment manufacturing business. In spite of this, they complied with the hypnotist's recommendation.

Amid disappointment, disillusionment, and infinite unhappiness, Ada gave birth to a third daughter. Had she given birth to a boy, perhaps things would have been different. Perhaps Harold or Ada might have had some reason to be a little more interested in that child, who turned out to be me, Myra Sturnberger nee Kaufman.

Oh, how I grew to hate that name and what it represented. When I met Teddy, the love of my life, I couldn't wait to marry him and say goodbye to Myra Kaufman forever.

Chapter Forty-four
KAT

I haven't had a day to myself in ages since meeting Stephen at Starbucks. I do really love Noah. I couldn't imagine a life without him, but honestly, you have to watch him constantly. He's up, he's down, he's climbing the walls, squirming and fidgeting, distracted from one activity to the next. The little imp runs circles about me; I cannot take my eyes off of him for a second. Who has the patience or energy for this? Between work and coming home to such a wildly spirited child, I don't have the luxury of ever taking it easy. At the end of the day, all I can think about is putting my feet up and catching some Zs.

Stephen thinks I should be putting more effort into my social life. "Start dating again" or "Go to a movie with a friend". My mother keeps urging me to pick myself up, dust myself off, and start anew. No, I cannot blissfully float myself off to *Never-Never Land* and act as if everything is all right. Try the "un-clinging" method when your monkey-toddler-child has been up four nights in a row with teething pains and you've had zero sleep!

My one good friend, Sheila, has been seeing someone steadily ever since we went to the speed-dating event together (he plain out refused to move on to the next female when the timer went off), but I am far from anxious to put myself up for grabs in that meat market again. All that I want to do lately is veg-out. Is that too much to ask?

Good old omniscient Myra has started to get on my case about me moving out: "I left the newspaper on the credenza opened to the real estate section." At the supper table, she's constantly inquiring about the progress I'm making. "Have you Googled it? Just type in clean, decent, two-bedroom apartment or small house to rent. Be sure to check out Zillow and Trulia as well."

"I will; I will," I moan back.

"I have many friends who are realtors. You can call any one of them to help you out."

"I will; I will," I respond with the keenness of someone undergoing a root canal.

"You're making her life too easy here. You should stop coddling her," I heard my father remark when he mistakenly presumed I was out of earshot.

I guess my parents' original intent to "be here to support you no matter what" has finally run out of steam. What's that saying about fish and guests stinking after three days? Noah and I must really be smelling up their joint!

It can't be just by accident that our meals are becoming less inspired and much more ho-hum. The dinners Mom has been providing of late have been reduced to the standard proteins and vegetables on a plate or take-out subs from the deli counter at the supermarket. Gone are the whipped-up, oh-my-God-these-are-so-delicious-and-amazing casseroles, soufflés, or frittatas. Thrown into the mix of things getting tired and out of hand are the many toys Noah is leaving all over the floor, exactly in position for Mom or Dad to trip over. I cringe each time I have to hear her cry, "I'm getting too old for this," when she stoops to pick up some plaything. *Oh, please do spare me the theatrics.*

If I have to be honest, I have noticed that some windows and sliding doors have been generously smeared with greasy imprints matching the size of Noah's hands. The walls in the kitchen and dining room have been scribbled on with crayons and markers. You don't need to be Sherlock Homes to identify who the culprit may be. The untidiness and disarray surely have to be bugging the hell out of my dad, who generally prefers everything to be in its proper place. *Has that come to include me and Noah as well?*

Despite these overt grumblings, I haven't been able to find an ideal residence. I'm not going to grab any old apartment or rental just because it's available.

My mom took a stab at me at the dinner table one night: "Buckingham Palace is already taken." It was just the two of us since Noah had been given an early dinner and bath and Dad had to work late at the office. "Do try to set your sights on something a little less perfect," she added, scrunching her lips and peering at me like she was the Queen of Hearts and I was poor Alice. If she had said, "Off with your head," it wouldn't have surprised me at all. Instead, she stated, "Oh, and the White House is currently occupied too, so I think you have to come down a notch or two with your list of prerequisites."

"Ha ha," I retaliated with a smirk. "You should try out for *America's Got Talent*."

"I'm not trying to be funny, Kat," came her deadpan response.

Why is she always judging me? Who made her holier than thou? What makes her think she has all the answers for fixing people's lives? Come to think of it, what did she ever do to improve her own mother's deplorable situation? I asked her this point blank and received a mouthful after she turned beet red and managed to stop stuttering. She related how she had told Nanny during one of her many illnesses and hospital stays that she was a battered woman. Nanny's response had been predictable.

"You know how stupid I am. I don't know what that means. I don't understand what you're saying."

"Mom, you're living under constant abuse. You have been all of your married life," my mom had pressed on. "Yes, you do understand. You're just too afraid to admit it."

Nanny had told my mother that she was too old to do or say anything different and refused Mom's offer to bring her for counseling, resigning herself to a lifetime of intimidation and unhappiness.

"Nanny was afraid Poppy would use his gun to kill himself or one of us if she ever left him," my mom had shared. "When your dad and I were first dating, his car was stolen from outside Nanny and Poppy's apartment building. Poppy had taken out his handgun and left it fully loaded on the seat by his side, telling Dad, 'We're going through Jamaica, just in case we spot the shits that took your car.' Daddy had gripped the handle on the passenger door, desperately praying to make it home in one piece and not caring if he ever saw his car again."

I sat motionless. Part of me had wanted to reach out to hug her, but I didn't.

"Kat, this is not what I wanted for myself," she said, clasping her hands together as her eyes again made contact with mine. "And I certainly did not want it for you. Neither one of us ever needs to be a victim or a martyr. What I witnessed and experienced, I fully understood it was bad, but I never wanted to perpetuate that kind of bad myself. You believe me, Kat? I would never hurt anyone unless it was absolutely necessary. You understand that, right?" When she finished speaking, she combed her fingers through her hair and kept on staring at me expectantly. She sure did look desperate.

"Yes, of course," I answered. "I think I understand what you're getting at."

"Some things go beyond our control, though. Things happen in spite of ourselves. I mean we choose it, but not really comprehending that we're choosing it to happen."

Okay. What's going on here? Please don't tell me that you're confessing to calling Sam again. I will strangle you with my two bare hands if you are. "You've lost me, Mom. Why don't you come right out and tell me what you're trying to say instead of speaking in circles?"

"Somehow Kat, while you were younger, I accomplished the very opposite of what I had set my heart on doing. By hoping to protect you from a similar fate as mine, I ended up pushing you away." She closed her eyes and sighed. "When I gave you the skirt, I sort of hoped it would make things right again. I wanted the skirt to help you distance yourself from Craig."

"The skirt? You're talking about that dirty old skirt?" *How in the world did she manage to dig that topic up?* "You gave me that to wear in a play! I assure you that Craig's leaving had nothing to do with that pile of scrap. Mom, I'm beginning to worry about you. You're talking much more nonsense than usual and it's freakin' me out."

"There's more to it; much more to it," she uttered, pounding the table.

"The 'it' you're talking about, does it have anything to do with why I'm reading your journal and stories?"

She nodded.

Okay. So now I'm getting somewhere. "Why didn't you insist on telling me these things before?"

"I really don't know," she said after clearing her throat. "I thought about telling you everything. I had tried, but no, not really. You were younger and it wasn't appropriate. I've kind of kept it hidden all these years." She began to do that thing that people do when they bite the cuticles around their nails even though no excess skin is hanging out anywhere.

I leaned in closer. "Mom, did you ever consider going for help? A good therapist could have helped you work through a lot of these issues. Perhaps now would be as good a time as any to see someone you can talk to about all of this."

Her head snapped back up as readily as a rubber band. *"Aren't you the pot calling the kettle black!"*

"You're obviously deeply troubled about something. Speaking to a professional about it might make a significant difference," I offered in as calm a voice I could muster.

"Well, that's exactly what I've been telling you. In your case, it would have made a significant difference too! Look at all the weight you've gained."

I could tell I was getting nowhere fast, so I decided to let the matter go. "Yeah, whatever."

"Kat, I believed that Craig was totally wrong for you, and I was devastated when you married him. It happened during a terrible, terrible time in our lives, and I felt completely drained and powerless to do anything about it. For the longest time, I sensed that ending your marriage must have been something you also had been wishing for, but you just didn't have the means to bring it about. Thankfully, Craig is now out of the picture. It's not too late, however, for you to do something to improve your own life right now."

"Weren't we just talking about you a second ago? How did the conversation turn back so suddenly to me?"

"Kat, move out."

"That's putting it bluntly. Noah's too much of a handful, huh?"

"No. It's time, Kat. Find a place within the next three months!"

"And you'll toss us out on the street?"

"You can't just stay with us forever. You deserve more."

Chapter Forty-five

When I returned to my bedroom, I decided to go through the contents of the infamous box once more—the one Mom had been adamant about me bringing to her house when Noah and I had moved in and had insisted I keep in my room. The first thing I noticed was the folded-up skirt, the one she is fixated on, whose image seems to be nailed to her brain. Who knows; maybe to a collector it's worth big money, but she won't come right out and tell me because she wants me to be the one to discover the surprise on my own? As a kid, anytime I wanted to know the definition of a word, instead of telling me outright, she would say, "Go look it up yourself; that way you'll remember it better." I hated that!

I lifted *the skirt* with both my hands, not sure if it was even safe to touch. It was pretty heavy, but then again there really was a lot of fabric. My great grandmother must have been a big woman. I stepped into it and looked at my image in the mirror.

The skirt gathered in excess sections around my hips but surprisingly, it didn't drag me down. I felt like a burden was lifted away from me, as if I was an ox being freed from a heavy, bulky yoke. Lines of worry and tension began to disappear from my face. I felt and appeared younger than I had in years.

I couldn't explain what was happening. It was as if some voodoo magic was taking place. The hem reached the floor, but nothing unusual looked back at me. This shabby, ratty garment had an inexplicable dignity about it that was obviously intriguing. I don't know how else to say this, so I just will: it was somehow calling to me. I started to hear words, but they didn't come from the outside and in through my ears. They seemed to arise in my gut.

Believe in yourself and all you are capable of becoming. Pretty hokey, right?

I checked to make sure that my mother wasn't hiding, playing a trick on me. After all, she has been eerily preoccupied with this skirt to the point of absurdity. The words I heard were so typical of what spouts from her mouth, but I was definitely alone. I know I was alone in that room! Could it be that Black Bubbe—Poppy's mother; the witch; the original owner of that skirt who had ostensibly saved little Myra and was the hero of her short story—was speaking to me from her grave?

Do not surrender that power to anyone else. Each one of us is a special gift to the world.

This brought tears to my eyes. What the heck was going on? Waterworks were flowing nonstop down my cheeks like a dam had just broke. Whoever was doing the talking had hit a sore spot. *Bam!* I felt so awkward and so silly, but all the pain and embarrassment I had endured in my marriage and tried to suppress came surging to the surface. I bawled and I bawled, standing in front of the mirror and wearing that ridiculous excuse of a skirt.

Had my mother seen me, no doubt she would have had me Baker Act'ed. "When you are able to curtail the hysteria," she would have ordered the mental health authorities, "please examine my daughter thoroughly for obsessive anger and neurotic weight issues."

I continued to stare at my reflection, taking in a few deep breaths.

It's time to move out, Kat. You can do it.

No; I didn't believe I could do it. I wish I had the confidence to step out from behind my parents' shadows, but I was too afraid. I was stuck. It's safer to stay in the nest than to fly off and crash to the ground. If I fall again, I don't think I will ever be able to pull myself together. Humpty Dumpty and me, we share a lot in common.

When Nathan died, I felt like there was no order or meaning to life. I had felt completely helpless and vulnerable, susceptible to the whim of the fates. That's probably why it had been so easy to surrender to Craig's bullying: so he could do my thinking for me. Now, I don't want to be controlled by anyone else ever again. It's a path I've been down before, and aside from giving birth to Noah, it took me in a totally wrong direction. Craig managed to kill most of my dreams, including wanting to believe I was somebody special.

I studied the skirt some more. My instincts told me there was something of importance being left unsaid. The color and cloth had been worn away mostly around the pockets, into which I inserted my hands. My right hand touched something soft and silky; was it a handkerchief that had been left inside?

Pinching my fingers together, I carefully extracted the item. There were several sheets of white onionskin paper folded over in two and tied by an old rubber band. The rubber band had decayed and its pieces fell apart in my palm. Cautiously, I opened up the sheets and discovered a hand-written letter in a language that was foreign to me. It was dated 1957, but was impossible for me to read. *Who wrote this? To whom? And why?* I slipped it into the zippered side pocket of my bag so I could review it later during a break at the office.

After dabbing my eyes with a tissue, I folded up the skirt, taking care as I did so. My state of mind was fragile, so I wasn't ready to discuss the emotional outbreak I had just experienced with anyone, let alone my mother.

Chapter Forty-six

Early the next morning, I spent a little time watching Noah ride his miniature fire truck on the sidewalk before I headed to work. One of his favorite things to do is sound the siren while I pretend to speak on the walkie-talkie. It was obvious that Noah was enjoying our moment together. The weather was perfect; wintertime in Florida can be glorious.

A cool, delightful breeze gently blew against our backs and Noah, topped in his fireman's hat, busily ran about spraying imaginary fires with his plastic hose. A helicopter hovered overhead. A flock of flying birds came to rest on the eaves of a neighbor's rooftop; their little bodies looked like notes on a sheet of music. The fronds of the palm trees gently swayed as Noah waved his hand to no one in particular. I looked down the street in either direction, but there was no one else around. A big smile stretched across his face as he focused on some distant object. He waved once more as he uttered "Bye-bye." I asked him who he was talking to, and Noah answered, "The man."

Noah's appetite was ravenous when we returned home, and he ate every morsel of his breakfast without fussing. He stubbornly refused, however, to get ready for school, insisting that he had to clean all the floors first with his toy vacuum. I carried him kicking and screaming to the car, having to deal with his out of control, temper tantrum the entire ride, which the *Sesame Street* tunes CD failed to mollify. By the time I dropped him off at his class, he had perked up as cheery and playful as a little puppy, ready to join his friends in the day's activities while I suffered from a pulsating headache and the worst case of guilt. *Am I really such a terrible mother?*

Lunchtime couldn't come soon enough at the office. All morning long, I had to study the photographs of a one-year old's body brought overnight to the emergency room at the Delray Hospital. The father kept insisting the baby had fallen down the stairs. "I don't know how she crawled out of her crib by herself, but she did," was his story. There was substantial bruising around the neck and on the arms. The mother barely spoke English; even so, she had seemed too afraid to utter a peep.

The detective on the case had observed raw, purple contusions on the mother's neck and arms as well, but she refused treatment. A thorough investigation was going to be conducted, possibly leading to criminal repercussions. My hunch was that the father would be serving some serious jail time if he didn't cop a plea and get his sentence reduced. Then he'd be out sooner than I'd like him to be, ready to pounce again on yet another defenseless, innocent victim. My stomach churned with anger and sadness for that baby.

I called my mom and between taking bites of a honeycrisp apple, I asked her if she was aware of a letter in the skirt. She was not. She told me she was in the middle of painting and had little time to talk, adding, "I just squeezed a dab of cerulean blue on my palette. I want to use it before it dries up. Plus, it is extremely annoying having to hear you munching in my ear. Why don't you call me back when you've finished eating?"

On my second call, I asked her if she could guess who wrote the letter. Again, she didn't know. I asked her if she knew what language it was written in. She asked me to read her some of the words while she washed off the paint from her brushes.

"Could you please turn off the water? Now *that* is annoying *me*. It's difficult enough just trying to pronounce these words. I don't need Niagara Falls roaring in the background."

"Is there any reason you're in a particularly bad mood today?" she asked.

"Nah. I'm at work; business as usual." I made a few stammering attempts at reading the letter, minus the clamor and racket at my mother's end.

"It sounds like Yiddish," she declared.

I asked her if she knew Yiddish well enough to translate.

"I don't know Yiddish at all."

I swiveled in my chair. The photographs of the dead child rested on top of the file. I opened the folder and slid them in. "Didn't you and Dad take an evening course a few years ago?"

"Yes, and we've forgotten every single thing we learned." I could hear the paper towel roll being spun and the soft tear of one section. I pictured her wiping her hands. She was probably wearing her oversized, blue chambray shirt that had become as splattered as a Jackson Pollock abstract. I would bet money on it that she also had flecks of yellow, blue, and white in her hair and on her cheeks. "Learning a foreign language is only good if you get to practice it regularly," she announced. "Why not take the note to your friend who teaches at FAU? Isn't she with the Jewish studies program there? She should be able to get it translated for you."

I thought about Craig and wondered if he had been capable of attacking Noah the same way the father had assaulted that poor baby. It made me shudder. Hearing my mother's voice at this time comforted me, made me feel grounded. It was one of the rare instances she didn't sound abominably cruel. "Great suggestion, Mom. I knew you were good for something! By the way, I don't want you to go on and on about this, but I just sent a letter to Stephen."

"About what?" she asked. "Hurry up and tell me because I have to clear away my easel and start making dinner." She sounded innocent enough.

I could have bet money that Stephen was in cahoots with her over this letter request. "He didn't tell you already?"

"No. I know nothing about it." There was no telltale change of pitch or tone in her voice. Her words did not come out faster or slower than usual. "Why did you send Stephen a letter? What is this all about?"

"He suggested that I put my feelings about what happened to Nathan in a letter. The point I want to stress is that I didn't email it to him, *I sent it through the mail.*"

"Sounds like an excellent idea," she said, her interest aroused. "But how come you decided to mail it? I didn't think you snail-mailed anything nowadays. Hold on a sec; I'm going to put something in the microwave."

I heard the buzz of something being nuked and waited for the long, continuous beep to end. I figured she was making herself a cup of tea. "I'm impressed that you know the lingo but that's not how the term is used. Anyhow, I don't know why I 'snail-mailed' it. I just did. Don't you think it's really strange that I sent a letter to Stephen and soon thereafter I find this hidden note in the skirt pocket? Isn't this some great, amazing coincidence?"

"Coincidences are the universe's way of sending you a message," she said in her grating told-you-so tone while cabinet doors were opened and dishes were rattled.

"I knew you were going to say that. I hope you're making something good for dinner."

"Vegetarian meatloaf for you, me, and Noah. The real cow stuff for your father, although I wish he would start eating a little healthier. Hmm; I wonder why I never found that letter before you did. Oh well. Kat, promise me you'll let me know as soon as you find out what's in it."

Arrangements were made to meet my professor friend early that evening during an off hour in her teaching schedule. I made a pit stop at her campus after picking up Noah, planting a generous number of kisses wherever his skin was exposed. After the sixth smack of my lips, he was playfully pushing me away. My friend made a socially acceptable fuss of him—the way people who don't have any kids typically react to someone else's: "Oh, isn't he a cute little boy? Now, where is that letter you were telling me about?" And then she told me that she would work on it within the next two weeks. It appeared to be easily something she could handle herself. If not, she would seek assistance from an associate in the language department.

The following week, while I was in my office perusing affidavits prepared on behalf of a daycare operator, I opened up an email from my friend, who was taking a break from grading papers. The translation, which could be found in the attachment, had not been too difficult a task to accomplish, and she was happy to hold the original letter in safe keeping until we could meet again. She informed me that the author of the letter was a woman named Leah.

Bubbe Leah's Letter:

I come from a family of transients; always moving around from one town to the next. If the laws were kind to us, we stayed for a while. When the laws changed and became bitter toward the Jews, then it was time to find a better place to live. Sometimes we were in Poland; sometimes we were in Russia. With every move came a new way to identify ourselves; we didn't have surnames back then. We were known by the last town we had come from, thus ensuring that young boys would not be counted more than once for each town's mandatory quota to serve in the army.

I grew up in a village not too far from the city of Vilnius, in the country now known as Lithuania. At times, uprisings would affect who governed us; we could stay in the very exact same place, but the country itself would change.

It was my father who named me Leah. He believed that his first child should have been a boy, and that God deceived him at the moment of my birth by substituting a girl in his son's place. Although not a very pious man, he knew the story of Jacob and Rachel by heart and how Leah took her sister's place as a bride to Jacob. Like many other Jews, my father ran a tavern and sold liquor to the local peasants. When too many of the peasants became overly drunk and misbehaved, my father would be blamed for bringing evil to the village and we would be forced out of our home.

As time went on, it became harder and harder for my father

277

to make a living from selling alcohol. New rules were passed that reduced the number of days the taverns could be open and also prohibited customers from buying their drinks on credit. What made matters worse, all of the patrons' past debts were eliminated as well. My father grew to be a very angry man. His struggles to make a living fueled his temper, which he unleashed regularly upon my mother and me.

"Not only has God cursed me with a daughter, but the girl has to be such an ugly one. When the time comes, where am I to find a man to take such a mise punim *for a wife? Will it be my burden to support her for the rest of her life? When will you provide me with my son? Ach, you are a lazy, dried up woman!"*

I felt badly that my mother had to bear the blame for my ugliness. She told me that true beauty was a reflection of God's nature. She said that it was measured by a person's spirit, and that I was endowed with an especially beautiful spirit, and therefore, could never really be considered ugly. She would bring me with her into the woods and taught me everything she knew about the plants that grew there. She had names for every tree, bush, and plant. Together, we would pick berries; she guided me as to the safe and poisonous varieties. She advised me on the herbs, wildflowers, and roots, teaching me how to soak them and use them to heal. I learned what was best for a burn, what to apply for an insect bite, what would appease poor digestion, and countless other remedies for different situations. She instructed me how to concoct solutions which would impact different areas of the human body.

I was into my ninth year when I noticed that my mother's body had begun to swell, and I surmised that she was again with child. My father's rants subdued and his temperament became almost benign. This was in spite of the lawmakers assuming all responsibilities for the sale and manufacture of liquor so my father was no longer permitted to own a tavern or produce any alcohol at all. Accordingly, Velvel, the ginger-haired butcher, allowed my father to work in his shop as an assistant. Velvel's wife, Basia, had taken ill and the butcher needed someone to cut and mince while he saw to his customers' requests.

I watched as the mound beneath my mother's breasts grew. She placed my hand upon her skin and let me feel the little one kicking inside. She told me the time was approaching for the baby's birth and she prepared me to assist in its delivery in case the midwife was called to some other village. Despite all of her tutelage, my mother could not train me enough to handle all of the horror that occurred. To my father's supreme delight, a baby boy was delivered and was eventually known as Yussel. My mother did not survive the childbirth; she died in a river of blood that drowned both her body and her spirit. The midwife arrived just in time to slit the chord; she grabbed the baby and ushered me out of the house.

I doted upon Yussel and spent as much time as I could

filling his head with stories about our mother. He was kind hearted and a good companion to me while I took charge of the house and managed the cooking. Yussel would sing alongside me; his voice was sweet and melodic. He observed me baking and darning while teaching himself how to fashion clothing from flour and potato sacks. Many starving cats and wounded animals would find their way into Yussel's arms and our home to be nursed back to good health.

Our father complained that Yussel was acting too much like a girl and talked about sending him to a proper heder where he would learn the trades and skills to make him a successful man. He had heard about the maskilim's *school in Vilnius, which was part of the Haskalah movement. It impressed him that less time was devoted to Torah, Mishnah, and Gemara and more emphasis was being placed on other subjects. He liked the idea that Yussel's education would give him greater opportunities to assimilate with the gentiles.*

My father was not a religious man; he believed that many wars and much strife had been caused in the name of religion. He brought home cow's meat from the butcher shop, but he also fed us pork chops and bacon.

I had heard that many young girls were being accepted to these new schools as well. Not only were they studying Hebrew, religion, and writing in Yiddish, but there were classes in arithmetic, art, and music. I begged my father to let me go as well and he told me that he had better plans for me. The day that Yussel left our home to travel to Vilnius is the same day that Velvel came to take me as his wife. Basia had died and Velvel had offered my father a portion of the butcher shop in return for my services. My feelings were never considered in this arrangement and I had no power to refuse the betrothal.

Velvel was a monstrous pig who pawed my body savagely without regard to my dignity or innocence; he exhibited more care while dissecting a dead cow into slabs of meat. After he finished lying on top of me, he would beat me for being an "ugly, cold fish, incapable of pleasing a man, and fulfilling a wife's duties."

I did not know what else I was supposed to do. Each night he would come to lay on top of me and I dared not resist him. As his lips slobbered over my mouth and other areas, I sent my mind into the woods, trying to recall the names and attributes of all the fruits and herbs my mother had told me about. I mentally recited each of the leaves, roots, flowers, seeds, resins, barks, and berries and recounted the specific amounts that distinguished them from being safe or toxic.

Velvel's attacks did not let up. He had an insatiable appetite for relieving himself in me. My only respite was during my woman's cycle. I would lie to him and say that the bleeding had yet to stop, so I would escape an extra day or two. Some months went by where I did not see any red spotting on my under garments. Slowly, my body was becoming thicker and more tender; I realized

I was with child. I was filled with dread and shame to be carrying Velvel's seed in me. I did not want to raise a child with him. Without a moment's hesitation, I began to plot my departure from Velvel's home and my unhappy life.

I had gathered many herbs and roots from the forest, but needed a place to store them out of Vevel's watchful eyes. The coarse gray blanket, which Velvel used for market day, was large enough to cover all the goods he hauled on his dray to the central square. I retrieved it from the stable, replacing it with a large rectangle made from sack cloths that I had pieced together.

From the blanket, I sewed a skirt with huge pockets. Into my right pocket, I placed all of my gatherings from the woods. The left pocket was intended for all of Velvel's and Basia's jewelry, which he kept locked in a safe box.

Next, I went about making Velvel's dinner. How delightful for him to have such a fragrant, spicy supper so unlike his usual bland meals. He was surprised to see me in such a cheerful mood at the end of his work day. He suggested that I keep the smile on my face long into the evening. He said it helped hide my ugliness. He enjoyed his food, even asking for seconds of the pea soup and veal stew. As he soaked up the last drops of gravy with the thick dark grained bread, his head hit the plate.

I followed my plan. I slid the loop of keys from his belt, opened the safe box, and stuffed my left pocket with the watches, rings, necklaces, and money from the box. Next, I took one of his butcher's knives and stabbed his body.

My first stroke was a little hesitant. Then the stabs became quicker and stronger in retaliation for all the many times he had ravaged my body. The blood spurted in every direction. I sliced through the furniture, slashing the cushions and crushing the chairs. I ripped the feather bed and poured wine on the bed linens. Who would not believe that an angry, drunken band of Russians had attacked this house and carried me off with them? These atrocities were commonplace; it wasn't safe for anyone to be a Jew in these times.

My journey across the continent was not an easy one, especially as the baby was growing inside of me. Fortunately, there were many making the same trek as me, and I joined Jews from Poland and Russia heading to England and America.

I paid for transport aboard a wagon belonging to one family, and they shared their provisions with me. My valuables remained hidden in my skirt, close to my skin. We were packed like fish in the boat that brought us across the English Channel, surrounded by stench, filth, and vomit. The family who were my traveling companions had decided to head to London; they had been told of a large Jewish population already there. I was afraid that I might be recognized by someone from my past, so I headed to Nottingham—a place not known to many of my landsleit.

I secured a room to rent above a baker's shop which was owned by an immigrant from Russia. In the months before my baby was born, I baked spiced cakes for the baker to sell. The English were curious about the spices that I mixed in the dough; the taste appealed to their pursuit of the exotic. The cakes and my strudels sold as soon as they were displayed, and the baker was happy to place a daily order for me to fulfill.

I delivered my boy with the help of an English midwife. He was healthy and very beautiful. He reminded me of Yussel, whom I sadly never heard from again. Years later, I learned that Yussel had been killed in the mass extermination which took place at Ponary in July of 1941. Before he had been ordered to strip naked of his clothes, he had been forced to wear a pink triangle on his armband.

I named my son Jack. It was a proper name for an Englishman. I did not want him to grow up branded as an outsider in society as I and my family had lived in Lithuania. I kept his reddish hair short and dressed him the way the other English boys were clothed. When he became old enough, I sent him to the public school where he could acquire the skills he needed to succeed in business the English way. I didn't care if he never learned to daven or quote from the Talmud.

Solly, the baker, disagreed with me. He said that I committed a sin by not requiring the boy to learn how to recite the daily prayers and know his Commandments. He tutored Jack in the afternoons while I waited on the customers. In the beginning, Jack appreciated the extra attention and thought his lessons were fun.

Solly and I would drink our afternoon tea together. Some evenings, I would invite him to join our dinner table. It became our routine to spend more and more time in each other's company. Solly proposed that we live together as man and wife; it seemed like a constructive suggestion. We received the rabbi's blessing under a makeshift chuppah. Although I wasn't so enthused about the name, which Solly told me he had made up, people soon became accustomed to addressing me as Mrs. Kaufman.

Solly insisted that I keep a kosher home and light the candles on erev Shabbos and the Jewish holidays. It didn't seem a lot to do to make him happy. As time went on, he became more frum and demanded that I regularly go to the mikvah and don a sheitel. He became stricter with Jack and talked about taking him out of his secular school. Jack began to resent Solly's interference in his life. I finally put my foot down and made it clear to Solly that Jack's education and future were not his business. A cold but civil distance grew between us in the home. We went about performing our chores, but there was no joy in it.

The bakery functioned on a regular routine and maintained a nice income. Many days, however, I became lethargic and irritable. Some afternoons, I would dabble with artificial gems, old belt buckles, and paste to make jewelry just to amuse myself. I was at the age that a woman's body begins to go through its "changes." Solly insisted that I consult with the rebbitzin to learn how to make my disposition more kindly and bearable for him.

There were herbs at my disposal that I could have administered, but I decided to seek a doctor's advice instead. To my shock, the doctor discovered I was with child. I did not want another child, especially at this late age, and so I did not share this news with Solly. I ingested the herbs and spices that would get rid of the baby. Nausea came, but nothing else occurred.

I had heard of women in the old village using knitting needles to terminate such a pregnancy. I jabbed the needle further and further up my private parts, but not one drop of blood or fetal tissue descended. Solly took note of my swelling belly and cautioned me to eat fewer cakes. It was at this point that I told him about the baby. He was ecstatic of course. He praised God for this magnificent gift. If it was a boy, he wanted to call him Hod, which meant "Glory of God."

Solly could not be budged from fussing over Hod. As soon as the bakery's doors were locked each night, he busied himself with his son. He told me many times that this son was to become something special. He brought even more intensity to overseeing Hod's education and upbringing than he attempted to do with Jack. Solly was merciless in making demands upon him.

There were times I actually feared for Hod's safety; he would beat the child for forgetting a lesson or for transposing words in a prayer. I tried to intercede as best I could, but Solly shut me out of both of their lives. He became sinister and unkind, telling me he did not want such ugliness around his perfect child.

Hod began to mock me with the very same harsh words he had heard his father use. Once more, my life had become unbearable.

I decided to use the herbs in the same way I had dealt with Velvel, adding an extra secret punch to Solly's afternoon tea. I wanted him to die a slow death; anything else would have aroused the suspicions of others around us. I feared that the police and the enforcement of laws in England would be more fastidious than in the old country.

As Solly became weaker, his kidneys began to malfunction and his body started to retain a lot of its fluid. He made an appointment to meet with the doctor, but circumstances made the appointment unnecessary. One morning, he fell off the ladder while going to the loft to retrieve a bag of flour for the bakery. Unfortunately for me and Hod, the fall did not kill Solly and our burdens multiplied.

Now Solly had become a cripple. He was wheelchair-bound, unable to work in the bakery, and unable to provide us with any income. I didn't want to run that bakery on my own. Why should I have? It was Solly's pet enterprise and just a mere diversion for me. I sold it without telling him first. This way it was done and finished. I knew he would have balked at the idea. He yelled that I had given it away for such a paltry price.

We had plenty of money in the bank to live on, but I miscalculated for how many years. There came a time, however, when there wasn't enough in the account to see us through the year. Jack was enrolled in his higher levels and refused to work outside of school. He claimed it would have been too much of a distraction.

So, I did what I needed to do. I brought my brooches and other decorative pieces to the market square in Nottingham and set up my display between the hardware carts and fabrics. I wanted my colorful gems to attract the eyes of all the female shoppers, which they did. It was a heavy load to schlep back and forth on the weekends, but I made enough money to keep our family well stocked in food.

Solly's scolding of Hod did not abate, and with this, Hod became nastier to me. My preference was for him to study accounting, like his brother had. Whenever I saw him drawing or sketching, I told him "Don't do with your hands, do with your brain." Hod replied that I was not one to give advice. Solly wanted the boy to become a great rabbinic scholar and demanded that he give full concentration to his holy studies.

When Hod was called up to read from the Torah on the day he became a Bar Mitzvah, Solly severely criticized him for what seemed to be a lack of dedication and a hastiness in his tone. The next day, Hod disappeared from the house. He was nowhere to be found. I reckoned this was Hod's attempt to be free from his tormentor. I could not be critical of him; it was the same path I had chosen for myself. Neither Solly nor I heard from our son for many years. Solly's condition continued to decline; perhaps too much tea drinking sealed his fate. When he died, I felt no reason to mourn his passing. I made a promise to myself to never use the herbs again unless it was absolutely necessary to do so.

The next time that I saw Hod, he was a full grown, swanky man with a very pretty blond woman on his arm. He called himself Harold, and he introduced me to his fiancée, Ada, who seemed kind and eager to please but did not appear to be his intellectual match.

It was obvious to me that Harold had definitely sought out someone with exceptionally good looks. It surprised me, though, that Ada wasn't a shicksa. Harold was much calmer and more polite than I ever remembered him to be. I couldn't tell if he had made a permanent transformation or was merely masking his true self for the woman's benefit.

Naturally, I had invited them to my house. As little and unassuming as my home was, I could still manage to put out a fine selection of strudels and tea and make the two feel welcomed. When he called to say they were on their way to Nottingham, I had asked Harold what flavor cakes his girlfriend preferred. Harold insisted, though, on meeting at the new posh hotel in the center of town, to which I needed to take a taxicab. His call came from out of the blue and sent me reeling.

They told me about their wedding plans and invited me to the celebration. I wanted to decline of course. I would feel out of place with the fine ladies and gentlemen from London.

289

The second big war had come and passed; luckily, the bombs had not reached my neck of the woods. With the news I received about Yussel, I feared for the loss of the entire Vilnius Jewish population. Dribs and drabs reached my ears about the Concentration Camps and those who perished there. Gone were all the cousins, aunts, uncles, and friends from both my mother's and father's families. Ada kept me informed about Harold's detail in Africa for the years that he was there. Jack never went overseas; he was an officer with the Secret Service Bureau.

My body was feeling the weight of its years, and I could no longer manage to sell my jewelry or take care of my home. I now needed the help of a walking stick in order to move from room to room. Ada was nice enough to ask me to live with her, Harold, and their three daughters; how my son felt about this arrangement was never shared with me.

I gave some thought to using my herbs to finish it all, and then decided I wanted to get to know my grandchildren. Jack, his wife, and their two sons lived in Manchester and I had not heard from them since the Germans surrendered in May 1945. They were well-to-do and comfortable being a part of the British upper crust. I believe that Jack was ashamed of me and his humble beginnings. He said I looked like a hag when he last saw me. I could tell that he wanted nothing to do with me.

I went to live in a place called Stamford Hill. I was given my own room and a mahogany wardrobe in which to hang my few clothes. It bothered me that a door led from my room out onto a terrace which overlooked the street. The lock on the door was broken, but Harold never got around to fixing it. Who was to say that a robber couldn't use this entryway to sneak into the house at night?

Really, it didn't matter which neighborhood i lived in because I never left the house. I surmised that there were vicious whispers about me in the other homes. People love to gossip and fantasize about things they know little of. Harold treated Ada like dirt, with much the same disdain as my father had treated my own mother and not too differently than how my own two husbands had mishandled me.

I felt sorry for her much of the time. She wasn't such a bad person. When Jules, the son Solly had abandoned, came from Russia penniless and starving, it was Ada who did her best to help him out. She would sneak food and money out of her house and bring it to him. Jules told Ada his story and about how Raisa had survived the war only to die months later, but Harold would have nothing to do with him. It repulsed Harold to know that Jules was a homosexual. I overheard Ada tell Harold that Jules was dying, suffering alone on a bare cot in an unfurnished London County flat. Even that did not motivate Harold to lift a finger to help. So much like his father, Harold was.

On the few occasions Ada ran away, I hoped she wouldn't be found. There were moments when I considered sharing with her my supply of herbs, but then thought better of it. She probably would have messed up the doses or blabbed about it to someone else, and we'd both end up being incriminated. That's when I decided to maintain my vow of silence.

Harold and Ada thought I was oblivious to the news about the plane crash that took place. I heard about it on the television when it happened and I heard the family whispering about it whenever I left a room. Jack and his wife were on the plane; not a trace was found of either one of them. How was I to mourn something that had already long disappeared from my life?

I knew that there were plenty who snickered about me behind my back. I was quite the mystery. The children said I was the "Black Bubbe." Did Esther and Joan not know that I hear them call me a witch? What harm could it do me? I've lived through and seen much worse. They should only know the truth of it! Perhaps they will learn my story one day, after I am long gone and buried.

The little one, called Myra, was the one who most got under my skin. She wasn't mean spirited like her two sisters; I felt sorry for her and for all the trickery and mocking she received. They called her an ugly pig; I knew what that felt like. Only she wasn't ugly at all; I could see she had that beautiful good nature. It was a mistake for Harold and Ada to have another child. Just as my father had reacted with me, they made no attempt to mask their disappointment when a third girl was born to them. I felt it my duty *to keep the little one under my wing. I did what I could to indulge her with playthings whenever Harold and Ada's backs were turned, but that was seldom the case. She soon forfeited whatever I had managed to give her.*

I am surprised that it has taken this long for me to outlast my welcome in this house. Everything has become too stale and beyond repair. My bloomers sag as much as my jowls, my stockings keep falling down, my muscles and bones are fatigued, and it is way too much an effort to bathe this useless body. I can see that Harold will never bring himself to discuss our past so we can mend the damage in our relationship. There is much too much anger in that man's heart.

I see him bullying his girls; as much as he craves it, he will never win their trust or respect. It pains me to have witnessed such destruction of what could have been so easily loved. In nature, growth is so effortless. Grass does not struggle to become grass. Trees do not grapple to become trees. Why then, have the men in my life erected such aggressive barriers against living with harmony and peace? Have the guns, tanks, bombs, diatribes, lashing out, sexual attacks, and verbal abuses gained them such a valuable prize? Was this acquired power so great? Some people make life so difficult for themselves while others make it so easy. The universe gives back exactly what is put forth.

I do not profess to be innocent and free of blame. After all, I killed not once, but twice, and soon, my death will be by my own taking. Whatever is left of my supplies will be enough to accomplish my final act. Where is that God that the Jews talk about and praise? Are you laughing while we insignificant humans are running around trying to make ourselves feel self-important? Where is your great morality? Is it written in books only to grow dusty on the shelves? Are your prayers memorized solely for the sake of pride and self-congratulatory achievement? Where are the rules that teach us what is good and keep us from acting bad? When I loved and knew I was loved, I didn't need your rules, but the world has yet to be such a place to foster and encourage such love. Not one of us is safe to indulge in this freedom.

I'm not looking forward to meeting again with Velvel, Solly, or my father—that is if my spirit is to end up in the same place as theirs. I am anxious, though, to greet Yussel and my mother once again. I know they will understand that what I did was out of desperation and despair. What other choices did I have? It is the same with Ada; she is bound to a life of suffering. Ach. Is this the only reason for which women were placed on this earth?

If I were a betting woman, I would place my money on the little one. She has a glint of defiance in her eyes. She has the potential to discover her own inner strength one day. She was born with a birth mark over her left thigh; that tells me she was designated for a special mission. Perhaps she will be the one to set things right.

Chapter Forty-seven

"So, the translation is finished and was emailed to me," I nonchalantly informed my mother over the phone. I was taking time out from a case involving a three-year-old who had been negligently left sleeping in the back seat of a school bus. The driver had locked the bus and parked it in a lot while she ran into the supermarket. The problem, once again, is that this is Florida—not that such behavior should be condoned in any other state. It was a sunny day and the temperature inside the bus rose to 113 degrees, causing the child to die from heatstroke.

"When did you get it? What was in it?" My mother's tone was just as eager as the words she expressed. "What have you found out?"

"Mom, either it was written by Bubbe Leah or by you. Has this been one of your really big, not-so-funny jokes?"

"Absolutely not, Kat.," she blurted out. "Let me turn off the TV. I want you to tell me everything Bubbe Leah had to say."

I filled her in as best I could. When I stopped speaking, I heard her sigh as if she were being crushed by an unbearable weight. She took a moment and then she said, "Sometimes I think that it is a matter of perception. We can all look at the same object and define it in a million different ways because we filter it through different sets of eyes, experiences, and perspectives."

"That's your response? That's all you're going to say?" I could feel my blood pressure zooming up past the danger level. "Here you go again Mom, speaking in generalities without letting on how you really feel. Not only do you come from a crazy, abusive family, but now we know your grandmother was a murderer. A murderer that went around killing people."

"Yes, Kat, that is the definition of a murderer, but she seemed to have some very valid reasons for doing so. In my opinion, she was a special woman who decided to take her fate in her own hands. The question is, what do we do about this now?" She sounded far more composed than I could ever have anticipated.

I thought about how distraught the bus driver had been when she found out what her actions had caused. She had become hysterical and kept screaming, "Let me die. I deserve to die." My heart went out to her as it did to the mother and father of that three-year-old victim. "Mom, you're amazingly calm for someone who just heard such an amazing story as this. But then again, you're not human, so why should I be questioning your behavior? She murdered her husband! No, make that *two* of them! And she killed herself. Make that three murders. Does Dad know anything about this?"

"How should he know? This isn't his family; it's mine."

"Oh yes. Yours is a stinking family in which abuse runs all the way back for generations. Please don't try talking to me about perspective and giving consideration to the circumstances. Abuse is abuse no matter which way you look at it, and although a murder may be justified, it's still a major act with major consequences."

I could hear my mother faltering for an appropriate response. There was a lot of "Well, er..." coming out of her mouth, but nothing more substantial followed. I said goodbye and hung up the phone.

The next call I made was to Stephen at his office. After he picked up, I threw a ton of information at him about Mom and Black Bubbe. He thought it was cool. That's just how Stephen is; he doesn't let anything serious get to him. Let me correct that: he never lets on that anything serious has gotten to him. He cautioned me not to take it too seriously either. He thought that the whole scenario was pretty funny. An old sack skirt hidden in a box with a deep dark secret inside the pocket. Either all of it was the truth, or my mom was having a really good time making this shit up.

Chapter Forty-eight

It has taken quite a while for us to adjust to our surroundings, but Noah and I now reside in a new apartment, which is in the same complex as a co-worker. She has a three-year-old son named Archie who is bright and outgoing, so Noah has a readymade playmate living close by. Luckily, we have worked out a sleep-over arrangement for the boys in lieu of hiring babysitters.

The indoor space is compact, but affordable and adequate for me and Noah's needs. On the walls, there is room for just one of Mom's paintings and a few contemporary posters I have chosen to hang in my bedroom. Noah's colorful drawings adorn the kitchen refrigerator door, the corkboard over his bed, and one entire wall of our shared bathroom. One of the pictures he tells me is of his family. "That's Mommy, that's Nana, that's Papa," he says, pointing to many squiggly lines and dashes. A blob of random circles in the corner is supposed to represent him.

Most of our furnishings were acquired from IKEA, which were put together by me and Dad in a much longer time period than the salesman had originally indicated was required. We might have finished a lot sooner if Mom hadn't returned earlier than anticipated from the trip to the ice cream parlor with Noah. Curiosity got the better of him, and he was touching every little screw, wrench, hammer, and bolt with his sticky fingers. Now that the assembly has been finally completed and absent the chaos and clutter, I have managed so far to keep everything in its rightful place.

As I am now the person in charge of my own finances, I've taken a firmer grip on my spending and Noah receives far fewer packages from internet purchases. What's nice is that he is just as happy as he was before. Some of Noah's biggest pleasures are pressing the elevator buttons and spotting the airplanes from our terrace.

By the side of the building is a grassy playground with slides, climbing bars, and some picnic tables. There's even a nice sized swimming pool, sufficiently fenced in and gated I might add, with beckoning Caribbean aqua-blue heated water and a giant wading area perfect for us to enjoy late afternoon splashes. Initially, Noah resented having to pick up and relocate a second time, but he is capitalizing on the great open spaces to run around in, which give him more freedom than he had in my folks' home. He does get to see Mom and Dad whenever they want to spend time with him, which has been quite often lately.

I've been socializing with my work pals on the weekends and have even been on a few decent dates. Mr. Perfect has yet to come along, but I'm not complaining. I realize that Craig never was nor could he ever be that person. The guys I've met so far have been down to earth and respectful. I want to love and be loved but not out of desperation. Ideally, I'd prefer to share a loving relationship with someone I can really trust. Trust is a big issue for me right now. Once you've had the dirt kicked in your face, it's hard not to suspect every guy of being capable of doing the same.

Noah made the leap from diapers to underwear shortly after our move. Without the worry of soiling my parents' home with accidental leaks, the training has gone amazingly smooth. He is very proud of his superman underwear; he now recites the alphabet, completes a wooden puzzle quick as a wink, and sleeps in a big boy bed.

Although we're still plagued by some sporadic bouts of anger and frustration, there are far fewer of them and Noah is more able to articulate what is really stressing him out. I've been working with a counselor on a regular basis, and she has also been teaching me how best to deal with Noah. The obvious exclusion in his family portrait did not go unnoticed and was the subject of one such session.

Sadly, Noah hardly ever mentions Craig's name to me anymore. It's been ages since he has heard his father's voice or seen him in person, although the court-mandated support checks regularly arrive right on time. I keep hoping that Craig and Noah will have a closer relationship one day.

For my part, I have absolutely no desire to ever see Craig again. The thought of having sex with him repulses me. I will never let myself sink that low with him or any other man like him. As much as I don't want him in my life, Noah is still his child and deserves to know more about his father. I have attempted to involve Craig in Noah's life by sending him updates on his progress and forwarding any invitations for events held at the school. I've emailed him asking when he would like to visit. Based upon the absence of any positive response, I guess Craig has no desire to be a part of his child's life other than what is compulsory.

Wednesday nights have become girls' night out for me and my mom. Who would have ever guessed that we'd end up paling around together on a regular basis? It had started right before Purim, when I asked for her special hamantaschen recipe. I knew that Noah would get a kick out of pinching the cut circles into delicious triangle cookies. He loves it when we practice cooking together. After each trip to the library, we scan the cookbooks we bring home and choose two new dishes to prepare.

My mom had suggested that I join her first in making the hamantaschen instead of her just telling me the ingredients over the phone. So, one evening, my mom and I formed the dough, loaded with butter, sugar, and cream cheese, into one solid form and placed it in her refrigerator until it became firm. A few days later and armed with flour-dusted rolling pins and perfectly-sized juice glasses for cutters, we were thinning portions of the dough to place on cookie sheets.

"Mom, you have flour in your hair," I casually informed her, brushing her bangs with my wrist and accidentally powdering her cheek with more flour. I began to laugh.

"What are you laughing about?"

"Nothing."

She stuck her hand into the Tupperware container, stroking her fingers across my face. "Two can play the same game you know."

Well, I'm not one to ignore a challenge. I grabbed the entire container of flour and dumped it on her head. She froze in shock, and for a split second, I thought she was going to pick up a bagel knife and slice me with it.

She screeched, "Kat, what did you just do?" and then the giggling started. Her first; me second. Laughing and sobbing, then sighing, and laughing uncontrollably again until we were both sitting on the floor peeing our pants.

"Kat, you and me, we've been through a lot, haven't we?"

"Yes Mom, we have."

She put her arms around me and gave me two loud, wet kisses on each cheek. "Oh, I have to tell you about the bracelets." Not waiting for me to respond, she rambled on about misplacing her two silver bangles. Each bracelet had a double catch, but each one had slipped off her wrist one evening apart. Mom had searched all over her house for the missing jewelry, sifting through her lingerie, pulling out all of her shoe boxes, and un-stacking the bathroom towels.

"I found the first bracelet on the floor under the middle of my car in the garage," she stated with more drama than I thought was warranted.

"Ah ha."

"The next evening, I found the other one right smack in the very same place."

"Ah ha. You must have not been that careful when you looked under the car the first time."

"Kat, you're missing my point." She sounded testy. "You're not listening to me. One fell off Saturday. The other one fell off Sunday."

"I don't see what the big deal is. You must have pushed them off your wrist as you were getting into your car and just didn't realize it. You should take them to a jeweler to have the locks fixed or made stronger."

"Nothing's wrong with them. They close perfectly and stay closed no matter how much I tug at them."

"Then what caused them to fall off?"

She jerked her head forward. "Exactly my point. Nothing!"

I turned to face her, aware that I was being drawn into one of her nutsy, mystical productions like a sailor being lured to a shipwreck by a siren. "Okay, I'll bite."

She became all animated as she commenced with her totally illogical, inane explanation. "The universe must definitely be sending me a message to do with my car, because that's where the bracelets ended up. I hadn't used my car for quite a number of days up to and including the times the bracelets went missing."

"Hmmm," I responded. "Hmmm," I repeated, this time rubbing my chin to show I was interested. "If I might be honest with you, I'd say your theory does seem a little far-fetched." That was all I said. I wish I had said so much more.

Chapter Forty-nine

My kitchen was in much better shape than Mom's when Noah and I made the hamantaschen with apricot, cherry, and chocolate chip fillings. More of the chips, however, went into Noah's mouth than in the cookies, but that was to be expected. He also ate a fair share of the baked cookies after they had cooled down. He complained plenty of a bellyache a short while after; no surprise there.

Noah brought ample samples of each flavor to school for "show and tell" the next morning. We had cut out circles of construction paper so he could demonstrate the folding and pinching method to his class. When I picked him up at the end of his day, he was in the mood for pizza, so we dropped by Antonio's, our local Italian restaurant, on the way home.

As we waited by the checkout line, someone tapped me on the shoulder. It took a while to associate the face with a name. I knew the person, but I came up short figuring out where I had met him before. His hair was curly and blackish brown, as were the pupils of his eyes, made even more intense by his thick eyebrows. Think Colin Farrell or Tom Cruise.

He wasn't overly tall, but he did tower over me by at least five inches. He kind of looked like he was from Boston or Ireland; one of the two. Don't ask me why I thought this. I presumed he must have just come from a baseball game because he was wearing sweats and a jersey that had been dampened at his armpits and back.

He pretended to be insulted. "That's very nice. I'm living in your house, and you have no idea who I am." It was his broad smile that gave him away.

"Oh, you live in our building. I'm sorry I didn't recognize you at first." *Awkward.*

The Canadian smiled. "Your old townhouse; I bought it from you, remember?"

Even more awkward!

He told me that he often stopped at Antonio's on his way home from work as he was now living in Florida full time and had shifted his office down south as well. *Why hadn't I noticed how charming the Canadian was before? And not too difficult to look at either.* We chatted a short while and exchanged contact info. I entered his phone number under C, for Canadian, too embarrassed to ask his name.

Later that evening, my phone rang after Noah had been tucked into his *Toy Story* sheets. I felt giddy thinking it might be the Canadian calling that soon. Noah and I had already read the two bedtime books he had selected. After his angelic plea for one more story, I had acquiesced before outing the light and wishing him sweet dreams.

I tapped the "Answer" tab on my cell phone and heard Dad's somber voice; he kept choking on his tears.

"Tell me. Tell me what happened," I begged. The memory of the calls from Nathan's passing flooded my mind. My knees buckled and I sank to the ground. "Dad, what is it?"

"There was a car crash in the intersection by Publix. Mom is in the hospital. It's serious."

Stephen, who it turns out, was standing right next to Dad, grabbed his phone and filled me in on the particulars. I called my co-worker, who called her niece, who drove over to watch Noah for me.

Much of that night, we paced the corridors and watched unfortunate people file in and out of the emergency area. It was frigidly cold. Mara kept supplying us with hot chocolate and coffee from the vending machines to help us keep warm. There was one boisterous, spaced-out patient who kept ranting and raving, needing to be restrained. A couple of armed policemen entered the triage area carrying a straightjacket. I heard violent screams continue from behind a curtained cubicle. "Get me out of here! Somebody help me! Let me go home!"

Ambulance sirens wailed as they approached the entrance doors. Gurneys were pushed and pulled, some with IV tubes clamped to their sides. The nurses, doctors, and orderlies scurried about their duties, hoping not to be interrupted by our anxious questions. The drone of CNN broadcasts emanated from every overhead television. The atrocities from the scenes of bomb sites and terrorist attacks made me avert my eyes. I tried to ignore the foul hospital odor that was intensifying my worst fears and carried me back to the dialysis wards of Nathan's illness.

Dad was called to the central nurse's station and relayed to us the message that we should all go home and try to get a good rest. Mom's condition was critical but stable. There was nothing any of us could do in the hospital to help. They would call us if any change occurred.

The next day, I tried to go through the normal routine of work and tending to Noah, but my mind and heart were heavy with concern for my mother. I wasn't ready to lose her. For several more days, Mom continued to be in intensive care. The rest of us felt as if the laws of gravity and planetary motion had been upended. Nothing was holding us in place. Our lives were no longer moving along in the ordinary way we had assumed they would; in the same way we had often taken them for granted.

Mom was heavily sedated and no visitors were allowed except for Dad, who kept a constant vigil by her bedside. When she did finally open her eyes and was able to speak, she told Dad that she had seen Nathan. "He looked wonderful. It was as if he were 21 or 22 years old, strappingly handsome and totally healthy. He was there to greet me. Ted, I wanted to stay with him, but he told me to go on back. I wanted to stay with him. I confessed that it was my fault he had died so young."

"Hush," my dad told her, stroking her hair and forehead. "Take it easy and relax. You don't realize what you're saying."

"No. I want to speak. I want to tell you what happened. Bubbe Leah had heard my plea and had taken care of the matter."

"Okay, I hear you. We'll talk about this some other time."

"You don't understand. She really was a witch. She really was a witch. God was punishing us—punishing me—for wishing my father dead. She did it. She heard my prayer and did it. I prayed to the skirt. The skirt; it's really a very powerful skirt. I wanted to stay with Nathan. I wanted to stay with him." She cried and cried, but Dad could not calm her down. Her sobs grew increasingly louder. She wailed over and over again, "I didn't want to leave him. He was my baby; my first child. It should have been me you buried; not him." A nurse came rushing into the room, but Dad indicated that he was in control of the situation.

"We need to let her cry. She's been holding it in for far too long."

Chapter Fifty

MYRA'S JOURNAL

My childhood was by no means a happy one:

In the 1950's in England, the majority of women did not work unless they needed to for economic reasons. How a woman behaved in her home as well as in public was mostly controlled by societal rules. Women were expected to be attentive mothers, subservient wives, and accomplished housekeepers. They were discouraged from wearing trousers, smoking cigarettes, and driving cars.

Divorce, in those days, was considered scandalous and sacrilegious, and was therefore never a viable option for my mother. She kept finding different means to escape from her life, the same way a rat in a maze will keep running to find its cheesy reward. To my knowledge, her exterior wanderings began when I was a baby and had yet to learn how to maneuver my way down the flight of stairs in our house. I can recall a lot of tumbling, knocks on the head, and tremendous relief when my body would come to a halt on the landing. There's no guessing at what age I taught myself how to descend unharmed.

Throughout my childhood, much of my clothing was ill fitting and soiled; my neck was often plagued by itching and red chafing marks. For many weeks in a row, my undergarments went unchanged and the knots in my hair were left to multiply. A short trip to the beauty salon one day (I vaguely remember my mother standing somewhere near the entrance) resulted in a pixie haircut to remove a mangled mess from my head and I was temporarily transformed from a wild, unkempt, little girl into a sparsely haired, pudgy one, resembling Robin Hood's pal Friar Tuck.

From out of nowhere, as I was engrossed in painting a paper doily one morning (one of the rare permitted activities), my mother said to me, "Put on your coat, Myra. We're going out." She brought me into a strange classroom in an austere, large brick building and then vanished. Joan came to find me in the emptied classroom at the end of the school day and tugged at my coat sleeve. "Move it, you fat ugly pig! It's getting late and I'm hungry," she had yelled. "Now I'm stuck with you every day."

I did not see my mother again until the next day when I was eating breakfast prepared by the *au pair;* she reemerged in the kitchen no less mysteriously than a rabbit plucked from a magician's hat.

On the occasions when my father would return from working in his dress factory and discovered his wife nowhere in sight, he sent his five brothers-in-law on a mission to locate their sister and bring her home. In actuality, she could never have traveled too far. Not licensed to drive a car, her journey had to begin with the 653 bus route, so her brothers would investigate every hotel within a fixed radius and they would inevitably hunt her down. Many times I have wondered what the clerks might have been thinking when they registered my mother, all alone and baggage-less, at these "get away" sites. Was it a common practice among women to seek refuge in these places?

One Sunday morning my father had been angrier than usual because he couldn't find his manicure scissors, blaming my mother for not returning them to their rightful place. Despite her denials, my father persisted with his accusation, becoming louder and more bellicose as my mother became more unhinged. His yelling and outbursts punctuated the air like exploding bombs in a war zone.

There was nothing my mother could do to calm him down short of producing the scissors, which she did not have. She begged him to leave her alone. From the perspective of a six-year-old standing in the hallway outside the kitchen where the altercation was taking place, it seemed like his booming threats and violent shoves were escalating to the point that he was going to kill her.

I opened the door to the closet carved out of the space under the stairwell, purposefully not pulling the string connected to the light bulb. I did not want to be discovered. I was afraid my father might kill me as well. This was a place where coal had been stored and spiders, bugs, rats, and mice ran around. I had never dared to enter this closet before. The screaming and sobbing continued on the outside, but I chose to stay in the pitch black with the vermin.

I next heard footsteps coming down the stairs. I guessed

they belonged to my ten-year-old sister, Joan. She must have brought the manicure scissors to my father, because she was saying she had found them by the sink in the upstairs bathroom. What followed next was the sound of heavy feet stomping up the steps. I did not hear my father speak or offer an apology. Each thump of his shoes pounded my head. I waited in the closet until I could no longer ignore the scuttling and nibbling going on about me. When I emerged, I found that Joan and my mother had left the house.

A few days after the scissor fiasco, my mother had beckoned me to join her. She was seated next to the kitchen table with her cosmetics case open and various jars displayed on the tabletop.

"Myra, we're going to do something that is going to make Daddy very happy," she informed me in an unusually cheerful voice.

I peered at her inquisitively, glad to receive the unexpected attention.

"He's going to love seeing you look so pretty," she continued, clasping and twisting her hands together. "I am going to make you look beautiful for him! Oh, this will be so exciting." Her enthusiasm was contagious and spilled into me.

After sitting me on a chair, my mother applied layers of creams and powders to my face. I cherished feeling the brush of her hand against my cheeks. *Don't ever stop. Please pat my cheeks some more*, I silently begged. So often, I had wanted to be hugged or touched by her to make up for the times when she was absent or busily moseying off in her own universe.

She picked up a shiny small tube, twisted the capsule to expose the color, and then painted my mouth with dark red lipstick. Some of it smeared beyond where it was supposed to be so spitting on her extended fingers, she tried to rub off the excess with her saliva, but I wished for that stain to stubbornly remain in place forever. After examining a selection of eye shadows, she decided on a shimmering, midnight blue.

"Close your eyes, Myra," she instructed.

I sat before her, imagining the two of us holding hands and skipping together in the countryside. I fantasized wearing matching navy and white polka dot dresses. The very ones I had seen two models wearing in a magazine ad.

When she whispered, "I'm almost finished," it saddened me. She used her pointer finger to scrape some rouge from a jar lid and made pink circles on the center of each of my cheeks. "This is going to be terrific," she had said, and I believed her. "Daddy's going to be so impressed when he sees how beautiful you look."

I didn't utter a sound. I hoped the beauty treatment would make my father say that I was a lovely girl instead of being a fat, ugly baby, as was his usual taunt.

I heard the driver's door of my father's two-toned Ford Zephyr slam shut. Next came the sound of his steps striding from the street curb, up on the sidewalk, and across our paved front walkway. I heard his keys jingle and the click of the lock on the front door. My mother's wink gave confirmation that something very special was about to happen. She pushed me forward, saying, "I want you to be the very first thing he notices when he comes in," before quickly retreating behind the kitchen door.

In walked my father, looking like the giant that chased Jack up the Beanstalk, only he was wearing a tan, cashmere overcoat. After he placed his felt fedora on the telephone table and his briefcase on the floor beside it, I noticed his flaring nostrils and his eyes zeroing in on me. He didn't bother to remove his coat.

"What in God's name have you done?" he hollered. It felt like his thunderous voice was drilling me into the ground. "You look absolutely stupid, you stupid, stupid little girl. You've made yourself up like a bloomin' hussy. This is what I have to come home to? I won't tolerate this. Not at all! How dare you? You should be terribly ashamed of yourself."

He caught hold of my sweater and dragged me over to the bannister. "Get upstairs and wash that crap off your face! It makes me sick to look at you." With the palm of his hand, he pushed my back. "Go on then. Get a move on! What the hell are you waiting for? And don't bother coming downstairs afterwards for supper. You won't be having any. You are a disgrace to this family. No wonder no one can stand having you around."

Chapter Fifty-one

Bubbe Leah's demise:

Concealed by the solid banister, I was kneeling on the stairs in the hallway, counting the number of petals in each color on the floral carpeting. Absent permissible play objects of any kind, at seven years old, I had become quite adept at keeping myself amused. Instead of one imaginary friend, I had created entire villages with my mind's eye and was not averse to conversing out loud with the people who populated them. One benefit of playing by oneself was that I could assume the role of any character I wished. Another was that everything was entirely invisible and therefore, not subject to anyone's censure or scrutiny.

Bubbe Leah was slumped on the chair next to the table where our one telephone sat. She looked sadder and more disappointed than usual. Her cane was tilted with its hook resting on her lap. Her laced-up shoes were placed far apart on the floor, raising the hem of her skirt to reveal her knee-length bloomers. Her thick stockings had fallen down because their elastic rims were all stretched out.

The previous night, my parents had been arguing again. This time, it had been about Bubbe. My father insisted she needed to be placed in a nursing home, emphasizing that the existing living arrangement could no longer continue. He was as adamant and unbending as ever, so my mother agreed to seek out an appropriate facility in the coming days.

I watched Bubbe Leah exhale, arduously lifting her shoulders up and down as if in resignation of her fate. With her right hand, she had taken what seemed to be a throat lozenge from her skirt pocket and placed it under her tongue. Pretty soon, she fell into a deep sleep. I next heard raspy, snoring sounds coming from her chest, but then she began to choke with her eyes remaining closed. Her cane fell to the floor. More sounds and foam emanated from her mouth, making it seem like she was about to vomit. Her breathing had turned into laborious pants.

I watched, undetected, as my mother ran to retrieve the metal "throw up" pan, which she placed beneath Bubbe's several chins. This was the same pan in which my older sister Esther used to nurse ailing birds so they could afterwards fly away. Esther and I shared something in common: we both envied those birds when we watched them escape to a healthier life.

Nothing, however, fell into the pan from Bubbe's mouth. There had been no bile or regurgitated food. A heavy *whoosh* arose from her body and then came silence; her head fell to her chest. Bubbe Leah had died.

A hubbub of activity then ensued in our home, but no one bothered to discuss or explain what had or was about to transpire. In accordance with the practice of *sh'mira*, a righteous woman entered our home to sit with Bubbe's body, which was brought to rest on the sofa in the living room. It was the *shomer's* responsibility to watch over and guard my grandmother's soul until the burial. When the *shomer* took a brief break, I snuck into the living room to peek at the body. I remember staring at the dark hairs protruding from the putty-colored, lifeless face.

Eventually, my grandmother's body was mysteriously removed from our home. Of course, there must have been a burial service where the body was interred, but I was not permitted to be present at the cemetery. I had been shuffled off to spend a week with one of my aunts and uncles. No one said a word about my grandmother's death there either.

Bubbe Leah's name was never mentioned again. Her body, her furniture, and all of her personal belongings evaporated. Not a smidgeon of her appeared to have been left behind. On my way to school one morning, I found her skirt sticking out of the top of a dustbin, placed by the curb outside our house. I checked to make sure I was not being watched and despite being terribly afraid of being caught, I grabbed the skirt to hide in the bottom of my dresser drawer.

Chapter Fifty-two

And then we set sail:

On my first day of Hebrew School, my teacher pointed to his club foot and said, "If you are not a good student, God will surely punish you. He'll give you polio, like me."

Taking a peek at his right foot, I saw that it was in a corrective shoe with a four-inch black platform. On his left foot was the same laced shoe but with a regular, thin sole. Not only was my teacher's warning daunting, but it left me confused as to whether the God he had been referring to was the same God I was being taught had created the world.

"Is there more than one God?" I had asked to no one in particular at the dinner table.

I received a lot of blank stares. Joan and Esther laughed. My mother looked away. My father was furious that the ketchup bottle was not with the other condiments, so my mother headed to the kitchen to retrieve it. I decided to rephrase the question. "Where is God exactly?"

"Where's God?" my father mimicked. "God is everywhere. That's all you need to know."

"Didn't God create the world?" I asked, this time specifically addressing my father.

"Yes, of course he did," he said, cutting into his fried steak.

I don't know why, but my thirst for an answer overcame any fears I may have had in asking the question, "Well, where was God before the world was created?"

"I told you, idiot, that God is everywhere!" Raising his voice even louder, he yelled, "Ada, I want the bloody ketchup for my chips while they're still hot. Move yourself!"

"If the world had not been created yet, God couldn't have been everywhere because there *was* no everywhere." This statement had made perfect sense to me. From my father's expression, I couldn't tell if he was exasperated with me or his steak was too tough to chew.

My father threw his knife and fork on the table and bellowed, "*Fanculo*! What I tell you is all that you need to know. God is everywhere. That's it! I don't want to hear another word out of your mouth about this or anything else. Don't go asking about things that don't concern you. Just keep your mouth shut and do what you're told! You were born solely to serve the whims of your family. For no other reason. For nothing else. Get that into your dumb head and keep it there!"

Joan and Esther glared in my direction. My mother returned to the dining room and handed my father the ketchup bottle without telling him the top had been unscrewed. He turned it upside down and shook it vehemently. The sauce went everywhere; it landed on his hair, on his starched, white shirt, on the embroidered tablecloth, on the lamp shades, and us.

"*Fanculo*! Not one word out of any of you!" he screamed.

I think all of our faces were blanched white, dreading the action he was going to take in response. Laughing was definitely out of the question. I sucked on my tongue and stared at the ceiling, picturing Noddy and Mr. Big Ears driving around Toyland. My father picked up his plate and sent it crashing to the floor before he left the room.

The following week, my mother handed me a pen, the center of which contained a plastic window where a two-dimensional ship sailed back and forth. "Take this to the Rabbi at Hebrew School," she advised, "and tell him that you can't be there anymore since you are going to America." It amazed me that she was able to fabricate such an excellent excuse.

One week later, however, I witnessed a loud, sorrowful parting take place between my mother and my five uncles at a massive train station. A train ride brought me, Esther, Joan, and my parents to a dock, along with seventy-five packed crates, included in which were two sets of draining boards and koshering tools in case they didn't have such items in America. We next boarded a super enormous ocean liner. That's how I found myself on the *Queen Elizabeth* about to sail across the great Atlantic Ocean.

Chapter Fifty-three

Nightmares:

Shortly after Bubbe Leah died, armies of gnome-like fiends would come peeling off the ceiling and walls in my bedroom. These terrorizing creatures would begin to pounce upon me as soon as my head touched the pillow. Their chant was always the same: "We are coming to take you away. Ha Ha. We are coming to take you away. Teehee." Each night in contemplation of these unwelcome visitors, I would be sieged by panic and my intestines would become painfully tied in knots. It didn't seem to matter to my attackers if I resided in London, England or in Brooklyn, New York.

In America, my designated bedtime coincided with the end of the *John Charles Daly and the News* television show, which was the signal for me to depart the living room where the rest of the family had gathered. My orders were always the same: to put on my pajamas, shut the door, and out the lights. Hearing John Daly's sign-off, "Goodnight and a good tomorrow," had the same morbid impact on me as a Passing Bell would have had in Medieval times when three times two strokes warned of a female's impending death. For me, walking into my bedroom alone was akin to climbing a ladder to the gallows with a rope around my neck.

I would hope against hope that my mother would exhibit some concern and rush to my side as soon as my nightly wailing and screaming reached her ears. I desperately wished she could bring some control to the terrifying internal chaos I was experiencing. I wanted so badly for her to make the blood curdling monsters disappear. Perhaps she could have given me a kiss on the forehead or read me a book to help ward off my nightmarish assailants, but that never happened.

"Leave her alone," my father would direct. "She's being a baby. She's acting childish. You spoil her too much as it is. She has to grow up."

Each evening, my bed and I would end up being sopping wet. I was eternally fearful of the dark, persistently petrified of monsters, but even more so deathly afraid of my father.

This devastating fear continued all throughout my teenage years—when I was propelled into a downward spiral of rebellion and self-destruction—and even into my adult life. Experimenting with drugs, overconsuming alcohol, and engaging in sex with casual acquaintances were my chosen means of escape from this living dread. Spinning out of control, I landed in places that were both sordid and dangerous.

In the middle of protesting the Vietnam War and dancing while substantially stoned in the fountains of Central Park, I began to hemorrhage and passed out. When I awoke in a hospital bed, I learned that I had miscarried. I didn't even know enough about my own body at that time to realize I had been pregnant. A nurse, who stood rigidly by my side and stared icily ahead, thrust a clipboard at me. It contained a Fetal Death Certificate for me to sign. I had no idea why it was relevant, but I did as I was told.

It was quite by chance that at eighteen years old I met the slim, good-looking, level-headed, highly considerate and intelligent Teddy Sturnberger at a party in a basement apartment. Deep down, though, I have always believed the universe had decided it was time to intervene and save me. He became the first stabilizing force in my life. As I entered the room, I spotted him seated on a chair by the landing. His long sideburns and flared jeans made him seem more of a hippie than he actually was. He looked up and his eyes told me he loved me and always would.

I eventually married Ted and gave birth to three wonderful children, but still that fear clung to me, haunting me, stifling me, gripping my shoulders, weakening my insides, and making me forever feel like an inferior, worthless human being. When my father carried on like a ferocious, wild lunatic, barking one day at my children in our home for no apparent reason, it was only then that I could muster the strength to finally confront him. I was determined to be the kind of mother who protected her children, unlike my own mother who had repeatedly declined to do so.

I stepped forward and told my father, "That kind of talk is not acceptable in this home," keeping my voice low as my legs continued to shake. This was all I said.

His reaction was one of total shock. His bulging eyes looked like they were going to snap out of their sockets. His nostrils flared and he became even angrier. Grabbing hold of my mother, who stood a few feet away, he pulled her toward the front door, despite her begging him to rethink the situation. With a tight hold on my mother, he shoved her into the passenger seat of their car. He sat down by the steering wheel and locked the doors. I could hear him muttering and cursing. "You ungrateful little shit! Who the fuck do you think you are?" He pressed heavily on the gas pedal, causing the vehicle to skid as he tried to swerve out of the parking spot. The car jumped off our driveway and lurched into the main stream of traffic.

For several weeks following, my father held my mother hostage in their home, acting not unlike the Ayatollah Khomeini of Iran with the diplomatic aides from the American Embassy. Joan and Esther, both married women with their own children, contended that any harm befalling our mother was a direct result of my actions. If she were to die, the guilt would lie squarely and solely upon my shoulders.

I believed that what I had said was right and appropriate, but it ran contrary to the way my family had dealt with our ongoing problem. For me, though, there was no turning back. Someone had to break the chain of abuse that seemed to have no end in sight. It was just a small step in a gigantic field of heartache, but it was a step nevertheless in the right direction.

This is when I turned to my paintbrushes and paints as a way to cope with the confusion and uncertainty percolating inside me. Patterns in a multitude of shapes and hues poured through my hands and out onto canvases. Many of the images contained cryptic information and repeating icons, much of which I did not understand and still do not to this day.

My sisters were quick to inform me that my mother's health was in rapid decline. "Call him up and apologize before it's too late," they urged. "He'll let her go once you make amends."

I chose not to make that call. "I did nothing wrong," I told them.

"What difference does that make?" Joan questioned. "This is just the way it has to be."

For the next few months, my mother's visits to hospital emergency rooms—which had been many during her marriage—now occurred with even more frequency than before. She underwent a continuous cycle of surgery, narcotic pain medication, and strenuous rehabilitation. I was precluded from visiting her. I worried that she had lost the willpower and stamina to carry on. I feared she would finally lose the battle.

One night I was feeling desperate. The latest news from the hospital was that my mother had taken a turn for the worse. I removed the box containing my grandmother's skirt from my closet and placed it on a table before me. Yes, I had stashed it in the suitcase with my clothes before we left England; no one had noticed. No one had even cared what I bothered to pack.

"Bubbe Leah," I prayed, "I am asking you to intercede on

Ada's behalf. It's time for you to do something about Harold. I understand you gave birth to him, but the time has come for him to go. Bubbe, do whatever magic you can. I am afraid my mother will die if she is not set free. She is a helpless, innocent victim. Please do what is right." I placed the skirt carefully back in its box and returned it to its resting place in my closet. I told no one about what I had prayed for. I kept it a secret, stowed away in the farthest corners of my mind.

A severe bout of coughing caused my father's stage-four lung cancer to be detected two weeks later. It was an aggressive cancer. Within ten weeks' time, he had died. That's how quickly he went. My mother was finally liberated.

Chapter Fifty-four

Dealing with the aftermath:

I could not allow myself to say *Kaddish* for my father. I didn't believe the man deserved it. For some, issues of faith and religion come easy. For me, it has always been a struggle. The rabbi at our synagogue reminds me often that the word "Israel," in Hebrew means to "struggle with God".

In the *Book of Lamentations*, it is written that, "Our fathers sinned, and are no more; it is we who have borne their iniquities." In *Exodus*, the second book of the Hebrew Bible, it is stated, "Yet he does not leave the guilty unpunished; he punishes the children and their children for the sin of the fathers to the third and fourth generation."

I have concluded that it was, therefore, my crime that caused Nathan to die. Nathan's illness came into his life solely as a punishment for my actions. *What did I do? Oh, what did I do?*

As a grieving parent, I will never come to terms with my child's untimely death or the suffering he had to endure. Sometimes, I fear there will be no end to my anguish and damnation.

I've asked for signs to let me know that my son is safe and now in a good place. Psychics have relayed messages from Nathan. I have been told that he is fine, that his body is no longer needed, and that he is no longer suffering. Nathan indicated he understood he had died when he recognized his grandparents and all the relatives that had been alive before him. He also tells me his illness had nothing to do with me and that I should let go of the guilt.

The psychics tell me that he's watching over all of us and how proud he is of Stephen's success. He told me to tell Kat not to be so hard on herself. He knows she loved him, and he continues to love her. "Let go of the anger, Kat," he says. "Let it go."

Chapter Fifty-five
KAT

Since the move, I have been reading my mother's journal in drips and drabs, but yesterday, I finally finished the last few pages. How could my mother possibly have believed she was responsible for Poppy's death? That's just plain ridiculous. There's no way Nathan's illness had anything to do with Poppy's death either. I don't believe things work that way. Perhaps it would be healthier for her to never have to see Bubbe Leah's skirt again.

I'm guessing that Mom needed to hold on to Leah's skirt for many reasons. On one hand, it was because of her guilt from the thought of killing her father. It could be that in some misguided way, she had to hide "the evidence." On the other hand, it represents Leah's extraordinary powers of healing and unconditional love. The knowledge that she was loved by Leah alone and not loved by anyone else is possibly what protected Mom throughout all of her rotten years.

I had to think long and hard about what I was going to do with the skirt, now that I had learned the truth behind it. My immediate reaction was to toss it into the garbage where it originally belonged or cut it up and burn the pieces. Would that be so terrible? Who needed to hold on to the remnants of such a sad saga?

Okay, I need to warn you: this is where I begin to engage in a little self-pity. Why couldn't my life story be like everyone else's? Not like the stories of the people I deal with in my job, but the stories of all the people that walk around with smiles on their faces and seem to be perennially carefree and content. What's with the poisoning, the pogroms, the abandonment, and death camps? Is it at all possible to ever move away from all of this misery? How do I do that? I'm not so certain if the past can ever be completely erased from one's mind. If it can, then I need to know specifically how to accomplish that.

Another question: is it the past that needs to be erased or my emotional attachment to it? If the past is totally eradicated, then there will be no fragments remaining upon which to build. Isn't one supposed to learn from history and prior experiences? I love Nathan with all my heart, but he is no longer with me, and I need to release all the anger connected with his passing. Craig and I made a mistake, but I do not have to be eternally bound by it. I never again need to be in a relationship that makes me feel so horrible and undesired.

The contents of my mother's journal and Leah's letter still spun around in my head. Yes, these were the stories of my ancestors and my family. There was no need for me to repeat them; I could do much better than that. All our collective layers of guilt, drama, and false suppositions needed to be put to rest for good.

I know that having Nathan in my life really changed me in

a positive way. I loved him dearly, and I always will. I miss his annoying put-downs, abrasive behavior, and sloppy wet kisses as much as I miss his effusive warmth, unique intelligence, cockiness, and great bear hugs. He definitely would have gone nuts over Noah had he had the chance to meet him in person.

I'll never admit this to Mom, but lately I've come to believe that Nathan has been watching over Noah and me. There are just so many times during the day that I'll sense his presence. A funny word he would often repeat will flash on my computer screen from out of nowhere, one of his favorite songs will start playing from my speakers, or his framed photograph on the counter will suddenly fall.

When Nathan died, I lost whatever self-confidence I thought I had; I think Nathan's been working all this time to help me get it back. On some crazy, mysterious level, I've even felt Leah's spirit doing the same. That incident with Mom's missing bracelets still gets to me. Surely, there's got to be something to that. Nathan or Leah had to have set up that scene as a warning. There's no other logical explanation for it. And then there's my mother's version of how she first met my father. She even wrote that it had to be some kind of divine intervention. Somehow, that account doesn't seem to be so implausible to me now.

In my religious studies, I had learned that all obsolete sacred writings and ritual objects should be preserved where they cannot be destroyed. They must be placed in *Genizot*—repositories typically provided by synagogues. Every few years, the contents of the *Genizot* are shrouded and buried in a Jewish cemetery as a sign of reverence and respect.

I bought packages of parsley, mint, basil, cilantro, and rosemary seeds at the garden store and asked Noah to help me dig a large hole for their planting in my parents' backyard. I wrapped Leah's skirt with her note in a white cotton pillowcase and placed it in the hole, covering it with a generous layer of fresh topsoil. Noah and I opened one package at a time and scattered the seeds into the hole. We made sure to add fertilizer and a sufficient amount of water. I promised Noah we would make something really delicious once the herbs grew strong and hardy.

Chapter Fifty-six

Still ailing from bruises and fractured ribs, Mom is making some progress in her recuperation from the automobile accident. Dad arranged for around the clock care, and Stephen, Mara, and I take turns stocking their refrigerator with grocery supplies and ready-made meals. I try to bring Noah often on my visits, and this seems to cheer her up the most. She claims that his kisses and hugs are the very best medicine in the world.

This is a new gig for Mom: graciously accepting lots of attention, which just so happens to be upbeat and constructive. More than just her body is being rebuilt.

"I understand a lot more about you than I ever did before," I told her as we engaged in our four o'clock ritual of sipping tea. We were seated on the patio by the table, neither one of us caught in the shadow cast by the overhead umbrella—the sun had moved lower in its trajectory for the umbrella to have fully done its job. I covered her lap with an orange handmade quilt; the same one that used to envelope Nathan, Stephen, or me when we were much younger and ailing from a cold or upset tummy but not too sick to join the rest of the family in the den. "Rather than instilling confidence, which parents are supposed to do, yours subjected you to so much trauma that you became afraid of doing lots of things, like even going down a baby slide with Noah at a playground."

"I was once left all by myself in an infant swing in a neighborhood park for hours," she uttered, her face saddening. She cleared her throat.

I pictured her as a little girl stranded, penned-in by a bar, the wooden square seat, and the metal chains to which she must have clung. When Noah's limit has been reached after a few sways back and forth in a bucket swing, he kicks his feet, rattles the chains impatiently, and bellyaches nonstop as he struggles to regain his freedom. For how long did that little girl's shoes have to dangle mid-air beneath her? Had she cried out for help? Had her feet begun to ache? Was there not a passerby who could have rescued her? Was there not some evil-doer lurking in the playground who might have snatched her up?

"Mom, you've been putting on such a false, brave front for as long as I've known you."

My mother placed her teacup delicately mid-center on the saucer. She took my hand in hers and stroked my fingers with her thumb. "It was just one more place Nanny had left me high and dry." She leaned in and softly kissed my knuckles. "I love you. You know that, right?"

"Yes. Without a doubt. I know that."

"Whenever I'm in a playground, it tends to rouse a ton of those horrible memories."

She sounded tired. I noticed grey circles below her eyes, drooping eyelids above them. She cleared her throat again, a little louder this time.

"When I first gave you the skirt, Kat, I wanted Bubbe Leah to alleviate all your pain and misery. I kept hoping that you would ask for some terrible fate to befall Craig and that Bubbe Leah would hear your wishes and act accordingly the same way she had done for me. But things had a way of working themselves out on their own somehow."

"Let's not talk about the skirt right now," I answered.

She pushed a smile onto her cheeks. "But when I'm better I would love to take Noah to the Pirate Ship playground and run around with him. That's something I can truly look forward to doing, even if it means going down a slide or two."

I nodded. "That's good to hear." I gave her a broad smile in return. "That would be wonderful if you could do that." I reached for two oatmeal cookies from a plate resting on the table. Handing her one, I added, "It's sad that unlike me, you never really had a role model; someone whom you would want to emulate growing up."

Tilting her head, she bit into the cookie. Her eyebrows rose inquisitively and a raisin tumbled down her chin and landed on her chest. "That's a nice compliment coming from you. I guess I should make myself vulnerable to car accidents more often."

Using a paper napkin, I gathered the raisin and dabbed away at crumbs lingering on her lips and chin. "That's not at all funny," I scolded. "Every once in a while, your weird attempt at humor emerges; you should definitely squelch it."

***

Since Mom's accident, I had completely forgotten about the meeting at Antonio's, but fortunately for me, the Canadian had not. When he phoned to meet me for coffee, his company name showed up on the caller ID. Detesting telemarketers, I was ready to let voicemail take the message, but thank God, at the last minute I changed my mind.

I felt like an idiot for still not knowing his name. He was being so warm and friendly, and I didn't want to come across as an insensitive ignoramus. Thankfully, when the doorman called to announce Josh Goldstein's arrival the evening he came to pick me up, yet another mystery was finally solved.

When Josh came for dinner the first time, he brought a pretty bouquet of flowers and a Thomas train for Noah. He raved about my new hairstyle and commented that I should always wear it that way. "Well, that is if you want to. I'm not saying you have to. It just looks pretty this way."

I let him stumble around in his awkwardness for just a short while, and then led him to the table. "I get what you're saying. I went to the beauty parlor today and decided to try something new. It's all right. I'm not offended in the least. I like my haircut too."

I learned about his life up north and his failed two-year marriage while a pesky Noah kept interrupting, wanting company to play with his railroad and cars. Josh took to the floor to build a train track with Noah sitting alongside him.

Now, the track set up on my living room floor has become far more multi-tiered and complex with depots, towers, bridges, and bypasses. Noah keeps a watchful eye over the configuration, ensuring that it remains intact for Josh's welcome visits.

Noah and I have not made a return trip to see Josh in our old townhouse, as I believe it would be far too confusing for Noah to handle. In the meantime, the three of us have paid some wonderful visits together to the zoo, street fairs, and museums. On the occasions when Josh has been in our apartment, he has been a willing guinea pig for my building repertoire of fine culinary dishes. He downs every morsel of food, and at the end of each meal smacks his lips and licks his plate—a pattern of behavior that Noah enjoys mimicking to the point of abandoned laughter. Even if Josh is being overly kind, I still take delight in hearing his compliments.

On occasion, Josh has to fly up to Vancouver on business. I miss him awfully while he is away. Sleeping alone isn't too bad, but I do miss our wonderful sex, our long pillow talks, and not having his cheeks to kiss in the morning.

Chapter Fifty-seven

Several months had passed, and we were solemnly observing Yom Kippur, which in my parents' home is taken very seriously. It is a day to fast and reflect upon our sins. Noah was lucky in that he got to spend the day with his friend Archie and his mother, who are not Jewish. I hoped he was eating enough for the two of us because I'm never a happy camper when I have to skip a meal. Josh had flown north again to spend the Jewish holidays with his Canadian family, whom he would like Noah and me to meet sometime soon.

The three of us were sitting in the living room still wearing our synagogue clothes, engaged in a philosophical discussion as to what religion really meant to us. Mom and Dad had removed their suit jackets; I had kicked off my three-inch pumps. My father is a stickler about the Day of Atonement, so there was no TV and no radio playing.

Somewhere in the middle of my mother's comment about "churches and synagogues being political institutions," I noticed a pretty antique crystal pitcher on the credenza.

"Is that the one your mother received as a wedding present?" I asked. "It's nice. I would like to have it when you die." As soon as these words came out, I realized my mistake. *You dope, she almost did just die in that accident!*

"I'll be sure to remember that, Kat," she answered, smiling in a way to indicate she wasn't bummed out by the inappropriate slip of my tongue. "Mara also happened to comment on it once before. I think perhaps Stephen and Mara would like it too."

"Well if that's the case; which paintings are you leaving me in your will, now that I've given you back most of the ones that were on loan?"

Before my mother had an opportunity to respond, my father said, "Kat, you seem to be pre-occupied with the concept of death. Surely, not eating for a few hours hasn't made you that morbid. Is it possible to have a conversation more pertinent to Judaism given the occasion?"

Okay, here goes. I shifted forward in my seat. "Dad, why do you feel so compelled to observe this holiday so strictly? Doesn't any of it start to look silly or anachronistic to you?"

"Not at all," he responded. "One of the reasons I maintain these traditions is to spite the drivers who wouldn't let me ride their buses years ago when I was in elementary school. It would be freezing cold up north with snow and ice covering the ground. I would approach the bus stop just like everybody else, and then the drivers would tell me, 'No way are you riding this bus with your phony pass. Put your money in the slot or take a hike, kid!' All the students from St. Vincent and Our Mary Sacred Heart Schools would shove past me without having to show their passes, but the bus drivers would refuse to acknowledge that the Hebrew School I attended was real. I never had enough money for the fare, so I mostly had to walk home in the bitter cold."

I found myself shaking my head, not in disapproval of those drivers but in disagreement with my father's way of thinking. "The bus drivers were wrong to do what they did, but Dad, is that alone enough to make you hold on to practicing your religion?"

"What about all the Jewish people who perished in the Holocaust?" His voice became slightly elevated. "I have to remain a vigilant and practicing Jew out of respect for them. I will not allow those deaths to pass silently into the annals of history. In my mind, my commitment to upholding the rituals gives their deaths some meaning."

"What about the gypsies and the Poles?" I asked, straightening my back. "The Jews were not the only ones to suffer in the Holocaust. Don't you feel a need to respect those victims as well?"

My father remained silent.

When I mentioned, "It bothers me how some people define the practice of their religion solely by references to the Holocaust and anti-Semitism," a disappointed frown clouded my father's face. He sat up in his chair and clasped his hands. I knew I had struck a nerve. His furrowed eyebrows and clenched lips pounded the message home even more.

"That's not what I said, Kat," my father defended, his voice atypically loud. "I like to belong to something. As a child, I was kept out of every organization I wanted to join. Being Jewish is also my culture. It helps me realize that I am not alone. It sets me on the right path. It teaches me to seek justice for all people; not just Jews"

It sounded a little to me like my father's Judaism was a default religion. If he hadn't been so ostracized as a kid and the stupid bus drivers had let him ride for free, then he might not be such an ardent Jew today.

For me, the issue of religion is not so clear cut. There are way too many archaic rules to be obeyed, stemming from too many made-up, incredulous Bible stories. Deep down in my gut, I also have to wonder what kind of God would have allowed Nathan to die the way he did. Promoting goodness and kindness: that's what a religion should be about. This is what makes sense to me, and these are the tenets by which I hope to raise Noah.

That being said, when I had stood that day in the synagogue for the *Amidah* and it was time to confess my sins, tapping my chest lightly with my fist, I also added these words:

"I forgive you Nathan for dying as young as you did. I forgive you Mom for seeming to be so insensitive to my needs in the past. I forgive you Craig for not being the kind of husband I hoped you would be. I forgive me for the mistakes I have made and for taking this long to finally let go of all this anger."

Chapter Fifty-eight

I am definitely over being a victim. There will be no more abuse tolerated by me in this lifetime, and I am happy to report that my relationship with Josh is still going strong. I'm even feeling younger and closer to my true age again, worrying less and enjoying more.

As a family therapist, I'm good at what I do, except of course when it comes to diagnosing my own ailments and dealing effectively with my mother, but that no longer seems to be an issue.

I've read loads of articles online and in psychology textbooks covering the topics of marriage and family counseling. In my career, I've come across all sorts of domestic situations and unusual household arrangements. Family matters are complex; there's no question about it. But this is what I've come to learn: families have unique dynamics which are both helpful and unhelpful, although there are patterns common to all families that may also repeat from one generation to the next. It is within the family structure that we gain our perspective by which to view life as a whole, some of which will be with prejudice and some with acceptance. This is how we discover the difference between right and wrong and good and evil.

We are all capable of change, however, and we each participate in different experiences, so the dynamics within a family never remain the same. No one's family life is perfect, but that shouldn't stop anyone from making theirs as good as it can be. While all family members share bonds and a sense of history, they bring strengths and weaknesses to the table. Whatever is good needs to be identified as such and be built upon. What is problematic needs to be confronted and corrected. In some cases, these challenges require a substantial amount of work, but with commitments of compassion, love, and respect, this is certainly doable.

It took a lot of nerve for my mom to stand up to her father. God bless her for finally finding the strength to do so. It halted a line of abuse that ran from Shlomo (Solly) to Hod (Harold), and from Harold to Ada, Esther, Joan, and Myra. Craig treated me with that same disdain and air of superiority. Why the women of my family had a tendency to be victimized I do not fully comprehend, but that doesn't matter. What matters now is that it will never ever happen again.

With practice, my cooking skills have drastically improved. There's an abundance of herbs growing beautifully in my parents' backyard, and I have experimented using them in some interesting dishes for Noah, Josh, and me. If some chefs are renowned for their special seasoning and ingredients, why can't I be one of them? After all, didn't my mother say something about it being in my blood?

Okay, I'm warning you, this is where my imagination begins to take off—something I guess I inherited from little Myra. I fantasize about one day starring in my own cooking show, in which I'd share some great recipes and herbal secrets for delicious meals and for healthy living. I might even throw some singing into the program too. It could be a cooking, singing, healing show.

Mom, in her new age voice, once mentioned that our shared human history is stored in our cells—that all the information we need to know is locked in our bones. She explained that music is the key to setting it all free. It has something to do with vibrations and waves and oscillating molecules at different speeds and frequencies. Don't get too hung up on trying to understand it fully; I certainly don't. In order to do so, you'd have to have your mind go off in circles way up in another hemisphere—kind of like some of Noah's sketches— and sometimes, when that happens your mind can get stuck up there for good. And that's the last thing anyone needs—*to get stuck anywhere. Tell me about it!*

But here's the part I definitely want to stress the most: the un-clinging, the sorting out, and all the forgiving that invariably every one of us mortals has to deal with needs to happen before we can each move on to wherever it is that we are meant to be going. Am I sounding a little too philosophical and convoluted? Well, yes, maybe.

Let me explain further. All of this, every last bit of it—the scraps, the pesky, clingy-on negative stuff that wears you down and makes you drag through your days so your life seems to have lost all meaning—has to be cleared off your plate before you can even think about hearing any music. The music I am referring to here is not the kind you hear on your iPod or radio. It's so much bigger than that. It belongs to the greater universe. It's what the entire enchilada is all about. Am I losing you? Oh, where is my mother when I really need her?

The bottom line is that I'm telling you now to let it all go. Do not hold onto your pain. Do not adhere to your anger. Do not be a martyr. Do not be a suffering victim. Take time out from your everyday life to go hike in the woods. Go hug a tree. Be soothed by the flowing waters of a lake, river, or ocean. Watch a butterfly flap its wings. Smell a rose. Count the clouds. You can use any or all of these methods to let go of your pain.

All of this is absolutely essential if you ever want to hear the very special all-powerful kind of music—the music that can get you to achieve the greatest high of all; that transcends everything. The kind that will empower you and guide you through all the ups and downs of your life and to hear it with an open heart, an unencumbered spirit, and an unfettered mind in just the way it is truly meant to be heard.

###

Acknowledgements

Thank you for reading my book.

If you enjoyed it, please take the time to enter a review on the website from where it was purchased.

***

I also want to thank the people who lent their support and advice during a challenging and lengthy writing process:

Fred Steinmark, Alyssa Hirsch, Vera Hirschhorn, Janyce Speier, Clara Schuster, Nikki Rae, Carol Killman Rosenberg, and Michele Matrisciani.

Sources:

1. Schoenberg, Shira. *Modern Jewish History: The Haskalah.* http://www.jewishvirtuallibrary.org/the-haskalah

2. Rabbi Ken Spiro. *History Crash Course #56: Pale of Settlement.* http://www.aish.com/jl/h/cc/48956361.html

3. O'Day, Rosemary. *The Jews of London: From Diaspora to Whitechapel.* http://fathom.lse.ac.uk/Features/122537/

4. University of California Press. (UC E-Press Collection 1982-2004). *The Russian City between Tradition and Modernity, 1850-1900.* http://publishing.cdlib.org/ucpressebooks/view?docId=ft4m3nb2mm&chunk.id=d0e8794&toc.id=d0e8248&brand=ucpress

5. Goldberg, Jacob. *Tavernkeeping.* The YIVO Encyclopedia of Jews in Eastern Europe. http://www.yivoencyclopedia.org/article.aspx/Tavernkeeping

6. Jesuit Social Services. *Understanding Families: Family Dynamics.* www.strongbonds.jss.org.au/workers/families/dynamics.html

7. Plone Demo. *How to Have a Good Family Life.* http://plonedemo.com/sample-content/parent/Have-a-Good-Family-Life

www.ingramcontent.com/pod-product-compliance
Lightning Source LLC
Chambersburg PA
CBHW030250270626
47156CB00021B/312